Dolphin Diaries™

SPECIAL EDITION BOOKS 1-3

Ben M. Baglio

Illustrations by Judith Lawton

SCHOLASTIC INC.
New York Toronto London Auckland Sydney
Mexico City New Delhi Hong Kong Buenos Aires

12 11 10 9 8 7 6 5 4 3 2 1   5 6 7 8 9 10/0

Printed in the U.S.A.   23

ISBN 0-439-80844-8

This edition first printing, August 2005

Contents

Special thanks to Lisa Tuttle

**Thanks also to Dr. Horace Dobbs at
International Dolphin Watch for reviewing
the information contained in this book**

You will find lots more about dolphins on these web sites

The Whale and Dolphin Conservation Society
www.wdcs.org

International Dolphin Watch
www.idw.org

Dolphin Diaries™

INTO THE BLUE

1

June 19 — nearly midnight.

I'm so excited! Tomorrow morning the dream comes true; we set sail for the adventure of a lifetime. After more than two years of hoping and planning, Dolphin Universe is finally happening. A whole year of watching and following dolphins!

Jody McGrath put down her pen and began to play with the tiny silver dolphin that hung from a fine silver chain around her neck. Although she knew it was unscientific to be superstitious, she couldn't help feeling that this little ornament, a present from her Italian grandmother, had brought them all luck.

Her parents were marine biologists who had long dreamed of taking Jody and her twin brothers on an oceangoing yacht, to observe as many different kinds of dolphins as possible. Their idea was to sail from their home base in Florida, tracking and recording dolphins, and hooking up with other researchers around the world. But although many organizations were interested in contributing to the project, Craig and Gina McGrath had found it hard to raise the vast amount of money it would take to turn their dream into reality.

Then one day the little silver dolphin had arrived in the mail, with a note from Nonna saying: *To bring you luck*. On that very same day had come an offer from PetroCo, a major oil corporation, to provide the remainder of the money needed to go ahead with Dolphin Universe.

One of her father's favorite sayings came to mind: "There's no such thing as a free lunch." Jody's smile faltered. She picked up her diary again and paged back to find what she'd written then:

Of course, there's a catch. If we want PetroCo's money, we have to take their pet scientist along, too, a guy called Dr. Jefferson Taylor. It doesn't make any sense, since Mom and Dad are happy to share whatever they find. Mom says it's because businessmen don't understand how science works and only trust people they pay themselves. Dad says they just want to make themselves look good, and it's better to have another hand on deck than have to put advertisements on the sails and name the boat after the oil company! No way! There couldn't be a better name for our boat than "Dolphin Dreamer"!

Jody wondered what Dr. Jefferson Taylor was like. It was strange to think that, although she still hadn't met him, after tomorrow she would be seeing him every day. She and her younger brothers were already friends with the rest of the crew: their captain, Harry Pierce; first mate, Cameron Tucker; the cook/engineer, Mei Lin

Zhong; and especially Maddie, Craig and Gina's assistant. From the beginning of the project, Maddie had felt like family.

Jody knew that Dr. Taylor had only recently arrived in Florida from California, but she wondered why he hadn't come to the party her parents had given last week to celebrate the launch of Dolphin Universe.

"I don't think Dr. Taylor is much of a party animal," her father had commented dryly.

Jody had pounced. "You don't like him!"

"I didn't say that, Jo," her father replied.

"He's a well-respected researcher," her mother said. "Careful, methodical . . ."

"Fussy," concluded Craig McGrath. "He probably didn't come to the party in case he got onion dip on his suit."

"Give the guy a chance!" Gina protested.

But Jody had seen her mother biting her lip to keep from laughing.

Oh, well, she thought. If my parents can put up with Dr. Jefferson Taylor, so can I. He can't be any worse than my annoying twin brothers.

Jody looked at the poster on her bedroom wall. It showed three bottle-nosed dolphins rising high out of the deep blue ocean, caught by the photographer just as they were flying through the air. Jody thought it showed what she loved best about these animals: their grace, natural beauty, freedom, and playfulness. But although it was her favorite picture, she was leaving it behind. She wouldn't need it on the boat, with real dolphins so close at hand.

It was thoughts like these that made sleep impossible. Jody shivered with excitement, impatient for the night to pass. She picked up her diary again. She began to flip through it, remembering how much had happened in the past year: helping her parents outfit the boat, learning to sail and scuba dive, taking courses in first aid and lifesaving, all on top of her regular schoolwork, projects, and time spent with friends.

There were only two blank pages left. She was eager to start a new volume on board *Dolphin Dreamer*. Maybe by then she would already have met her first wild dolphins! The idea of keeping a "dolphin diary" had come from her father. He had told her many times about the summer he'd spent as a boy with his grand-parents in Ireland, how he'd watched dolphins from the shore and kept a diary — which he'd shown her.

Jody had loved reading it. She had especially liked the sketches he had made of the dolphins and other wildlife. Craig McGrath could have been an artist if he hadn't become a scientist. A school project based on that diary had won a statewide competition, and Craig had gone on to study marine biology in college.

Jody had inherited her parents' fascination with dol-phins. To her, there was nothing more interesting on earth than the playful, intelligent, mysterious creatures who belonged to the group of sea mammals called cetaceans. The chance to travel with her parents and share in their research really was a dream come true.

Of course it meant leaving school and her friends, but she would stay in touch with them via the Internet. And there would be no escaping schoolwork while they were at sea, no matter what her little brothers might think! One reason Craig and Gina McGrath had chosen Maddie out of all the graduate students who had applied for the job of their assistant was that she had trained as a schoolteacher and would be able to make sure that Jody and her brothers didn't fall behind in their studies.

But this was the start of summer vacation, with more than two months of glorious freedom stretching ahead! Jody was getting out of school a little early because of Dolphin Universe — her friends would still be stuck there for another week. She had said good-bye to them today, and they had promised to think of her tomorrow.

A soft knock at the door made her jump. The door opened and Gina McGrath poked her head in. "Oh, sweetheart, you're not still up?"

Jody smiled ruefully. "I can't sleep!"

Gina smiled back and came in with her arms outstretched. Jody jumped up and gave her mother a big, warm hug.

"I know how you feel," Gina said softly in her ear. "But try to get some rest. We've got a busy day tomorrow."

"Okay, I'll try," Jody replied. "Good night, Mom."

She climbed into bed and dutifully shut her eyes, as her mother put out the light.

* * *

The next thing Jody knew, Sean and Jimmy were marching through her room making enough noise for a small army as they whistled and shrieked and shouted, "D-Day, D-Day, D-Day!"

Dolphin Day!

For once Jody was too excited to get mad at them. Today of all days she didn't want to sleep in. She jumped up and rushed to get ready.

By nine o'clock the McGraths were at the marina just outside Fort Lauderdale. It was a beautiful day, already hot beneath the blazing sun, but with enough breeze to stir the rigging. Jody loved the familiar clanking sound made by the metal lines knocking against the masts.

She hurried along the narrow wooden jetties among the many boats of all sizes, her heart thumping with excitement as she caught sight of the elegant *Dolphin Dreamer*. She — for some reason, boats are always called "she" — was a beautiful two-masted schooner. The gleaming white fiberglass prow was decorated

Our home for the next year!

with a picture of two leaping dolphins, painted by Jody's father.

Of course, the twins were there first, swarming over the decks with bloodthirsty cries, pretending to be pirates. Jody felt like yelling with excitement herself, but she managed to quietly follow her parents.

"Those boys," sighed Gina. "I hope they'll calm down."

"If they don't, I'll drop 'em in the drink. That'll cool 'em off," Craig said, shifting the weight of his bags.

"They'd probably love it. They'd love to walk the plank," said Jody.

"A plank!" Her father winced comically. "I knew we'd forgotten something!"

Harry Pierce was waiting for them on deck. He was a tall, strongly built man with a weathered face and thick, closely cropped graying hair and beard. Jody had heard he was divorced and had a daughter her age who lived with her mother in West Palm Beach. Jody guessed that he must miss his daughter very much.

"Welcome aboard," Harry said, in his gruff English accent. He reached out to take Jody's bags. "We're all present and accounted for now."

"Dr. Taylor's arrived?" asked Gina, as she clambered nimbly aboard.

"He's getting settled in down below," Harry replied. Then he turned to Sean and Jimmy, bellowing, "Come on, boys! Look lively!" But his kind blue eyes were twinkling.

Sean and Jimmy responded immediately, rushing to stand at attention.

"Help your parents and get these things stowed below," Harry commanded.

"Aye, aye, sir!" Both boys spoke at once.

Jody stared in astonishment as her brothers each grabbed a bag and took it away without the slightest protest.

"They never obey me like that," Craig complained.

"Ah, but you're not the captain," said Harry with a wink. "I've explained the rules of the sea to them."

Jody carried her own bags belowdecks to her small two-bunked cabin. Her brothers were sharing an identical cabin next door, but Jody was lucky enough to have her cabin all to herself.

She spent some time busily unpacking and stashing things neatly away in the wall lockers. Though not normally so tidy — there were always far more interesting things to do with her time than putting things away —

Jody had been told that it was crucial to be tidy in the cramped confines of a boat. In an emergency, everyone on board had to be able to move swiftly and not be at risk of tripping over things. And in a storm, anything not properly stowed away could become a dangerous flying object.

When she'd managed to unpack everything, Jody emerged from her cabin eager to find out what was going on. She spotted Maddie standing in front of an open storage locker, checking off items against a clipboard.

Maddie, an attractive young African-American woman, was dressed in a white T-shirt and shorts that made her dark good looks even more striking.

"Have we got everything we need?" Jody asked.

Maddie grinned at her. "We've got everything on the list — if that's not everything we need, don't blame me!"

Passing through the main cabin, Jody paused to peek into the tiny kitchen — or galley, as it was called. She found the ship's cook putting away fruit, vegetables, and other fresh produce bought that morning. "Hi, Mei Lin," she called.

The small, slender Chinese woman turned. "Good

morning, Jody. You look happy. Your face is shining like the sun."

Jody felt her grin grow even broader. "Really? Well, I am happy. This has got to be the absolutely best day of my life!"

A small frown line appeared on Mei Lin's face and she murmured something in Chinese.

"What's that?" Jody asked curiously.

"Don't tempt fate," Mei Lin replied. "In China, it's very bad luck to talk too proudly. It attracts bad luck."

"Oh, that's just a superstition," Jody said. But she realized, as she spoke, that she was fingering the little silver dolphin at her neck as if it could keep her luck good.

"Jody!" Her mother was calling from the deck. "There's someone here to see you!"

"Oh, I'd better go. See you later, Mei!" Wondering who it could be, Jody scrambled up the stairs. As soon as she emerged, blinking against the blazing sun, she heard the sound of many hands clapping, and voices cheering, "Jo-dee, Jo-dee!"

Her heart gave a thump. She shaded her eyes and gazed up at the dock. Her jaw dropped in astonishment. There, in a long line, were all thirty-two of her classmates, and Mrs. Kilpatrick, her teacher.

Eager hands stretched out to help her cross from the boat to the dock, and a babble of voices broke out as everyone tried to say something to her at once.

"Quiet, class, please! One at a time!" Mrs. Kilpatrick's voice carried, calming them a little.

Jody's best friend, Lindsay, stepped out of line to hug her.

Jody thought now of how hard it was going to be not to see Lindsay every day, not to hear her voice on the phone whenever she wanted. "I'm really going to miss you," she said. Her voice squeaked a little at the end, and she swallowed hard.

"Me, too," whispered Lindsay. "Promise you'll e-mail me whatever you're thinking about, not just the web-site stuff that everybody can read."

Jody nodded. "You, too. Keep me up on what's happening."

"Here, I got you a going-away present." Smiling, Lindsay handed Jody a silver-wrapped rectangle. "Go on, open it."

Jody tore off the paper to find a book with a sky-blue cover embossed with a silver dolphin. There was no title; when she opened it, she discovered it was full of blank, lined pages. A new dolphin diary — much more special than the plain notebooks she'd bought to use on the trip. A lump in her throat made it impossible to speak. Shutting her eyes against the threatening tears, Jody hugged her friend again.

From behind her came the unmistakable whooping cries of Sean and Jimmy, while from the other direction came answering shrieks from their friends.

"Sounds like Mrs. Bacon's class has arrived," said Lindsay. She grimaced as the two boys raced past. "I don't envy you being trapped on that boat with the gruesome twosome."

"I don't envy myself, either," Jody agreed. "But Dad says the experience will make them more responsible. He says they'll surprise me. I'll let you know if they do!" She rolled her eyes at Lindsay, who responded with the same disbelieving look, and suddenly they were giggling helplessly as they hugged each other one last time.

More people were arriving at the marina to see the launch of *Dolphin Dreamer*: friends, sponsors, well-wishers, and reporters, including a camera crew from the local TV station WDOL. The station logo included a leaping dolphin, and it had been one of the earliest supporters of Dolphin Universe.

Melissa Myers, a glamorous reporter Jody had seen on television, was standing just a few feet away, carefully positioned so that the camera shot would include *Dolphin Dreamer* in the background as she spoke about this historic occasion. Then she gave Gina and Craig a chance to say a few words.

"Dolphins are fascinating and intelligent creatures," Craig began, gazing earnestly into the camera. "And we humans have always been very interested in them. My wife and I feel that the ideal way to study creatures of the sea is by living there, among them. Ideally, we'd have a submarine as well as a sailboat, but I'm afraid that, even with the generous sponsorship of PetroCo, our budget didn't quite stretch to that!"

Jody grinned. Around her, people were laughing appreciatively.

Gina McGrath took over the explanation. "We hope that we'll learn a lot by observing and recording the wild dolphins that we meet on our journey," she added. "But we're just as interested in the work that other people are doing, and we've scheduled visits all over the world with people who are studying or working with dolphins." Gina paused for Craig to continue.

"It's our plan to create a network among the 'dolphin people' of the world," Craig said. "Everything that we discover will go into a Dolphin Universe database. By sharing this information, we hope that not just scientists, but ordinary people will benefit. Anyone who is interested can visit our website."

Jody was so caught up in listening to her parents that she didn't realize that someone was talking to her until she felt a soft shove against her arm. Jody looked up in surprise to see a girl about her own age, taller than she was, with wavy, shoulder-length fair hair and a bad-tempered expression on an otherwise pretty face.

"I said, which one is Harry Pierce's yacht?" the girl repeated irritably. "Or don't you know, either?"

"Do you mean *Dolphin Dreamer*?" Jody asked.

"I don't know what the thing is called," the girl replied impatiently. "But Harry Pierce is the captain."

Jody pointed. "That's our boat, right there."

The girl gave a put-upon sigh. "I didn't ask about *your* boat. I want my *father*'s yacht — my father is Captain Harry Pierce."

"Oh! You're . . ." Jody searched her mind for the name of Harry's daughter. Brittany, that was it. "You're Brittany?" she asked. "Gosh, it's nice to meet you at last! I'm Jody McGrath — Harry works for my parents. It's their boat, actually . . ." Then, seeing the girl's frown deepen, she felt awkward. This prickly stranger wouldn't thank her for pointing out her mistake. Jody rushed on. "But you've come to the right place. Harry will be so pleased that you've come to say good-bye! I'll go tell him."

Brittany stared at Jody with distaste. "I didn't come to say good-bye," she snapped. "For your information, I'm sailing with my father to the Bahamas."

Jody couldn't believe what she was hearing. "But — you can't — I mean — look, somebody's made a mistake."

18

"Not me." Brittany raised her chin haughtily. "My mother doesn't make mistakes. She's very well organized. She would never have gone off to Paris without me if she hadn't arranged for me to have this vacation with my father. I would have rather gone to Paris, frankly, but she said I owe it to my father. He never spends any time with me. I've hardly seen him in two years. Anyway, it's only for a few weeks." She reached down and hoisted a designer-label carryall onto her shoulder.

Jody noticed she had two other bags as well.

"If you're not going to go and tell my father I'm here, you could at least help me carry something," Brittany said impatiently. "Or do you expect me to get all of this onto the boat by myself?"

2

June 20 — 11:10 a.m.

It looks like I might have a new bunk mate. Her name is Brittany — and she's a pain in the neck! Harry seems to be phoning around half of Florida, trying to find someone who will look after his daughter — but so far, no luck.

Big surprise!

When she came on board, Brittany gave her father a letter. It was from Brittany's mother, saying sorry about the short notice, but she had to rush off to France (she didn't say why) and thought it would be great for Brittany and her father to spend some time together. She also said

20

that Harry's description of his new job sounded like "an ideal learning experience" for Brittany.

All this was news to Brittany. She didn't know anything about Dolphin Universe. Her mother had just told her she was having a vacation in the Bahamas!

Harry said that his ex-wife must think that he could sail their daughter to the Bahamas anytime, no problem. But of course he can't — he's on Dolphin Dreamer to do a job, like everyone else. And though Dolphin Dreamer will be stopping off at the Bahamas, it won't be for quite a while yet.

Then Mom and Dad said that if push came to shove, one more passenger wouldn't cause any hardship, and there was even a spare bunk! No hardship? Maybe not for them, but that "spare" bunk just happens to be in my cabin!

But they're right, of course. It would be a disaster for Dolphin Universe if Harry had to pull out at the last minute to look after Brittany. Better to put up with some spoiled little rich girl for a few weeks than have to delay the whole journey. At least, I hope it will only be for a few weeks. . . .

Just heard Harry call to cast off. That's that, then. He mustn't have found anyone to take Brittany. We're off — and Brittany is coming with us.

Jody closed her diary, put it under her pillow, and rushed back up on deck. The press and some of the crowd were still there, cheering and whistling. Jody's school friends had said their final good-byes and returned to school earlier, but Brittany's arrival had delayed the scheduled departure time.

As Jody glanced at Brittany, she felt a pang of guilt for not wanting her around. Brittany's mother had lied to her daughter and left her. That was awful.

Jody decided to go over and try to make Brittany feel more welcome. But as she got closer, Jody could hear Brittany was still arguing with her father.

"Why can't you take me to the Bahamas *now*?" Brittany asked Harry yet again, as *Dolphin Dreamer* motored gently through the maze of the marina, toward the open sea.

Cameron Tucker had taken over the helm to allow the captain a chance to talk to his daughter. Maddie and Craig were standing by, waiting for the order to hoist the sails.

Jody decided to keep out of the way. She had been looking forward to this day for so long, and all she wanted to do was to enjoy it. But she couldn't help hearing every miserable word.

"Dr. McGrath said your schedule is flexible. You're not expected down in the Florida Keys for a week — or even more. Why can't we go to the Bahamas right now? Please, Daddy. *Please* . . ." Brittany's voice was sweet and wheedling.

"Brittany, what would be the point of that? Your mother isn't there, and I can't leave the boat and stay with you. I have a job to do, whatever you or your mother may think," her father replied. He was fidgeting and kept looking away, obviously deeply uncomfortable.

"I can stay in a hotel. I've got my own credit card, you know. Mommy wouldn't mind. I can look after myself!" Brittany said, proudly tossing back her long fair hair as she said it.

"Don't be ridiculous," Harry snapped. "You're only

thirteen." He took a deep breath, then spoke more calmly. "And I know your mother feels the same — if she thought you could look after yourself, she wouldn't have left you with me."

"I wish she hadn't!" Brittany cried.

So do we all, Jody thought. She gripped the side rail and stared at a passing boat being mobbed by a flock of seagulls.

Harry kept his temper. He didn't say what Jody was sure he was thinking, that he agreed with his daughter, too. Instead he spoke quietly, trying to calm her. "I only wish your mother had been honest with both of us when — "

"Mommy *was* honest with *me*!" Brittany interrupted. "She's always told the truth. *You're* the liar! You *could* take me to the Bahamas — you *could*! — *and* stay with me there. I don't know why you won't! You just don't want to — you've always been horrible to me!" Jody thought she sounded near to tears.

"Brittany — " Her father sounded concerned now.

"Leave me *alone*!" With that finally shouted word, Brittany vanished belowdecks.

Her father stood there for a few seconds, then turned to walk slowly in Jody's direction. Jody saw that the captain, usually so calm and certain, looked upset.

Harry spotted her then, and his weather-beaten face went a shade redder. "Did you hear all that?" he sighed.

Jody blushed, too, and nodded.

"I hope she'll settle down," Harry said. "Of course, it's hard for her — she must be feeling let down by her mother. But most kids would love a chance to spend the summer sailing on *Dolphin Dreamer* — don't you think so?" he asked anxiously.

"I can't think of anything better," Jody said honestly.

He nodded, still uncertain. "I'd always hoped my daughter would like sailing. I wanted to teach her when she was younger, but her mother could never see the point of it." He sighed again, shook his head, and moved away.

Jody went to join her brothers, who were leaning over the side, too busy talking to each other to have noticed the argument. "What're you looking at?" she asked.

"Jellyfish!" they both shouted.

Jody looked down into the frothy water where a Portuguese man-of-war floated like a pink, crested football. Three other smaller ones clustered nearby. She was suddenly aware of silence: The drone of the engine had stopped.

"Ready!" called Cam.

With a flap and a sound like a sudden, deep breath, the sails caught the wind and filled. They were sailing! Jody listened to the slap of waves against the side of the boat, and felt the sun's heat on her bare arms. She leaned out into the wind, breathing in the fresh, salty tang of the air, and narrowed her eyes against the sun's glare.

The marina and the traffic around it were receding, and already the land seemed far away. Jody felt as if she had entered another world where petty problems — like Brittany's bad temper — didn't matter. She sighed deeply. The ocean was working its magic. If Brittany would come out, instead of lurking below, she would feel it, too. She was bound to cheer up and act better, Jody thought optimistically.

She looked around at the others. Harry had taken over at the helm, looking more relaxed in his role as

captain than he had as Brittany's father. Jody's own father was discussing something with Maddie, while
Cam, who stood nearby, was gazing at her with a wistful expression on his face.

Gina was rubbing sunscreen onto Sean's freckled
face, while Jimmy waited his turn. The twins were red-
headed and fair-skinned like their father, which meant
they had to take extra care in the sun. Jody thought she
was lucky to have inherited her mother's Mediterranean complexion, which tanned instead of burned.

Everyone was on deck except Mei Lin, Brittany, and
Dr. Jefferson Taylor. Jody still hadn't met their new
crew member. In the uproar surrounding Brittany's unexpected arrival she had forgotten all about him. She
wondered where he was.

Just then, like an answer to her question, a pinkish,
balding head poked up out of the hold, reminding her of
a turtle coming out of its shell. After a cautious look
around, the owner of the head emerged onto the deck.
He was middle-aged and overweight, puffing a little, as if
even pulling himself up the few steps was more exercise than he was used to. Dark glasses hid his eyes, and

he was smartly dressed in a navy-blue short-sleeved shirt, white trousers, and expensive deck shoes.

"Dr. Taylor," Gina called. "Please come and join us. Can I offer you some sunscreen?"

Jefferson Taylor gazed around and touched the top of his bare head. "I can tell that I'll need a hat."

"Yes, a hat is a good idea if you're going to be in the sun for very long," Gina replied. "But you could sit there, by Jody, in the shade. I don't think you've met my children yet, have you? That's my daughter, Jody, and these two are Sean and Jimmy."

Dr. Taylor nodded rather stiffly. "Pleased to meet you, Jody. And you . . . er . . . boys."

"I'll bet you can't tell us apart," crowed Jimmy.

"I don't approve of betting," Dr. Taylor said rather primly. "However, I am a scientist, and the essence of science is observation." He whipped off his dark glasses, revealing a pair of brown eyes with surprisingly long, thick lashes. He thrust his head forward, right into the twins' faces, making Sean flinch, although Jimmy held his ground and stared back.

Dr. Taylor just looked, silent and unblinking, for several long seconds. "As I thought," he said. "There are distinct differences in the freckle pattern. Anyone who cared to look closely could tell you apart. Easy to miss at a distance, of course. I suspect behavioral differences would be of more practical use."

"What does that mean?" demanded Jimmy.

"In this case I would guess that you, Sean, are slightly more cautious. And you, Jimmy, are the troublemaker!" Dr. Taylor emphasized his words by pointing his stubby forefinger.

Gina burst out laughing. "You've got that one right!"

Dr. Taylor smiled, replaced his dark glasses, and turned away. "Of course. Now, if you'll excuse me, I'm going to get my hat."

The boys stared after him, mouths open. Jody couldn't hold it back any longer and began to giggle uncontrollably.

"Differences in the freckle pattern," Gina murmured, and then she began to laugh again. "Maybe we should call them Spotty and Splotch?" She leaned against Jody, and they both giggled hysterically as the two boys scowled.

Jody leaned over the side of the boat and gazed at the seemingly endless expanse of flat blue water. Almost two hours had gone by, they were well out to sea, and she had yet to see a single dolphin. She felt bored and disappointed.

It just didn't seem possible. More often than not when she'd gone sailing with her parents they'd seen dolphins. Sometimes it was just a leaping figure in the distance, but often they would swim right up to the boat. They weren't shy creatures and there were lots of them in the coastal waters around Florida — where they were now. So where were they all?

"You know what they say about a watched pot?" Jody turned to find her mother smiling at her sympathetically.

Jody sighed. "They say it never boils — but that's not true. The water will boil when it gets hot enough, no matter how many people are watching."

"Ooh, that sounds like a scientific observation worthy of Dr. Jefferson Taylor!" Gina McGrath's dark eyes twinkled with mischief.

Jody couldn't help laughing. "It's just so frustrating! I've been looking forward to this day for so long, and . . ." She shrugged, unable to find the words to express her disappointment.

Jody saw that her mother understood.

"I know, sweetie," Gina said. "We all feel the same. Luckily, we've got as much time as it takes for the dolphins to find us. It's a funny thing, but I've found that when you're looking hardest for dolphins is when you don't find them. It's when you're thinking about something else that they suddenly pop up. So why don't you think about something else . . . like the skyscraper of sandwiches that Mei Lin is putting together down in the galley? If we don't start eating, we're going to have a storage problem!"

As soon as her mother mentioned the word "sandwiches," Jody realized how hungry she was. "Well, you can count on me to help!"

Gina touched her shoulder. "What would really be helpful would be for you to go tell Brittany it's time for lunch."

Jody's heart sank. "Sure," she agreed.

Jody felt apprehensive as she turned away. She hoped the other girl would have cooled down by now, but it seemed like a bad sign that she was still sulking in their cabin rather than coming out and trying to make friends.

Jody made herself sound cheerful as she breezed in. "Hi, Brittany, Mom says — "

"Don't you believe in knocking?" Brittany, huddled in a corner of one of the bunks, glared angrily.

"Not on the door of my own cabin," Jody said, frowning.

Brittany groaned. "Oh, that's just perfect — I have to share a room!"

"Yeah, I was pretty thrilled when you turned up, too." As Jody spoke, she saw how red Brittany's eyes and nose were, and realized she must have been crying. She felt ashamed of herself for sniping at the poor girl. It must be awful to feel nobody wanted you. "I just came to tell you it's lunchtime." Jody spoke gently now. "Why don't we take our sandwiches on deck? Maybe we'll get lucky and see some dolphins."

Brittany snorted. "What is it with dolphins all the time?"

"Didn't your dad explain?" Jody asked.

Brittany shrugged. "About your parents' job, yeah. I know they study dolphins, and they're going to be traveling around the world meeting other people who study dolphins, and gathering all the information together and stuff like that. Boring! Why should I care about it? *My* dad's a sailor, but that doesn't mean I have to like being stuck on a boat for weeks and weeks!" Her eyes glittered with the threat of more tears.

Jody sighed. "Fair enough," she said. "But I love dolphins because they're wonderful, not just because my parents study them for a living. I'm part of Dolphin Universe, too. I've been working to help make it happen for more than a year." She leaned forward, eager to make Brittany understand.

But the other girl only snorted again. "You're just a kid — I'll bet you're younger than me."

"I'm twelve — the same age my father was when he first started studying dolphins," Jody defended herself. "He says — "

"Oh, who cares," said Brittany abruptly, getting to her feet. "Did you say it was lunchtime? I'm starving."

Brittany's rudeness smarted, but Jody tried not to mind. When they reached the galley, she introduced Mei Lin to Brittany. "Mei's our cook and chief engineer."

"That sounds like a weird combination," Brittany said, her mouth twisting with scorn.

"Well, I was an engineering student back in Beijing," Mei Lin explained patiently. "But when I came to America, I couldn't afford to continue my studies. My English was terrible then, too," she added, making a face. "But better now," she smiled, as she began to slice a loaf of bread into thin, even slices.

She continued her story. "First, I got a job as a cook at the marina, where I got to know Harry. But I was always helping people fix their cars and, as word got around, people asked me to fix their boats, too. Then Harry came into the marina one day and told me about this job. I thought it sounded like fun!"

Mei Lin looked down at the pile of buttered bread in front of her. "What kind of sandwiches would you like? Tuna, cheese, ham, or peanut butter and jelly?"

Brittany seemed to relax at Mei Lin's soft manner. She asked for tuna, even giving the cook a quick smile as she thanked her.

Jody and Brittany took their tuna sandwiches and large plastic cups full of iced tea onto the deck. The afternoon was hot and still. The boat did not seem to be moving at all. Cam was at the helm, a bored expression on his face.

"Any dolphins yet?" Jody asked him.

"Nope." Cam shrugged his broad shoulders.

"Have you tried knocking on the side?" Jody asked. Then she added for Brittany's benefit, "Dolphins are attracted by sound, so if there are any in the area they might come over to see what the noise was about."

Cam grinned, his even teeth brilliantly white in his tanned, handsome face. "Oh, I leave all that technical stuff to the experts, you and your parents. Harry just hired me to help him sail the boat — even when there's not a breath of wind."

"Why don't you use the motor?" Brittany asked.

"No point wasting fuel," Cam said. "It's a mighty big ocean, and we're not exactly going anywhere anyway."

Brittany frowned. "What do you mean, we're not going anywhere?"

"Jody could probably explain that better than me," he said.

Jody felt her stomach clench nervously as Brittany looked at her. She remembered Brittany's argument with her father that morning, and didn't want to stir it up again. She tried to change the subject. "Cam, aren't you having lunch?"

"I'm okay, Jody, thanks. Maddie's bringing me something." Cam gave her a wink.

"What did he mean, Jody?" Brittany demanded.

"Just that we're not going straight to a place," Jody replied. "We're looking for dolphins. If we find a group of dolphins we'll probably follow them for a while."

"And if we don't?" Brittany glared at Jody as if she had her to blame for her troubles.

"Oh, we're bound to!" A high, wailing cry made Jody break off and look up. She saw a flock of seagulls over-

36

head, calling to one another. One flew very low, nearly brushing her head with its wings, and Jody ducked.

Brittany laughed. "That bird doesn't seem to like you," she said.

"I think it wants food," Jody replied. She tore off a bit of crust and tossed it into the air. Immediately a shrieking, midair bird battle erupted.

"You shouldn't have done that," Cam said. "Now they'll *never* leave us alone!"

Three birds landed in a row on the side of the boat, very close to the girls. They stretched their necks, turned their heads, and peered at Jody and Brittany with bright, greedy eyes. Three or four other birds swooped overhead.

Cam stood up and waved his arms aggressively. "Go on, get outta here, shoo!"

The seagulls on the side left their perch, but their places were immediately taken by others.

"Eat up quickly," Cam advised. "Those greedy birds won't leave until there's not a scrap of food left in sight."

"I'm going inside," said Brittany, and left.

Feeling a little foolish, Jody wolfed down her sandwich.

"One ham on rye with mustard, and a pickle on the side," Maddie sang out, emerging from below. She held a blue plastic plate high above her head, balanced on the palm of one hand like a truck-stop waitress.

Jody opened her mouth to warn her about the birds, but it was already too late. Seeing its chance, the nearest gull left its perch and swooped on the sandwich, seizing one corner and flapping away with the top slice of bread. Shrieking angrily, the others followed it into the sky, all struggling for a share.

Maddie stared after them, openmouthed. She had only just managed to keep hold of the plate. "Well," she said. "That's one they never warned us about in waitress school! How do you feel about an open-faced sandwich?"

Cam laughed and took the plate to examine the leavings. "Fine — if I get a chance to eat it! Maybe I'd better go below for my lunch . . . if you ladies wouldn't mind taking the helm?"

"Oh, I think I could probably manage on my own at *this* speed," said Maddie, taking his place.

The seagulls returned to circle the boat briefly but, sensing there was nothing else to steal, they soon flew away.

The rest of the day passed slowly and uneventfully. Jody even found herself yawning, tempted by sleep in the peaceful heat of the day, but she was determined not to give up her dolphin watch. The thought of another encounter with Brittany also kept her on deck until Harry finally announced that, as there was so little wind, they might as well take in the sails and put down the anchor for the night.

Jody was disappointed that her first day of dolphin-watching hadn't been more of a success, but dinner was soon announced and she went below to join the others.

Mei Lin had made tagliatelle bolognese. "In honor of Dr. Gina," she said.

Craig pretended to be miffed. "What about honoring the Irish side of the family?"

The cook looked worried, obviously not realizing he was teasing. "Oh, Dr. Craig! Please excuse me! I understand what is Italian cooking. But I don't understand what is Irish cooking — "

"Mei, I was only teasing," said Craig. "This is a wonderful meal."

"But I am serious," Mei said. "I would like to learn how to cook Irish food."

"In that case, you'll have to find somebody else to teach you, because I'm the Microwave Man," Craig said with a grin.

"Shall we have some music?" suggested Harry as everyone started eating. He hovered over the CD collection that had made up a major part of his luggage. "In keeping with the Italian theme of the evening, I suggest *La Traviata*."

"Oh, Daddy, not one of those awful operas! It's not even sung in English!" moaned Brittany.

"You don't have to understand the words to enjoy the music," Harry said firmly.

Jody paused with her fork halfway to her mouth as the captain's mention of music triggered a memory.

She knew that the Ancient Greeks had discovered that dolphins had a love for music. She had read a story once about dolphins being attracted by the playing of flutes. And for the past year at school she had been learning to play the recorder, an old-fashioned wind instrument a little like a flute.

All of those thoughts came together to give Jody a brilliant idea, and she couldn't wait to try it out. "May I please be excused?"

Her mother looked at her, surprised. "There's still dessert to come."

"I know, but there's something I want to do before it gets dark," Jody replied. She looked pleadingly at her mother, who nodded permission.

Jody dashed back to her cabin and dug out her recorder, then hurried up on deck.

Outside, the sun had set, but there was still light in the sky. It was twilight, that hazy, blue hour that was Jody's favorite time of day. It was when the air seemed most like water, when she could imagine herself diving upward into it, to fly as easily as swimming. Away from the noise and artificial lights of the land, the atmosphere was peaceful and dreamlike, a time and place where wishes could come true.

Jody settled down, cross-legged, on the foredeck and raised the recorder to her lips. She played the first tune she'd learned and then stopped, peering out at the water for some response. Nothing. She tried "Greensleeves." Then the "Skye Boat Song." Still nothing.

Jody decided to tackle something a bit more difficult — one of the classical pieces her teacher had given her to work on while she was away. She didn't want to go below for the sheet music, so she played from memory. It was a struggle to get the notes right. When she made a mistake, she started over again. Then again.

She was concentrating so hard on the music that she forgot all about her reason for playing it. Utterly absorbed, she came to the end and as she was sitting quietly, the silence was suddenly broken by a sound like a squeaky door hinge.

Jody caught her breath. The gentle creaking noise came again, rising in pitch, almost like a question. She stood up and leaned over the starboard bow, straining

42

her eyes to see. Nearly all the light had drained out of the day by now, and although she thought she saw a dark shape in the water, she couldn't be absolutely sure — until it leaped straight out of the water, and she saw the unmistakable curving bulk of a dolphin, so close she could almost have reached out and touched it.

As it went under, a spray of seawater showered her. Jody laughed with delight. The dolphin poked its head up. It seemed to be smiling at her. Jody knew this was just the shape of the beak and mouth — all bottle-nosed dolphins look as if they're smiling, even when they're unhappy. All the same, she felt this one really *was* happy. She couldn't help feeling it was as pleased as she was by this encounter.

"Did you like the music?" she asked. "I was playing it for you. Do you want some more?"

The dolphin responded with a whistle followed by a series of rapid clicks and pops.

"Okay." Jody raised her recorder to her lips and played the passage she had struggled with before. This time, it came out perfectly.

When she'd finished, there was a moment of silence. Jody gazed down and the dark gleam of the dolphin's eye met her own. She felt a shock of connection. She *knew* this dolphin was as curious about her as she was about him. Her heart pounded with excitement.

The dolphin suddenly arced away from the boat, diving through the waves.

"Oh, don't go!" Jody cried. But as soon as she spoke, she realized her new friend wasn't leaving at all. He

Dancing Dolphin

44

came racing back again, expressing his happiness through speed and a series of exhilarating leaps. Jody felt like doing the same thing. She wanted to jump right into the water with him.

"Jody, we're waiting for you. Don't you want dessert?" It was her mother, standing in the hatchway.

"Mom, there's a dolphin here!" Jody called back excitedly.

Spray showered her as he darted away.

"It's too dark to see," Gina objected.

Jody held her breath, listening for the sound of the dolphin — but he had vanished into the night.

"Come in now, Jo. Time to look for dolphins again after the sun comes up," her mother said firmly.

"I'll be there in a minute," Jody called, and saw her mother go back inside.

The seconds ticked by as Jody stood alone on the deck, hoping the dolphin would return. But there was no sight or sound of her new friend.

"Please come back tomorrow," she whispered, and then, full of excitement and hope for the morning, she went below.

Dolphin Diaries

June 20 — bedtime.

My first sighting!

1. Bottle-nosed Dolphin (Tursiops truncatus)

Dark gray, with lighter gray underside. No obvious markings or scars noticed. Age unknown (Dad thinks fairly young, probably over four — since otherwise he'd be traveling with his mother's group — but under ten). Sex unknown (but I think he's a male).

3

June 21 — 8 a.m.

He was still there this morning. I came up on deck first thing to see, and he was swimming around the boat. When he saw me, he came right up out of the water and practically stood on his tail. It was the weirdest thing — it felt like he had been looking for me and was really excited to find that I hadn't disappeared overnight. Wouldn't it be funny if he's studying us, just like we're studying him? Maybe when he gets back to his pod they'll be talking about "Human Universe" and complaining about how hard it is to study creatures that have to stay on dry land and almost never get into the water.

" Jody, your breakfast is waiting," Gina called from the hatchway.

Jody looked up from where she was writing in her diary on the deck. Her mother sounded exasperated. Jody realized this was probably not the first time she'd been called. Still, she couldn't pull herself away from the fascination of her new friend. "Mom, there's a dolphin here," she explained.

Gina joined her daughter and gazed down at the dolphin who was swimming in lazy circles just off the port bow. "How many are there?" she asked.

"Just this one," Jody replied. "He was here last night." She couldn't stop smiling.

"And no sign of any others?" Gina asked. "That's odd. Dolphins nearly always travel in groups, even if they're very small ones. You don't often meet lone dolphins, especially not away from a harbor."

"Isn't he great?" Jody sighed happily.

Gina pursed her lips thoughtfully. "I wonder how he'd respond if one of us got into the water."

Jody caught her breath with excitement. "Oh, Mom, could I?"

"I meant me, honey," Gina replied. She bit her lip rue-fully. "I'm sorry, but this seems like a good opportunity to check out the camera and get some footage off to WDOL. Then if there are any glitches we should be able to straighten them out before we sail too far away from Florida."

Jody wasn't giving up just yet. "Okay, but I could come in *with* you, couldn't I?" she said eagerly. She had received her junior scuba diving certificate three months earlier and couldn't wait to use her new skill. "I promise I won't get in the way, and —"

"Another time." Her mother sounded firm.

"But why?" Jody tried not to whine, but it was so dis-appointing.

"Several reasons," her mother replied briskly. She ticked them off on her fingers. "One, we might scare him off. Lone dolphins are usually fine with lone swim-mers, but two might seem too many. Two, although dolphins aren't known to be aggressive toward people, there have been the occasional incidents when people have gotten hurt. Remember, this is a wild animal. Three, accidents can happen, and even though you know how to handle yourself in the water, I'd be tempted to keep an eye on you when I need to concentrate on my work."

Jody sighed and gave in to the inevitable. "Okay."

"You'll have your chance soon," Gina promised. "Now, come down and have something to eat."

Everyone was enthusiastic about Gina's plan — everyone, that was, except Brittany.

Her eyes narrowed and her face tightened with displeasure. "You mean we're just going to sit here while Dr. McGrath takes pictures of some fish?"

"It's a dolphin, Brittany," Jody corrected her. "Dolphins are mammals, not fish."

"I don't care what it is," Brittany snapped rudely. "I thought we were supposed to be sailing to Key West, then going on to the Bahamas. What is the deal? If it doesn't matter where we are, why don't we just go to the Bahamas now? There must be loads of dolphins there."

Her father, who was sipping a second cup of coffee, frowned, then said slowly and clearly, "Brittany, I've already explained to you. *Dolphin Dreamer* is not your private pleasure cruiser. This is a scientific expedition, and our schedule is set by the scientists, not a spoiled teenager."

Brittany jumped up from her seat. "Thanks a lot," she shouted. "I never asked to come with you. I don't want to be here. So why don't you just drop me off some-where . . . anywhere . . . the sooner the better!"

Jody saw Harry clench his jaw tensely, then take a deep breath and relax his face again. "Brittany, you know very well why not," he said calmly. "I hope we're not going to have to go through this every day. The sooner you accept the situation and make the best of it, the better."

"The sooner I get away from you, the better!" Brit-tany cried. "I want to go home!" Then she burst into tears and stumbled out of the main cabin in the direc-tion of her cabin.

There was an embarrassed silence.

Finally, Harry Pierce spoke. "I'm sorry about that," he said. "Brittany's had a bit of a rough time what with her mother and me splitting up. . . ." He waved a hand vaguely, looking miserable.

"Have you been able to get in touch with Brittany's mother?" Gina asked, her voice gentle.

Harry shook his head. "Her cell phone is still switched off. Maybe she didn't take it with her. I've left an urgent message for her at the hotel in Paris where she usually stays, and also a long e-mail explaining how impossible this situation is for all of us. I'm sure she'll be in touch very soon, to make some other arrangements, but in the meantime . . . I'm afraid you're stuck with Brittany."

"You mean she's stuck with us," said Craig gently. "Life will be easier for us all if we can convince her that we're really not so bad. Jody, you'll have to be our goodwill ambassador. Try to make friends with her."

Jody nodded unhappily, wondering how to get through to somebody who wouldn't listen, somebody who didn't care about anything she found interesting, and who had made it clear she didn't like her.

"Now let's get this show on the road," said Craig briskly, and the mood in the room changed to one of excitement.

Up on deck, Gina pulled on a wetsuit. Although the water was warm, it would protect her from jellyfish stings and other potential hazards. While Jody watched, wishing she was the one suiting up, Craig helped her mother fit on her weight belt, buoyancy vest, and dive computer.

Craig then checked the air gauge. "You've got a full tank, but let's keep this first time down shallow and short," he suggested. "Half an hour okay?"

"Sure." Gina grinned, putting fins on her feet. "I don't want to wear out my welcome with our finny friend."

Maddie was lowering the hydrophone — an underwater microphone — over the side of the boat into the water. The object was to record dolphin sounds, but the hydrophone often picked up lots more. Jody had been surprised to learn that the underwater world was far from silent; a lot of fish made noises.

Cameron emerged from the hatchway carrying the video monitor. "Where d'you want this, boss?" he asked Craig.

Gina arched an eyebrow. "You're going to be watching what I film on deck?"

"Naw, there's a Miami Dolphins game I want to see," Craig said, straight-faced.

Jody giggled and Gina laughed, too. "Well, I hope we don't find out the hard way that the monitor's not as waterproof as the camera!"

Harry glanced at the small flags called telltales fluttering in the breeze, and then peered over the side where the water was growing choppier. "Wish we'd had a bit of this wind yesterday," he said. "But you'll be all right."

"Just don't splash too much," said Craig. "I hate being disturbed when I'm watching football."

Gina made a face at him, then fitted her mask snugly on her face and put the air regulator into her mouth. She entered the water with a great stride off the dive platform. Then, when Gina had signaled that she was okay, Maddie handed her the camera, in its bright yellow waterproof housing.

Jody's heart pounded with excitement as she leaned over the edge and watched her mother's gentle descent below the surface. Sean and Jimmy jostled for position beside her, but Jody hardly noticed. She was watching the silvery stream of bubbles rising up as her mother sank lower. In her mind, she, too, had left the surface for the beautiful, mysterious underwater world. But the way the sunlight hit the waves, and the darkness of the deeper water, made it hard to follow her mother's progress. As Gina descended farther, she became a murky figure to Jody. Jody could follow the rising stream of bubbles only with her eyes, focus on the bright yellow case of the camera, and try to imagine her mother's movements.

Jody gazed around in search of the dolphin, wondering what he would make of this visitor to his world. He had been cruising in gentle arcs around *Dolphin Dreamer* all morning, only occasionally zooming off at a high speed. Jody wondered if he was inviting them to give chase for a game of tag. Dolphins were known to be playful creatures. But where was he now? Then she saw the large, smooth, streamlined shape of the dolphin streaking along beneath the surface, heading straight for Gina.

Jody caught her breath, suddenly nervous. It was such a big animal! Seeing it approaching her mother, she knew that all it would take was a careless switch of the tail, or an accidental bump, for damage to be done. If the air regulator got pulled out of Gina's mouth, or if she were knocked unconscious, she'd be in serious trouble.

But just as it seemed that the dolphin was about to hit Gina, he veered away, shooting past her with a simple flex of his powerful body. Jody let out a relieved breath, seeing that there had never been anything to worry about. The dolphin had been in total control. It must have known to the inch — or less — how close he could come without actually touching his visitor.

"Echolocation, remember?" said her dad, as if he'd read her mind. "Even in deep, murky water, dolphins don't bump into things."

Jody nodded.

"Echo-what?" said Sean, frowning.

"Echolocation," Craig repeated, smiling. "It means finding out where things are by using sound instead of sight."

Sean still looked confused.

Their father explained further. "Dolphins find their way by making a sound that bounces off objects around them and comes back to the dolphin as an echo. From hearing this *echo* the dolphin knows the *location* of whatever the sound waves have hit."

"I get it," said Jimmy, nodding. "It's like bats using radar."

"Cool," said Sean. But he still looked puzzled. "Are dolphins *blind*?"

"Oh, no," said Craig. "It's just that sound is more useful to them underwater — but they can see all right! Have a look at that one, eyeing your mother!"

Jody gazed down into the water to where her mother was hovering, kicking her fins against the currents to stay in roughly one place as she aimed the camera at the dolphin.

He was watching her with what looked like friendly interest, lying horizontally in the water, barely moving; facing Gina at first, then turning to lie on one side and gaze at her with one eye.

Jody wished she could get a better view, but with the

wind chopping the surface, and her mother following the dolphin farther away from the side of the boat, it was hard to see anything in detail.

"Hey, kids, you ought to come see this — your mom's getting some great pictures!"

At their father's call, Jody, Sean, and Jimmy all left their spots at the side to watch on the monitor instead.

The dolphin's head almost filled the screen as he seemed to smile directly into the camera. Jody caught her breath in wonder. Her mother must be so close to him! Close enough to touch . . .

As she thought this, the dolphin loomed larger as the camera drew even closer, and then Gina's hand came into view. Jody held her breath, watching as the hand reached for the animal, but before contact could be made, the dolphin slipped away. He didn't go far. He might not be willing to be touched, but he was obviously too curious about Gina to leave.

The dolphin circled, then rolled on his side. Then he rose up until he appeared to be standing on his tail. Jody wondered if he was imitating Gina's upright, two-legged stance. It was annoying not to be able to see everything. She wished she could be there, under-water, alongside her mother.

"It would be more interesting if we could see Mom, too, and know what the dolphin was reacting to," she said. "Somebody else should be underwater with them."

"And I think I know who you think that somebody

Mom meets Apollo

should be," her father said teasingly. He patted her shoulder. "You'll get your chance, honey, don't worry. I didn't pay for your scuba diving lessons for nothing!"

Dr. Taylor had been standing back, just watching without comment. Now he said in his rather formal way, "May I ask what you are hoping to learn by this exercise?"

"Excuse me?" said Craig.

"Why is Dr. McGrath filming this particular dolphin?" Dr. Taylor asked.

"Because it's there," Craig said jokingly. Then, with an expression almost as solemn as Jefferson Taylor's round, moonlike face, he went on. "I'm sorry, I didn't mean to be flippant, but didn't you read the Dolphin Universe prospectus? We are here to record our observations on all the dolphins we come across. Our video footage, still photos, and sound recordings will then form a database, which will be available to all interested researchers."

Dr. Taylor rubbed his chin. "Ah, yes . . ." He seemed

to be thinking hard. "Er, I will be conducting research, too, while we're at sea, of course. PetroCo will expect me to contribute something special. Yes, indeed . . ." Nodding to himself, the scientist wandered away.

Jody saw her father roll his eyes, and she was sure that Maddie was hiding a grin as she bent to turn up the sound on the hydrophone.

Although the meeting between her mother and the dolphin had appeared to be silent from Jody's position above, now she could hear a steady stream of low clicks and occasional high-pitched squeaks. These sounds wouldn't carry into the air above, but no doubt her mother would hear them in the water.

All too soon, the half hour was over, and Gina returned slowly to the surface. The dolphin followed, poking his head up through the waves and whistling at her.

Pulling away her mouthpiece, Gina spoke to the dolphin, "Don't worry, you haven't seen the last of me!" She handed the camera to Craig, and the twins stretched out eager hands to help by taking her fins before she climbed up the ladder back onto the boat. "I could have stayed down a lot longer, you know," she said wistfully.

"Sometimes I think you were a dolphin in a previous life," Craig teased.

"This wind is too good to miss," said Harry. "Do you need to stay here any longer, or can we get under sail?"

"That's fine with me," said Gina.

Craig nodded at the video equipment. "Just let us get this stuff down below. Maddie, we'd better pull in the hydrophone, too, if we're going to be traveling at any speed." He turned back to his wife. "The picture's beautifully clear. Wait'll you see it."

Jody hung over the side and gazed at the dolphin. He seemed to be still waiting for something. "That was my mom," she said. "Next time it'll be me, I promise." She turned, tensing as she saw Brittany come lurching onto the deck.

"I feel awful," the girl groaned to her father. She looked pale, almost greenish. "Can't you make the boat lie still?"

"It'll feel smoother once we're actually sailing, love,"

Harry promised her. "We'll get going soon. . . . Wait! Where are you going?" he called, as Brittany stumbled away again.

"Back to my cabin to lie down," Brittany replied.

"You'll feel worse if you go below," he warned her. "Honestly, love, the best thing if you're feeling seasick is to stay on deck, in the fresh air."

"You'd better not be making that up," Brittany muttered.

Jody decided she didn't want to be around if Brittany was going to keep complaining or start being sick. With one more fond look at the friendly dolphin, she went below.

She found her parents in the main cabin with Dr. Taylor and Maddie, getting ready to review the video.

"There, look, he's mimicking my posture," Gina said. "Now, you'll see the camera angle change . . . that's because I rolled onto my front to see if he'd do the same — and he did. He was great. Even though he wouldn't let me touch him, he was really interacting with me."

"We should think of a name for him," said Jody.

Dr. Taylor looked surprised. "Oh, surely not?" he said.

"What's wrong with that?" demanded Gina. "It's a good suggestion."

"Well, people name their pets," Dr. Taylor replied, "but that animal is not a pet. If you give it a name, you'll start imagining that it has a personality. Very unscientific."

"I'm sorry, Dr. Taylor, I have to disagree," Gina said. "Scientists who study animals often give them names."

Despite her mother's careful tone, Jody could tell that Gina was annoyed.

"It makes it easier to talk about them without confusion," Gina continued. "I know we're only talking about one dolphin now, but in a few days —"

"But surely numbers would do just as well for identification and wouldn't encourage the wrong attitude toward the dolphins," Dr. Taylor argued heatedly. "They are scientific subjects to us, after all. They're not our friends."

Now it was Jody's turn to disagree. "As far as I'm concerned, dolphins *can* be friends."

"Personally, I've always liked names better than numbers, and most people find them easier to remember," said Craig easily.

Jody smiled gratefully at her father.

"And I think Jody should choose a name, since she was the first to meet him," Craig concluded. "So do you have any ideas, honey?"

Delighted, Jody gazed at the dolphin on-screen. The underwater camera offered her a closer, clearer view than she'd had yet. For the first time, she noticed that the gray tones of his skin were not quite as uniform as they first appeared. There was a distinctive marking on the upper right side of his snout; an odd, curving shape that reminded her vaguely of an old-fashioned harp.

The harp made Jody think of music: of her recorder, which had first attracted the dolphin to the boat; and of the Ancient Greeks with their flutes. In the fifth grade, her class had done a unit on Greek mythology. She remembered the stories about the gods, and how each god had special characteristics. Suddenly, the perfect name slid into her mind . . .

"Apollo," she said.

"Apollo," Craig repeated, looking pleased. "The Greek god of music. That's right — aren't there stories that he took the form of a dolphin sometimes?"

Gina nodded. "Well done, Jody. It's a good name."

Dr. Jefferson Taylor said nothing.

4

"Excellent. I think we can send it to the TV station just as it is," Gina decided, after reviewing the underwater video footage she had taken of Apollo.

Dr. Taylor cleared his throat loudly. "Ahem . . . I think *I* should say something on the tape," he said.

Jody saw the surprise on her mother's face at this suggestion.

"Even *I'm* not doing an introduction," Gina explained. "The pictures speak for themselves. And the station manager at WDOL said they only want a minute or two of something light to tack onto the end of the news."

Dr. Taylor looked uncomfortable, then persisted. "I really do think I should mention that your video was made possible by my company's sponsorship," he said. "That's what I'm here for," he ended, looking a little embarrassed.

Jody saw her parents exchange a resigned glance, knowing that they couldn't really refuse.

"All right, I'll tape you," Gina agreed reluctantly. "But we'll have to keep it short. And the TV station may cut it anyway," she warned.

Dr. Taylor pretended not to hear this comment. "Now, where should I sit?" he asked, nervously straightening his collar and smoothing the little hair he had left. "Which do you think is my best angle?" he asked.

Jody couldn't stand to watch anymore. She had an idea. "Hey, Mom, is it all right if I use the new digital camera to take some pictures of Apollo? Then I can post them on the website."

Although she was looking strained from dealing with Dr. Taylor, Gina managed to smile at Jody. "Of course, sweetie," she replied. "You know how to use it."

"Just don't drop it in the water," Craig warned playfully, as Jody got the camera from its storage compartment.

"As if!" Jody answered.

She climbed up through the hatchway onto the deck, keeping a firm grip on the camera. She was careful where she put her feet, knowing how easy it would be to lose her balance on the unsteady surface of the rapidly moving boat. But though Jody was prepared for the changes underfoot as the boat lifted and fell against the waves, there was no way she could have been prepared for Brittany.

The other girl came charging across the deck, her face red with anger. Her seasickness had clearly disappeared. Jody saw that she was headed for the hatchway, and quickly moved to one side, out of her way.

As Brittany passed Jody, she gave her a deliberate, hard shove.

The push knocked Jody off balance. She would normally have kept on her feet by flinging out her arms, but she was clutching the camera tightly in both hands, and so she fell heavily onto her backside. "Ow!" she cried.

Cam hurried over to her. "Are you all right?" he asked, bending down to help her up, concern in his green eyes.

Jody took the hand he offered and got back onto her feet. "I'm okay, thanks," she said. She was more shocked than sore.

"That girl is a menace," said Cam angrily. "Yeah, I saw what she did." He shook his head. "Harry is trying his best. But she's impossible. If he tells her to do something, she'll go and do the opposite. I don't know how he keeps his temper."

Jody sighed, wondering how they were going to manage. "Somebody has to make her see that this boat is too small for her to go around acting like a three-year-old," she said.

"And soon!" Cam agreed, his voice grim.

"Is Apollo still around?" Jody asked, eager to change the subject.

"Who?" Cam looked puzzled.

"Oh, sorry," Jody smiled. "The dolphin — I've named him Apollo," she explained.

Cam shrugged. "Not sure," he said. "I've been busy with the equipment."

Jody went to the side of the deck and looked out over the sea. The wind whipped her hair about and chopped the water into hundreds of whitecaps. She saw several other yachts in the distance, nearer the shore. The brisk breeze made the sun's intense heat bearable; it was a glorious day for sailing. Behind her, she heard Cam commenting approvingly on their speed.

Where was Apollo? Had he felt abandoned when Gina left the water and they all went belowdecks? Jody wondered. Or had he lost interest when *Dolphin Dreamer* sailed on?

Her father came up beside her, muttering, "If I'd heard a lecture *that* dull in college, I would have dropped out. I hope Jefferson Taylor isn't going to insist on chipping in with his two cents' worth *every* time we send something to the media." He gave a gusty sigh. "Any sign of your friend?"

Jody shook her head, frowning with disappointment. "Do you think he's gone away for good? I wish now I'd stayed on deck and talked to him more."

She leaned out again, staring forward and narrowing her eyes against the bright sunshine. There! Was that him? Holding her breath, Jody saw the distinctive, finned shape of a dolphin, sleek and shining, as it glided through the water to one side and just ahead of the prow of *Dolphin Dreamer*, lifted and propelled by the wave that the yacht made in its progress.

She gasped with delight. "He's bow-riding," she cried.

"Which side?" Craig was immediately interested.

"Starboard!" Jody scrambled up to the forward deck for a closer view. Her father followed and they stood together gazing down at the dolphin. Jody could almost feel Apollo's pleasure in his "free ride" on the wave created by the boat. "It must be like surfing," she said. "Why do they do it?"

"Why do people surf?" Craig laughed. "Because it's fun."

Jody raised the camera. Just as she was framing a picture of the swimming dolphin, Apollo suddenly leaped clear of the wave he'd been riding. For one brilliant moment the dolphin's powerful, supple body hung in the air, and Jody pressed the shutter. She knew it would be a great picture. Then Apollo plunged back into the water.

Jody hastily pulled the camera close to her chest to

Apollo in action

keep it from getting splashed. "Thanks, Apollo," she called, laughing. "That was perfect!"

She took a few more pictures, and then gave the camera to her father to take down below.

"Don't you want to look at what you've taken?" he asked.

"Not yet. I'd rather watch the real thing!"

"A wise choice," Craig said with a grin. "I'm going to rescue your mother from Doctor Dull. I'm sure she'll want to come to see what Apollo is up to."

But when Gina came out on deck with her husband, Dr. Jefferson Taylor came, too.

"Mmm, a solitary bow-rider," he said. "I've read about that. But I had believed that was group behavior."

"Well, dolphins do usually travel in groups," Gina said. "We don't know whether this one is just temporarily separated from his group or if he's a loner."

"We might come across Apollo's school anytime now. Then we'd know," Jody suggested.

"Yes, we might," Craig said. "But it doesn't seem very likely now. Given the speed we're traveling, I'd expect to lose Apollo in the next couple of hours. The home range of the bottle-nosed in Florida is usually less than fifteen square miles."

"Don't they ever leave their home range?" Jody asked.

"Well, sure, for food if the fishing gets sparse," her father agreed. "And sometimes males will go in search of females, or migrate to another group with a different home range. And there might be other reasons why a dolphin would travel — we don't know as much about them as we'd like to think. But I've never heard of a dolphin leaving his home range to follow a boat. Not even a boat with someone as sweet as you on board."

Jody managed a weak smile in response. She reminded herself that Apollo was a wild creature, and only the first of many that she would meet. Yet she couldn't help feeling there was something special about him. She hated the thought of losing her new friend so soon.

"On the other hand," said Gina — as Dr. Taylor, looking thoughtful, left them and went back below — "some bottle-nosed dolphins have been tracked making regular journeys of more than one hundred eighty miles. We don't know where this one's come from, or where he might be going."

"I know where I'm going," said Craig. He patted his stomach. "Down below, to see if it's time for lunch yet."

"Coming, Jody?" her mother asked.

Jody looked out at Apollo, still enjoying his effortless ride on the bow wave. "I'll come down later," she said. "I just want to watch Apollo for a little longer."

As her parents left, she leaned against the rail on the prow and gazed down at the beautiful marine animal. Admiring the sleek lines of his body, she longed to sketch it, and wished she had a pad and pencil.

Hearing footsteps, Jody glanced around and was surprised to see Dr. Taylor heading her way. She looked away again, hoping he'd change his mind, but he came to stand immediately beside her and peered over the side.

"Still there," he muttered to himself. "Good. Now, just stay put, dolphin, so I can get you . . ." As he spoke he raised his hand, holding something that reflected the sunlight with a fierce, metallic glare.

Jody turned and stared. Her heart lurched in horror

as she saw not a camera in Dr. Taylor's hand, but a gun! And he was aiming it directly at Apollo.

"No!" she screamed and threw herself at him with all her might. He staggered, grunting, and rocked back on his heels, nearly losing his balance. He clutched desperately at the rigging with both hands to save himself. He had missed his shot, but he just managed to keep hold of the gun. Jody heard it clank against the stainless steel lines, and she was frightened. He might still use it on Apollo — or on her.

The sunglasses had slipped down Dr. Taylor's nose, and his watery brown eyes, angry and astonished, stared at Jody.

"I won't let you shoot him!" Jody cried passionately. "I won't let you hurt Apollo!"

"What on earth are you talking about? You crazy little girl —" he gasped breathlessly.

"What's the problem?" Craig came hurrying over to the forward deck, alerted by Jody's scream.

"Your daughter nearly pushed me overboard!" Dr. Taylor spluttered.

"He was going to shoot Apollo," Jody said, her eyes

appealing to her father for help. She saw his eyebrows go up as he noticed the gun.

"I had no idea anyone would be carrying a weapon on board, Dr. Taylor," Craig said grimly.

Squinting in the bright sunlight, Dr. Taylor straightened the sunglasses so they covered his eyes once more. He moved cautiously out of the rigging and displayed the gun, lying in the flat of his hand, to Jody's father. "This is not a weapon," he said stiffly. "Perhaps you don't recognize it, Dr. McGrath, because it is the very latest model. But if you examine it you will see that it is, in fact, a very sophisticated tagging device. And it cost a lot of money," he ended, glaring at Jody.

Craig took the instrument and whistled. "I've heard about these," he said.

Jody felt her own shoulders relax. She supposed she ought to apologize to Dr. Taylor, although she was still a little suspicious. "Sorry for pushing you over, Dr. Taylor," she said politely. "How does it work?"

Dr. Taylor grunted a grudging acceptance of Jody's apology, then explained how the tagging device worked. "It fires a dart, fitted with a microchip," he began. "Once embedded in the dolphin's flesh, the microchip provides information about the animal's movements."

"Embedded in the dolphin's flesh!" Jody repeated, dismayed. Perhaps she'd been right not to trust Dr. Taylor, after all. "Doesn't it hurt the dolphin?" she asked.

Dr. Taylor shrugged, as if he hadn't thought of this before. "I bought the equipment from a very reputable company . . ." he blustered.

"But dolphins have very sensitive skin, you know!" Jody insisted.

"Yes they do, honey," Craig agreed, putting a comforting arm around Jody's shoulder. "And some of the earlier methods of tagging probably did cause the dolphins some discomfort. In fact, some people still argue against any such tagging," he added, looking at Dr. Taylor.

The scientist's round face went even redder.

"But," Jody's father continued, "I think Dr. Taylor is right about this latest method — the darts are so tiny that the dolphin will feel only a tiny jab."

Jody trusted her father's judgment. But she didn't

think Dr. Taylor should be let off so lightly. "Would you let somebody shoot one of those things into *your* flesh?" she asked him.

"I wouldn't object," said Dr. Taylor loftily. "If it was in the interest of science, I would gladly agree to the slight discomfort."

Jody imagined a room full of scientists tracking Dr. Taylor's movements. She saw her father's mouth twitch and knew he was thinking the same thing.

"Well, now we've got that cleared up," Craig said, with a wink to Jody, "why don't we all go below for some lunch?"

"But what about my tagging?" said Dr. Taylor.

"Well, to be honest, I don't think it'll be much use here," Craig replied bluntly. "We'll soon sail out of the dolphin's range before you've had time to pick up any useful information on the tracking microchip."

Dr. Taylor sighed. "I hadn't thought of that," he said sorrowfully, as he followed everyone down to the galley.

Although Jody tried not to show it, she couldn't help

feeling cheered by the fact that Apollo had escaped being tagged.

"Never mind," said Gina to Dr. Taylor, as she was told about the recent drama on deck. "There'll be other chances. Here, have some of this chicken salad."

Dr. Taylor frowned, but accepted the plate she handed him. "Of course," he said. "And better ones. I'd rather track a dolphin that's part of a school, anyway."

After lunch, Jody settled down at her computer. Brittany had taken herself off, out of sight (and hearing!), to their cabin, and the twins were deeply absorbed — for once — in some computer game on their own computer at the other end of the main cabin.

Jody enjoyed the peace and quiet, looking at her pictures of Apollo and choosing the best one to post on the website. She also wrote a description of what she'd seen, and then wrote a long e-mail to Lindsay. She filled in her best friend on everything that had been happening, especially enjoying the chance to let off steam about Brittany and to describe her first encounter with a wild dolphin. Jody wished Lindsay could have been with her, and for the first time she realized just how much she was going to miss her friend.

That afternoon passed swiftly and peacefully. Then, toward evening, the motion of the boat changed dramatically. The smooth sailing had ended; it felt as if they were being dragged roughly over a very rocky road.

Jody couldn't concentrate with all the jouncing and bouncing. She was logging off her computer as Brittany came reeling out of their cabin, groaning loudly. She looked positively green.

"I'm going to be sick!" she cried loudly.

Maddie had been working across the table from Jody. She jumped up as soon as Brittany appeared and spoke sympathetically but firmly. "Get up on deck. I'll come with you. In fact, let's all go. We'll all feel better and we could ask Harry if it's possible to change course to find a gentler motion."

But when they emerged on deck, it seemed a different world from the clear and brilliant day Jody remembered from earlier. Dark clouds lowered overhead and lightning flared against the sky behind them.

Harry was far too absorbed in the demands of steering the boat through such a rough sea to pay much attention to the woes of a seasick crew.

When Maddie asked if he could change course, he shook his head grimly, and spoke above the noise of the rising wind and sea. "I've just changed course," he said. "We need more speed, not less!" He broke off to shout orders to Cam and Craig. Then, turning back, he added, "I'm sorry you're finding it a bit rough, but it would be worse if we took a different direction." He took a deep breath and gazed ahead. "There's a big storm on the way," he explained, "and we've got to try to outrun it."

5

Jody was immediately caught up in the excitement of the attempt to outrun the storm. The sails billowed, then swelled tautly as they came into the wind. *Dolphin Dreamer* surged forward, almost flying, as light and fast as a dream.

Brittany, beside her at the rail, already looked better, her seasickness helped by the smoother motion of the boat and the fresh air on her face. Jody was glad for her. She'd been seasick herself a few times, and it really was no fun.

Jody gazed out to sea, wondering where Apollo was, and if dolphins were even aware of storms. Probably the weather on the surface wouldn't make much difference to their lives.

She gasped as she was suddenly drenched with water. But it was fresh, not seawater. It was rain. Fast as the *Dolphin Dreamer* had flown, the rain clouds had been faster.

"Prepare to come about!" shouted the captain, giving the command to change course. Cam, Gina, and Craig scrambled to obey, slackening the sails. They hadn't managed to outrun the rain. Now the squall was so fierce that they could hardly see any distance ahead. It wasn't safe to keep going.

"You girls get below!" Maddie shouted as she rushed forward to help Cam reef the foresail. Taking it down would reduce their speed.

Jody's heart lurched and she clutched the rail to save herself as the deck pitched sharply beneath her feet.

Brittany cried out in fright. "What's happening?"

"We're going to heave to," Jody said. "That means

we're stopping — as much as we can. We'll drift a little, but we have to batten down and ride it out."

"Passengers below!" bellowed Harry from the helm. "Now!"

"He means us," said Jody urgently, putting one hand on Brittany's shoulder. "Come on. We're in the way."

"No! I'm not going!" Brittany shouted, setting her jaw stubbornly.

Cam was right, thought Jody. Brittany just wouldn't do anything her father said. She decided to try another angle. "You can't want to stay out in this awful rain! Come below where it's dry."

Brittany already looked as if she couldn't get any wetter. She shook her head stubbornly. "I feel sick when I'm inside. I'm staying right here." She straightened up, as if to emphasize her words, and moved toward the center of the boat.

It was the wrong move. Jody — an experienced sailor — had seen that Cam was releasing the boom, the long horizontal pole that supported the mainsail and enabled them to change direction. She heard his shouted warning — which Brittany was too absorbed by her own problems to notice. The heavy boom was swinging in their direction, straight for Brittany's head.

There was no time to explain. Jody grabbed the other girl by the arm and yanked her to one side. A split second later the boom swung by, narrowly missing them.

Brittany stared at Jody through narrowed eyes, then lashed out at her, reacting as if Jody was attacking her instead of trying to save her.

Jody tried to dodge Brittany's blow, but just then the boat heeled over sharply, pitching her forward. She flailed around for something to grab hold of, but there was only Brittany. And as Jody grabbed her again, Brittany's face blazed red. She shoved Jody away as hard as she could. Jody staggered backward and, with a feeling of complete disbelief, she felt herself go flying overboard.

It happened in an instant, yet on her way into the heaving sea below, time seemed to stretch out. Jody had time to feel shocked that it was really happening to her, to feel angry at Brittany, and annoyed at herself for being so careless! She also managed to hold her breath before she plunged below the water.

Quickly, Jody struggled back to the surface, pulse racing, adrenaline coursing through her system. She was a strong, experienced swimmer, and — like the rest of her family — Jody had practiced what to do if this ever happened.

Of course, in the practice sessions the sea had never been as rough as this, and it hadn't been raining so hard she could scarcely see.

But, as scared as Jody felt, at least she wasn't injured . . . and surely Brittany would have alerted everyone to what had happened. Her parents and the rest of the crew would already be looking for her. They'd locate her very soon, then Cam would attach the ladder, and she'd be back on board. All she had to do was keep herself afloat and stay near to the boat.

But where *was* the boat? She should have been right next to it, but she couldn't see it. All of a sudden Jody was completely terrified. She was lost!

Gasping for breath, her heart pounding, Jody strug-

Overboard!

gled to stay calm, remembering how her dad had emphasized the importance of keeping a clear head in a
crisis. The boat *couldn't* have disappeared. She must
have gotten turned around while she was underwater,
that was all.

Blinking hard against the blinding rain, and trying to
keep on top of the waves that threatened to submerge
her, Jody paddled around in a circle, searching desper-

ately in the featureless gray water for the shape that meant safety.

There it was! But it was so far away! Jody felt a sinking feeling in her stomach. She knew that she couldn't stay where she was and wait to be found. Her family would never see her from that distance.

Grimly determined, trying not to think about the difficulty of it, Jody began swimming toward *Dolphin Dreamer*.

Swimming was hard work in the rain and wind, and the waves all seemed determined to push her back. Jody managed to kick her shoes off. They were still-new sneakers that she hated to lose, but in the water they were heavy, making it harder to swim. Feet bare, she took a deep breath and plunged on. She kept her head down and swam steadily and fast as if in a grim race. But every time she stopped to get her bearings, *Dolphin Dreamer* seemed as far away as ever. What was going on?

Jody's heart sank as she finally realized the boat had still been moving when she fell overboard, and even with the sails all stowed, it was still likely to drift. As fast as she was swimming toward it, the wind and currents were taking it farther away. It must be moving much faster than she was. She was never going to catch up to it.

Jody nearly burst into tears of terror. But she didn't have the energy to spare. She *couldn't* give up now, she just couldn't. She had to hope that Brittany really had raised the alarm, and that her family would be looking for her — though she couldn't see any sign of that from the boat. By now, people should have been hanging over the sides, looking for her, calling her name.

Jody tried calling to them. "Help! Help!" Her voice sounded terrifyingly small in the vast waters, and when she opened her mouth to call a third "Help!" a wave splashed against her face. She gagged and choked on the salt.

The rain was still coming down in sheets, making it hard to breathe or to see. She prayed that the boat might be moving toward her instead of away. They *must* be looking for her, they must! Maybe she hadn't really been in the water as long as it seemed.

Gasping, panting, desperate, Jody forced herself to keep swimming toward *Dolphin Dreamer.* No matter how hard it was, she would just have to keep going. She would get there eventually. She was exhausted, but she wouldn't give in.

Then Jody saw something which turned her blood to ice. A dark, curving fin cut through the waves . . . vanished . . . then appeared again a few yards away. *Shark.*

She tried desperately to think of what to do, but the only advice she could remember — get out of the water — was utterly useless to her now. Sharks were deadly, but unpredictable. If this one wasn't hungry, it might simply swim past her. But if it *was* hungry, she wouldn't stand a chance.

The fin vanished . . . then appeared again, closer. Jody clutched the silver dolphin on her necklace tightly between thumb and forefinger. If she had ever needed luck in her life, it was now. The fin vanished.

Beneath the water, Jody felt something bump against her legs. She gave a yelp. She couldn't help herself. But then, as she felt the gentle pressure against her legs, she realized that what she was feeling wasn't the rough hide of a shark, but the smooth skin of a dolphin. "*Apollo?*" she breathed.

The distinctive head of a bottle-nosed dolphin broke through the surface. It *was* Apollo! Jody was immediately awed by just how big the dolphin was, close-up. Her mother had estimated Apollo's length as almost three yards. But it was one thing to watch at a distance while her mother swam with Apollo, and quite another to be in the water herself with such a large animal.

Jody wasn't scared, though. How could she be? This was Apollo. She looked him right in the eye. It was large, round, brown, and shining with unmistakable intelligence. There was something about the dolphin that made Jody feel peaceful. For a moment she almost forgot the danger she was in.

Apollo nudged her hand. Jody was amazed. He had avoided her mother's touch, yet he was inviting *her* to touch him. He moved to bring the dorsal fin on his back under her fingers.

Jody suddenly guessed what was being offered. "You'll tow me back to the boat?" Scarcely daring to believe it, she flung her arm around the dolphin's smooth, streamlined back, hooking her hand around the dorsal fin as a means of hanging on.

As soon as Jody was in place, Apollo began swimming — a gentle, powerful motion that pulled her rapidly through the water.

Although Jody realized Apollo was moving slowly by dolphin standards — probably out of concern for her — the sensation of being pulled through the waves by such a gentle, yet powerful, force was exhilarating. Jody began to grin. After the terror of the last few minutes, the delight she felt now was making her giddy. She knew she was safe, now, with Apollo.

Blinking against the slackening rain, Jody saw *Dolphin Dreamer*, seeming to grow larger by the second as she drew closer. Everyone was on deck, leaning over the sides, most of them in brilliantly colored rain gear.

They were all looking for her. When she was close enough to see her mother's desperately worried face, Jody cried out, "Ahoy!"

As Gina saw her daughter her expression changed to amazement, then lit up with an almost disbelieving joy.

Apollo took Jody to the side of the boat where the ladder had been hung out.

"Thanks, Apollo," Jody said, feeling her heart thud with relief. She seized hold of the ladder and began to climb up. Suddenly, it was all too much. She came to the end of her strength. Her legs started trembling and one foot slipped on the step, but before she could fall, her father's strong arms grasped her and he lifted her up and into the boat as if she weighed no more than a baby.

"Thank goodness," he murmured, holding her close. "Thank goodness you're safe."

Explanations waited — by Craig's order — until Jody was washed and dried, snugly dressed in a comfortable sweatsuit, and curled up on a seat in the main cabin with a steaming mug of soup provided by Mei Lin. Everyone except Cam, who was taking the watch on deck, gathered around.

Jody felt a little flustered at being the center of attention. Everyone was staring at her as if she'd performed a miracle, when really it was Apollo who deserved all the credit.

"I can't believe we almost lost you!" Gina said. She clutched her daughter's free hand as if she would never let it go again. "Thank goodness Brittany saw you go overboard and raised the alarm. What if no one had seen?"

Craig nodded. "That could easily have happened. Things here were pretty chaotic around then. The Genoa ripped while we were reefing it, and then — as if a ripped sail wasn't bad enough — one of the shrouds snapped! I thought we were going to lose the mast. Believe me, nobody had time to notice who was there and who wasn't," he ended seriously.

Gina shuddered, then flashed a warm smile of thanks at Brittany. But the girl was staring down at her feet and did not respond. Gina turned to Jody. "So what happened?" she demanded, squeezing Jody's hand. "I thought you kids had all been told to get below. How did you happen to be on deck, never mind go overboard?"

As Jody hesitated, Brittany suddenly came to life. Throwing her head back she declared, "It was an accident! Jody pushed me — to get me out of the way, so I wouldn't get hit in the head — but I —"

Jody leaped in. "Yeah, that's right! We were just about to go below when I noticed the boom heading for us, so I pushed Brittany out of the way — and then I was trying to duck the boom myself, so I wasn't paying attention when the boat suddenly heeled — and whoosh, I went right over the side! It was a complete accident." She stopped, breathless.

Brittany stared at Jody, shocked, her mouth still open. And then, as she realized that Jody had saved her again, the color began to creep back into her pale cheeks. "Yeah, thanks, Jody," she murmured quietly.

It seemed that Brittany was thanking Jody for saving her from being hit on the head by the boom. But Jody knew that Brittany was also thanking her for keeping her out of a great deal of trouble. "You're welcome," Jody replied. But she gave the other girl a meaningful look, and hoped Brittany would understand it: *I didn't rat on you, but you'll have to shape up.*

"Now tell us about the dolphin, Jody!" urged Sean.

"Yeah!" said Jimmy. "Tell us how he towed you! Did you really think he was a shark?"

6

When they were alone in their cabin that night, Brittany spoke in a voice Jody hadn't heard her use before — ashamed and nervous. "Thanks again for not telling on me."

"There wasn't any reason to. I'm not mad at you." Jody spoke honestly. In fact, now that the shock had passed, all she could think of was how wonderful Apollo had been. She almost felt grateful to the other girl, but she certainly wasn't going to tell her that, in case she got the wrong idea!

Brittany stared, wide-eyed. "But I could have *killed* you!"

"But you didn't," Jody pointed out. Then, curious, she asked, "What *did* you intend to do?"

Brittany collapsed onto her bunk and gazed pleadingly at Jody. "I just got mad. I just wanted to teach you a lesson, not . . ." Her voice trailed off and her face went pale as she thought again about what might have happened. "I didn't think. I was scared when I saw you fall over the side! I could hardly believe it."

Jody decided to take advantage of Brittany's guilty feelings. "Look, Brittany, things are different at sea. You may not like it, but everybody on board has to obey the captain. You have to do what Harry says — not because he's your dad, but because he's in charge of the boat. He has to make the decisions about our safety. If the crew starts arguing with him, or takes their time about following orders, it could be a disaster. Do you understand?"

A stubborn expression flashed across Brittany's mouth, but then she nodded. "I guess . . . while we're on board." Then, all in a rush, she said, "And I promise I won't push you or hit you again. It was a babyish thing to do, and I never thought it could be so danger-ous!" She took a deep breath. "I'm sorry."

It was clear that apologizing did not come easily to Brittany Pierce.

The morning dawned bright and still. The fierce squalls of the night before weren't even a memory in the achingly clear blue sky. The adults discussed their options and decided that, rather than motoring in to the nearest port, they would stay put and make their own repairs to the boat. This was unlikely to take more than two days. If they found they needed any replace-ment parts, they'd head for Key West.

Jody was glad. Now she knew they were still in Apollo's home territory, and she could look forward to spending more time with her new friend. Although she couldn't spot him in the water around the boat when she looked before breakfast, she had a feeling that he wasn't far away. Surely he would turn up before long.

"May I go swimming this morning?" Jody asked her mother over breakfast.

Gina smiled. "You mean you didn't get enough of being in the sea yesterday?"

"Nope. Do you think that means I'm half dolphin?" Jody teased.

"I think it means you're half mad, like the rest of this crazy family." Gina laughed and leaned over to hug her daughter.

"So is that a yes?" Jody pressed her mother eagerly.

"Sure, why not?" Gina looked across the table at the twins, who were as alert as puppies at the mention of a walk. "I think we all might enjoy a swim this morning, before it gets too hot."

Sean and Jimmy whistled and cheered their approval.

Even Brittany looked a little brighter at the idea of a swim, although she turned to Maddie to ask, "Is it really safe to swim out there?"

"If you're not a confident swimmer, you should wear a life vest," Maddie suggested.

"I'm an excellent swimmer," Brittany protested. "We have a pool at home, and I swim every day."

"Well, then, you'll be fine here. The sea looks practically as still as a swimming pool this morning." Maddie smiled warmly and laid her knife and fork on her empty plate.

"But what about . . . sharks and things like that?" Brittany asked, lowering her voice a little.

"We won't go in if there's any sign of sharks," Maddie assured her. "And we can ask Cam to keep a shark-watch from the deck."

"Race you!" said Jimmy to Sean.

Gina held up a warning hand. "We'll meet on deck in our swimming things in one hour, not before." She pressed on over the noisy groans of the twins. "Nobody is going in the water before their breakfast has had time to digest. We don't want anybody getting cramps."

Jody spent the time updating her diary about the exciting events of the day before. Then she quickly changed into her swimsuit and went up on deck.

As she emerged from the hold, Jody heard something that made her heart beat faster. First there was a whistle; then a series of rapid, stuttering clicks and pops — the unmistakable sounds of a dolphin. "Apollo!" she cried joyfully, rushing to the side where her parents were standing.

At the sight of her, Apollo whistled again and leaped into the air. As the spray rained down on her, Jody laughed with delight. "How long has he been here?"

"Less than a minute, honestly," her mother replied. "I was just going to call you."

"Can I go in with him? Please?" Jody looked hopefully at her mother.

At that moment, Sean and Jimmy erupted out of the hold, wearing matching fluorescent orange swimming trunks and goggles, yelling with excitement, their bare feet slapping the deck. They launched themselves off the side, knees up — to splash bottoms down like a couple of human cannonballs.

Gina winced and sighed. "Of course you can."

Craig had peeled off his T-shirt. "I'd better go and keep an eye on those two."

Watch out dolphins — here comes trouble!

"I'll join you in a minute," Gina agreed. She turned to look at the hatchway. "Oh, good, here come Brittany and Maddie."

Jody was too excited about another chance to swim with Apollo to wait another minute. She fitted on her goggles. Then, taking a deep breath, she dived off the side of the boat.

After the heat of the sun, the water was cool and welcoming as Jody sliced cleanly into it. It was a different world down here, the world the dolphins knew as home. Underwater, the sounds of her brothers' yells were muffled. She saw their pale legs kicking and waving in the dim, greenish water, like the tentacles of some strange creature. She turned her head, and there, only a few inches away, was Apollo. He gazed at her sidelong, out of one eye.

Jody ran out of breath and had to shoot back to the surface to breathe again. Apollo poked his beak out of the water, continuing to watch her. This time there was no pounding rain to blur her vision. She saw him more clearly than ever before. For the first time she noticed the little dimples on his head that marked where his ears would be.

"Hi there," she said quietly. "I'm really glad you came back."

She reached out to stroke him, and he let her. His skin felt smooth and finely ridged beneath her fingertips. She was careful to avoid the blowhole on the top of his head.

He dipped below the water and rolled onto his back, letting her stroke his paler belly, almost as if he were a cat or a dog.

"Hey, that's just like Fluffy used to do," said Jimmy.

Jody was startled. She had been so absorbed in Apollo that she hadn't noticed her brothers approach. Apollo rolled again and disappeared beneath the surface.

Taking a deep breath, Jody sank down and went after him. But speed was so natural to the dolphin that he shot away out of sight in an instant. Jody flailed around for a few more seconds, trying to see where he'd gone, then gave up and surfaced again.

"Where'd he go?" asked Sean.

Before she could reply, up popped Apollo.

"I want to touch him," Jimmy said, and began to swim toward the dolphin. Although the twins normally did things together, Sean hung back, saying nothing, looking thoughtful.

But Apollo wouldn't let Jimmy near enough to be touched. He shot away with a simple, effortless flex of his body.

"How can he go so fast?" Sean asked.

"Their bodies are perfectly designed for speed — streamlined and very powerful," answered his father. "There's no boat that can match them — and, believe me, boat designers have tried to learn from dolphins! One of the reasons they can go so fast is that the dolphin's body constantly changes shape while swimming. And their skin secretes an oil that helps reduce friction, helping them to glide through the water."

"That must be why his skin feels so smooth," said Jody.

Jimmy pouted. "I want to feel it. Make him let me," he begged Jody.

"He's not my pet, Jimmy. I can't *make* him do anything," Jody said reasonably.

"He gave you a ride yesterday," Jimmy pointed out.

Jody shrugged. "That was his decision," she replied, and began to swim away from her brother.

Jimmy scowled. "Aw, I want him to give me a tow! How'd you get him to?" A cunning look crept across his face. "I know! Like this!" He began to flail and splash and sputter. "Help! Help! I'm drowning! Help me, Apollo!"

"Knock it off, Jimmy," Craig said sharply. "Any more of that, and you're back on the boat."

Jimmy's clumsy acting did not fool Apollo. Gazing around at the remarkably still water, Jody caught sight of the dolphin swimming beneath the surface, not far away. He must have been aware of Jimmy's antics, but had decided to ignore them. She filled her lungs with air and dived down.

Apollo swam to meet her and they gazed at each other for a long moment underwater. Then he moved closer and nudged her hand. She stroked his nose. He made a soft clicking noise and opened his mouth. Jody stared at the small, sharply pointed teeth that lined his jaw, before he clacked it shut again. His clicks became more rapid. She had the sense that he was trying to say something to her, but what was it? Would she ever understand? A desperate need for air forced her to return to the surface.

As Jody came up, she saw that her mother had also entered the water, although there was no sign of Brittany or Maddie. This seemed odd, but Jody had no time to think about it, because just then she felt something nudge the back of her knees.

It was Apollo, of course. What was he doing? Jody gasped, astonished, as she felt herself being pushed and lifted from below. Her legs slipped over either side of the dolphin's sleek hide; her arms flailed for balance. She found herself sitting on the dolphin's back. She was riding Apollo!

It was like a dream, like the best dream Jody had ever had. She sat straight and tall and fearless, gripping the animal with her knees, letting herself be carried. It was absolutely magical!

Jody saw the amazement on her parents' faces as

they treaded water and gazed at her. She heard the shouts of the twins and Maddie was calling something from the deck of the boat. But they all seemed very far away, in another world entirely, as she was carried smoothly and swiftly over the water, in a big, arcing circle around *Dolphin Dreamer.*

It ended some timeless minutes later, with Apollo dropping a little lower in the water. Jody knew somehow what he meant and loosened the grip of her legs, slipping down and then letting him swim away.

She swam idly — still half in a dream, still feeling the wonderful sensation of being carried along by the fast, powerful animal who had chosen her for his friend. She felt blessed, enchanted. She drifted onto her back and floated there, gazing up into the blue, blue sky.

7

June 22 — 11:50 p.m.

This has been the most wonderful day of my life.

Brittany's asleep. I can hear her snoring in the bunk below. I should really be sleeping, too, but I'm still excited — I got to ride Apollo! I can't stop thinking about it and wondering what it meant.

Dr. Taylor thinks that Apollo must have been a performing dolphin who was taught that riding trick before being released into the wild. But I don't think that's true. I'm sure he's a wild dolphin. If he'd been trained to come to people, why didn't he let Jimmy or Mom touch him? Why only me?

Into the Blue

Dad says there are stories going back to ancient times about special friendships between dolphins and humans. Young boys used to ride on the backs of dolphins in the Mediterranean. I remember reading about a girl in New Zealand who swam every day with a friendly wild dolphin who eventually let her ride him.

Brittany never did come swimming with us. I don't know why. She got very huffy when I asked. She said she preferred to talk to Maddie, who's "really cool." I guess it's good that there is at least someone on board who Brittany will listen to, but even when Maddie dived into the water, Brittany stayed on deck.

I wonder if Brittany could be scared of dolphins? But that's just crazy. Maybe she has confused them with sharks — after all, she did think they were fish. I tried to find out, but she just got nasty. She's keeping her promise not to push or hit (so far!) but she still doesn't like me, and she sure lets me know it.

In the morning, while Brittany was still sleeping, Jody dressed hastily in a clean T-shirt and shorts, grabbed her recorder, and left. There was a smell of fresh coffee wafting from the galley, but no sign or sound of anyone else until she reached the deck, where she found her father.

"Hi, what are you doing up?" he asked in surprise.

"Same as you?" Jody lifted her face to the sun and sniffed the fresh, salty air.

He shook his head. "It's my watch. Everybody else is still asleep. It's still very early, you know."

"Oh. Well, would it disturb anybody if I practiced my recorder?" she asked.

Craig smiled. "A little dawn music would be lovely. Think you could whistle up a wind?"

Jody cocked her head, looking puzzled.

"It's a sailor's superstition. When it's calm, you're supposed to be able to raise a wind by whistling," her father explained.

"I won't whistle, then," she said fervently. "I hope it stays dead calm for days and days and we can just stay here and do some scuba diving. I haven't had a chance to dive yet, remember."

"Do you think Apollo would have given you a ride

yesterday if you'd had your scuba gear on?" Her father gave her a teasing grin.

Jody laughed. "No, probably not! But if you really want to know about dolphins you have to get right down under the water with them — to see life the way they see it, don't you?"

"Hmm, I couldn't have put it better myself," said Craig, his blue-gray eyes sparkling with mischief. "In fact, I think I may have put it exactly like that at some point. What a lucky man I am, to have a daughter who listens to me!"

Jody wrinkled her nose. "Well, now you can listen to me for a change." She waved her recorder like a wand at her father, then went up to the forward deck.

She'd intended to sit exactly where she'd been the first time Apollo had responded to her playing, but what she found lying there made her stop and stare down at her feet in surprise. It was a small blue-gray fish about twenty inches in length; nothing extraordinary about it except for the magnificent, iridescent wings attached to its sides — a flying fish!

Jody tucked her recorder under one arm and picked up the fish. She felt it quiver in her hands. It was still alive! Quickly, she tossed it over the side, then ran back to tell her father.

Craig nodded, unsurprised. "I've thrown back half a dozen this morning. Later on we might want to keep them to eat."

"Do they taste good?" Jody grimaced, not sure she would want to eat something that looked like that.

Her father grinned at her. "Depends on how hungry you are."

"They don't really fly, do they?" Jody was curious.

"No, but they can glide — up to about a hundred yards. Their wings are really fins, which they keep tucked against their sides while they're swimming. If they're chased by another fish, or sense danger, they launch themselves upward, taxi across the surface of the water, and then take off and glide to safety." Craig stuck his arms straight out to show what he meant.

Jody stared at the sea, shining in the early sun. "Could they have been chased by dolphins?"

"I guess so. But I haven't seen any," he said. Jody's

shoulders drooped. Craig patted her back. "Go on, go play your flute."

"It's a recorder, Dad," Jody corrected him.

"Whatever." Craig shrugged his shoulders, then gave Jody a little wave as she left him to return to the fore-deck.

She played the few pieces she knew by heart, gazing out to sea all the while. But no matter how hard she looked, there was no sight of a dark fin in the distance, and no head poked up out of the water to whistle back at her. An idea slipped into her mind, making her un-happy. What if she never saw Apollo again, and he had known all along? What if that fantastic ride had been his way of saying a special good-bye?

There would be other dolphins, she knew, but she couldn't believe she would ever meet another one who would be as special to her as Apollo.

By the time she gave up her solo concert — bored with repeating the same few pieces — a breeze had picked up, ruffling her hair and clanging the halyards against the mast.

When Jody joined the others belowdecks at the

breakfast table, she wasn't surprised to hear Harry Pierce proposing that they should set sail again, to take advantage of the wind, as soon as possible. The necessary repairs had been made, and there was no point in just sitting around, especially if there were no dolphins to study.

The prospect of moving on seemed to cheer everyone else. But Gina must have sensed Jody's unspoken sadness, for she touched her hair and murmured, "If it's not too rough this afternoon we'll do some diving — how's that?"

"That would be great," Jody said, and meant it. Even if Apollo wasn't around, scuba was one of the coolest things she knew how to do. Almost as good as riding a dolphin!

The morning passed slowly. Mei Lin was baking bread. Jody had wanted to help, but Brittany had got in first, and there wasn't room in the tiny galley for more than two people. It was her brothers' turn for a sailing lesson from Harry. Jody was feeling left out and bored when the shout came from her father on deck, "Dolphins off the port bow!"

Jody bolted for the hatchway.

On deck, she hurried to join her father at the rail, where he was gazing out to sea, along with her mother and the twins. What she saw took her breath away.

It was a whole school of dolphins, moving so rapidly that it was impossible to say how many there were. Thirty? Fifty? More? Dark fins dotted the waves, and sleek, leaping gray bodies leaped here and there, back and forth. It was an amazing sight!

The twins were shouting with excitement. Jody made room for Maddie and Cam, who'd also come rushing over. Even Dr. Taylor had come up on deck to see what all the fuss was about.

Harry Pierce, at the helm, gave a roar of laughter. "Honestly, if I didn't know better, I'd say you were a bunch of tourists!"

Through her excitement, Jody felt guilty, and she saw from the rueful look her parents exchanged that they felt the same.

Jimmy said, "We're going up front, okay?"

"Forward," said Sean. "The word is forward."

"Go ahead," said Craig. "But be careful. I'm not sure

I'll be able to convince Harry to go back for you if you fall in."

"I'm going down for my camera," said Gina. "This is just too gorgeous."

Jody stared in wonder as three dolphins all leaped out of the water in different parts of the group, slapping the water with their tails, then diving down again.

"What are they *doing*?" Only when Brittany spoke did Jody realize the other girl had also come on deck, and was now standing between her and Dr. Taylor.

"They're feeding," Craig replied. "At this distance it is hard to be certain, but I would guess that they've trapped a school of fish. They do that by forcing the fish upward against the surface of the water. Some of the dolphins will be swimming back and forth underneath, to keep the fish trapped, while others take turns snatching a mouthful. Still other dolphins will chase back any of the fish that manage to break away."

Gina returned with her camera and began filming. Under the captain's skillful control, they were sailing nearer to the dolphin group.

Lunchtime for dolphins.

"Why do they jump up and slap their tails?" Brittany asked. "That wouldn't stop the fish from getting away."

Jody was curious about this, too. Perhaps it's joyful behavior, she thought, a way of expressing excitement at finding so much food.

Her mother gave them a more scientific explanation: "Slapping the water makes a loud, sharp sound," she said. "Loud noises frighten the fish, making them gather together into a tighter ball, instead of trying to get away."

"So dolphins aren't just these totally sweet and friendly little angels," said Brittany.

"Of course not," objected Dr. Taylor, sounding shocked. "Dolphins are predators. They are hunters."

Jody knew Brittany's comment was aimed at her. "They have to catch the fish to live," she said defensively. "They have to eat, just like we do. But they only kill fish and squid and things like that," she added, eager to impress upon the other girl that dolphins weren't to be feared.

Jody had noticed two or three seagulls hovering

over the feeding dolphins. More appeared, out of the blue, until there was a screaming mob of birds darting toward the water, then flapping up again, sometimes with fish in their beaks.

"Hey, look, the birds are stealing the dolphins' lunch!" Cam laughed.

"Not exactly," said Craig. "Some of the fish try to escape by leaping into the air — those are the ones the birds pick off. Plenty for all. You'll often find seabirds following a school of dolphins, just waiting for a chance like this."

After a few more minutes, the birds flew away and the dolphins began to leave. Feeding time was over. Jody and the others watched as the sleek, leaping gray-finned bodies swam farther out to sea and were gradually lost to sight.

Jody sighed. She had been holding her breath, hoping the dolphins would come their way. She wondered if Apollo had been part of that big group. She knew that one of the reasons dolphins traveled in herds was that it made hunting easier. They could get more fish by working together than they could alone. It would be a hard life for Apollo if he was on his own.

For lunch there was fresh warm bread, cheese, and gazpacho — a cold vegetable soup.

Between hungry bites, Jody paused briefly to ask, "Mei, did you ever see dolphins when you were in China?"

Mei Lin nodded. "Once, only. But it was not like your dolphins. I was lucky enough to see a baiji."

"What's a baiji?" Sean demanded.

"It's the rarest dolphin in the world," Craig explained for the benefit of all. "It's found only in parts of one river in China."

"Really, Mei Lin?" said Gina in surprise. "You actually saw a baiji?"

"Yes, I think so. I was only a little girl at the time, and it was early in the morning and very misty. I was traveling with my parents in a boat on the Yangtze River. I heard a sound like a sneeze from the water, and I looked over the side and saw a smooth, grayish animal with a long, skinny nose swimming away. My father said this was one of China's national treasures. But later I was told by someone else that it could not have been the baiji that I saw. It must have been only a porpoise, because the baiji are too shy to let themselves be seen. I don't know. My father was not an expert. But I like to think we saw a baiji."

"You were very lucky if you did," said her mother. "It's been a protected species since 1975, but there are probably less than fifty left today. The Yangtze is one of the busiest waterways in the world, and as the baiji won't live anywhere else, there's not a lot that can be done to save them."

Gina's words made Jody feel gloomy. She knew that all over the world cetaceans — both dolphins and whales — were at risk, but usually there was something that could be done to help the various species to survive. Commercial whaling could be stopped, destructive fishing methods changed, pollution controlled. People's efforts could make a major difference. The oceans were vast, and most dolphin species numbered in the thousands. But for an animal whose habitat was restricted to a part of one river, the future did not look bright. Even declaring it a protected species was probably not enough.

There was only one thing that could have cheered Jody's gloomy thoughts — and it actually happened.

"Dolphins approaching! Port *and* starboard sides!" Harry's voice came bellowing down from the deck, like a foghorn.

The McGraths and Maddie abandoned their food and made a dash for the deck, Jody ahead of them all. At the front of her mind was one thought: Apollo! Has he come back?

8

There were six bottle-nosed dolphins swimming around the boat, poking their heads curiously out of the water and jostling for position, as if for a better view. One would suddenly dive down and disappear for a moment, only to appear a moment later on the other side of the boat. They also nudged the boat with their beaks, and one rubbed sidelong against it as if he had an itch.

"Do you see your friend out there?" Craig asked Jody.

Was Apollo one of the six? Jody frowned uncertainly,

and leaned out over the side, trying to get a better view.

The dolphins didn't make it easy for her. They were in constant motion, diving and resurfacing, swimming back and forth, slipping in and out of sight. They were all practically identical — at least, from her position on deck she couldn't tell them apart. Maybe if she was closer she would be able to see that one carried that funny, curving little mark on the side of Apollo's beak. But if he *was* one of the group, Jody felt sure he would draw attention to himself in some way, maybe give her a special greeting.

These dolphins, although they were vocalizing, clicking and whistling and blowing, seemed to be talking to one another, not to her. She shook her head regretfully in answer to her father's question. "No, I don't think so."

"They're all very similar to Apollo," said Craig. "They seem to be roughly the same age, the sort of group I would expect to find him spending most of his time with after leaving his mother."

"What age would that be?" she asked.

"For the bottle-nosed, it's about four years," her father replied. "The younger ones travel with their mothers' group."

"Do you think these are all boys?" Jody asked curiously.

Her father shook his head. "Probably not, if this is a group of sub-adults, as I think. They're the dolphin equivalent of human teenagers — a gang of friends hanging out together, boys and girls. Older adult males tend to travel in smaller groups, and adult females usually rejoin their mother's group. But sometimes adult males will be found with groups of mothers and calves. It's almost as hard to predict a bottle-nosed group as it is to describe the 'typical' human family!" He grinned.

"And of course, they'll gather together in the hundreds sometimes, to cooperate in a hunt, or if danger threatens," Gina put in. "People do that, too. If we weren't part of human society wouldn't it seem just as difficult to explain?" She lowered the hydrophone over the side of the boat into the water, to record the sounds the dolphins made.

Jody loved listening to the clicks, pops, creaks, and

whistles that seemed so full of meaning. She firmly believed dolphins had their own language, and she had a dream that someday she would be able to understand it. She knew that researchers had been working on the puzzle for ages, and that most had decided that dolphin sounds were more like birdsong than any human language. But history was full of experts who had been proved wrong. Maybe when she grew up she would design a computer program that could translate "Dolphinese" into English!

Dr. Jefferson Taylor hauled himself out of the hatchway onto the deck. He was not wearing his sunglasses, but had put on a wide-brimmed straw hat. He was carrying a small canvas bag. He paused, removed a handkerchief from his pocket, and mopped his face, sighing, "I'd really like to rest for a little while after that delicious meal," he said. "But I'm afraid I'm someone who just can't rest if there's work to be done!"

He strolled over to the side. "Ah, a nice-sized subgroup this time," he said with satisfaction. "Dr. McGrath, I trust there won't be any objection if I tag one of these specimens?"

Jody tensed anxiously. She felt like shouting at him that they weren't specimens, they were dolphins, but she felt her father's hand rest warningly on her back and she kept quiet.

She saw her parents exchange a glance. Gina said, "Of course, that's fine. But as Craig mentioned to you before, we are on the move and we can't guarantee to stay within the dolphin's range."

Dr. Taylor frowned. "I realize that, but I do need to at least try to do some research myself, you know. Otherwise, my employers will think I'm treating this trip like a vacation!" He laughed nervously.

Gina sighed. "Go ahead, then."

Jody couldn't stop herself. "You will be careful, won't you, Dr. Taylor?"

Dr. Taylor sighed impatiently. He didn't look at her. "I have been assured . . . er, Jody . . . that the firing of the dart will cause only the slightest discomfort to the animal," he said. "In fact, it may not feel anything at all, since I intend to put it into the fin, which is made of cartilage." He set his bag down on the deck and reached inside.

"Why don't you go below, Jody?" said Gina gently.

Jody bit her lip and shook her head. She was determined to stay and see what happened with her own eyes. She wanted to know if a dolphin was hurt or frightened by what Dr. Taylor did.

Finding the gun, Dr. Taylor checked it. Then, steadying his elbow against the side, he took careful aim and fired. The gun made a sharp, snapping sound and then a high whine as the dart shot out.

The dolphins responded immediately, disappearing beneath the water, the entire group moving as one. From the hydrophone amplifier came the sound of rapid, high-pitched chattering — as if, thought Jody, the dolphins were all exclaiming and asking one another what had just happened.

"I couldn't see whether or not you hit one," said Craig.

"Neither could I, but I'll tell you in a minute," said Dr. Taylor. He bent down again, creaking like one of the dolphins, and replaced the gun in his bag. Then he took out something that looked like a palm-sized computer. He pressed a couple of keys, checked the display, pressed again, and nodded, satisfied. "Bingo."

Jody could still hear the clicks and squeaks coming from the hydrophone, so — although she couldn't see them — she knew the dolphins must be near, as the hydrophone's range wasn't very wide. She leaned over the side and gazed down into the water.

Deep in the blue, there was a shadowy shape . . . two . . . three . . . six! Jody broke into a grin. Below the water, the dolphins were still following the boat; one or two lazily kept pace, while others shot forward, flipped over, and came back to swap places. Eventually, in five or ten minutes, they would have to come up for air, but they were in no hurry.

"What do you see?" asked Gina, leaning close. "Ah," she said. "I guess he didn't scare them off. The water certainly is clear today. And it doesn't seem as deep here. I wonder . . ."

Jody turned to look at her. "What are you thinking?"

Gina smiled. "What do you think I'm thinking?"

"I know what *I'm* thinking: that this would be a great place to dive!" Jody exclaimed happily.

"You could be right." Her mother nodded, returning her smile, then examined the brilliantly blue water again. "It looks to me like we might be getting close to the Florida Reef. It's the only living coral reef in the United States and it's what makes the water off the Keys such a paradise for divers. I'll go and check the navigation charts just to be sure, and I'll have a word with your father and Harry."

A few minutes later, Harry was giving orders to heave to, and Jody hurried below to change.

Brittany was in their cabin, painting her nails dark purple. She stared at Jody. "Are you actually going into the water with a whole *herd* of those animals?"

"If they stick around, I am," Jody replied.

"You must be crazy," Brittany said flatly. "I can't believe your mother is going to let you do that. After what she said . . ."

"What? What did she say?" Jody was bewildered.

"I overheard her warning you a while ago. She said that dolphins were wild animals and you couldn't trust them. She said there had been accidents, and people had gotten hurt." Brittany tossed her wavy hair back from her face and stared accusingly at Jody.

"Yes, *accidents*," Jody stressed. "Dolphins don't hurt

134

people, not normally. It's people who hurt dolphins. And I guess sometimes if people get too rough with them, then the dolphin might feel threatened and get rough back to defend itself. Mom just meant that you have to respect wild animals. Don't do things they might misunderstand. Let them come to you, if they want. You can't force them."

Brittany looked down and blew on her nails. "Oh! So it was, like, really smart of you to make that dolphin give you a ride."

Jody's jaw dropped. "I didn't *make* Apollo do anything, Brittany! It was all his idea."

"Sure." Brittany smirked in a self-satisfied way.

Jody opened her mouth to argue, but then she stopped. She couldn't force Brittany to believe her. She shrugged. "Have it your way."

On deck, Jody and her parents discussed their dive plan. She was glad to see the dolphins were still hanging around the boat.

"They may head for the hills when they see us coming — scary-looking critters that we are, with our tanks and regulators and fins!" Craig warned jokingly.

Jody nodded, but she had a feeling the dolphins would stick around out of curiosity. Dolphins seemed utterly fearless creatures to her. They would even head-butt sharks! It was only human beings who had ever posed a threat to dolphins, and yet, despite years of being captured, hurt, or killed, dolphins went on trying to make friends with people.

Craig insisted it was his turn to use the camera. "I'm sure our viewers would rather see two lovely mermaids than watch me flopping around."

"I wasn't planning on having you on camera, darling," his wife said dryly. "And our sponsors won't appreciate it if you produce a home video of your wife and daughter. I don't even want it switched on unless you're pointing it at a dolphin."

Jody went through the drill carefully with her parents: checking her tank and regulators; running through the few simple hand signals they would use to communicate underwater, indicating if there were any problems or that it was time to return.

She felt extra alert, excited by the prospect of entering the dolphins' territory on their terms. Although it had been wonderful to swim with Apollo, without scuba equipment she hadn't been able to dive very deeply, or stay underwater for more than a couple of minutes. This time, although she knew she would still be weak, slow, and clumsy in comparison with the dolphins, at least she would be able to stay in the dolphins' underwater world longer, and start to understand them better.

"Do you dive, Dr. Taylor?" Gina asked.

"I'm afraid I can't," he replied. He pointed to his head. "Trouble with my ears, you see."

He didn't sound sorry, Jody thought. She wondered if he even *liked* dolphins. But she had better things to think about. It was time to dive.

The dolphins moved away from the boat as Jody and her parents entered the water, but they did not go far. They were obviously curious about these visitors. They hung in the water, barely moving . . . just watching.

Clearing her ears, Jody sank down through the clear

blue water. She added some air to her buoyancy vest and her descent slowed. She hovered, trying to imitate the dolphins' posture and to keep as still as they did. It made her think of some silly game where the first one to move was "out."

Suddenly, one of the dolphins darted forward. It shot straight toward her. Jody tensed, half expecting a collision, but the dolphin came to a halt right in front of her. Its beak was just inches from her mask.

The friendly bottle-nosed face seemed to smile at Jody. She noticed the stream of silvery bubbles rising from the blowhole on the top of its head. After a few seconds the dolphin dropped a little lower in the water to circle her. The beak came questing forward, but never actually touched her. Then, with a push of its flippers, the dolphin moved away.

Jody decided to go after it, kicking with her own rubber fins. But even though the curious dolphin had seemed to be moving very slowly, she couldn't catch up with him.

As soon as Jody gave up the chase, two other dolphins appeared — one on either side of her. They kept pace with her, slowing when she slowed, but keeping just out of her reach. They were playing some kind of game, she decided.

Jody moved toward the dolphin on her right. He immediately moved away — out of reach, but only just — keeping the same distance between them. And at the

Me and my bodyguards

same time that Jody pulled away, the dolphin on her left moved toward her. It was almost like a dance!

The thought gave her an idea. She began to swim in a zigzag pattern. The two dolphins copied her. She went up and down as well as from side to side, trying all sorts of different movements. Although she couldn't watch them that well, she was pretty sure that they were both keeping up with her crazy routines.

Jody looked around for her mother and saw that she was hovering in the water not far away, face-to-face with the smallest dolphin. She noticed that bubbles were coming out of that dolphin's blowhole, too, and she wondered if the dolphins were imitating the rising stream of bubbles that accompanied all scuba divers. Then she caught a glimpse of her father swimming along on his side, pointing the video camera in its bright yellow waterproof shell.

And now, for your entertainment: Jody McGrath and the Dancing Dolphin Duo! she thought, waving to him and pointing at herself. Then she swam lower, toward the seabed.

The other two dolphins suddenly appeared out of

nowhere right in front of her. One of them shot down to the ocean floor, rooted around in the sand with its nose, and then emerged with a prize in its jaws: a starfish!

This seemed to be the signal for a new game. Excited clicking and chattering noises came from all around. Jody's dancing partners abandoned her and rushed toward the one with the starfish. But it shot away and the others chased it.

Jody could only stare after them, wishing she could play, too. But she didn't have the speed for this game.

Four dolphins all ganged up on the one with the starfish. For a few moments there were five tumbling, whirling bodies in a cloud of bubbles. Then the turmoil broke up. One of the dolphins streaked away, coming back toward Jody.

She saw that this one — she couldn't tell if it was the same or a different one — carried the starfish. It swam above her — she saw the paler belly — and then it suddenly swooped down and dropped the starfish.

The starfish drifted down through the water until Jody stopped its progress by catching it in her hand.

What now? she wondered. They were all watching her, waiting for something. What was she supposed to do? She didn't like the idea of trying to outswim them with it, and being mobbed by all six dolphins. But it was useless trying to throw it for them; it would go no distance before drifting toward the bottom.

Then one of the dolphins moved away from the others and swam toward her. It swam very close, on a level with her hands, close enough for her to touch — and then it opened its mouth.

Jody stared at the regular, triangular teeth that lined its jaws. Then, very carefully, she placed the starfish between them.

The dolphin gave a series of rapid clicks as he closed his mouth gently on the starfish. Then he flipped over on his back and shot rapidly away, with his friends in noisy pursuit. This time, they all rose upward, giving Jody a unique, dolphin's-eye view of their activities.

Jody kicked off from the bottom and swam upward, wanting to join them. But she was too slow. It was like a baby trying to join in a football game, she thought. Humans could play with dolphins only when the dolphins were willing to make the game slow, simple, and gentle enough for the land-living creatures to keep up. But as she trailed after them, Jody thought she was incredibly lucky to be allowed to come so close to these wonderful, graceful creatures in the sea.

All too soon, she saw her mother's signal to return to the surface. Playtime was over.

June 23 — bedtime.

Watching the video Dad took of me playing with the dolphins, I could see things I didn't notice when I was underwater. Those two that were swimming alongside me began to move their tails in a funny, jerky way. Dad pointed it out. He said maybe they weren't just keeping pace with me, but were trying to imitate the way I swam. Were they making fun of me? Dad said no, probably they were trying to understand what it felt like to be me — just like I try to imagine sometimes, when I'm swimming underwater, that I'm a dolphin.

I decided to give them all names. Maddie suggested we stick with the Greek myths for inspiration. So, the one that reminds me the most of Apollo is Artemis, since she was Apollo's twin sister in the legends. The biggest one — Dad thinks he must be around three and a half yards long, and he's the most powerful-looking in the group — is Poseidon. Poseidon was the god of the sea, and the dolphin was sacred to him. Poseidon had a son called Triton, so that's what I've named the smallest dolphin in the group. The one carrying the micro-transmitter in his fin (you can see a piece of bright blue plastic sticking out) is Hermes, because he was the messenger of the gods. Our Hermes will carry messages about where the group is in relation to us.

Then I was stumped and couldn't think of names for the last two. They look absolutely identical and don't have any markings to suggest special names. Sean said they were twin dolphins, and weren't there some famous twins in Greek mythology? So those two are Castor and Pollux, the Gemini twins.

Poseidon, Triton, Hermes, Artemis, Castor, and Pollux have all disappeared, but we know from Dr. Taylor's

*transmitter that they are only two or three miles away —
or maybe more now, or less. They don't stay in one spot
for long but are always on the move. Even when they
sleep they only "catnap" for a short while, resting near
the surface. According to Mom, some researchers think
that dolphins sleep with only half of their brain at a time!*

*Still no sign of Apollo. I can't help thinking he'd be
happier if he were part of a group like the one we saw today.*

First thing the next morning, as usual, Jody ran out
onto the deck to look for dolphins.

Maddie stopped her as she passed, to give her a flask
of freshly brewed coffee. "Could you take this up to
Cam?"

Cam, who had spent the past two hours on watch-
duty, looked pleased to see her, even though Jody sus-
pected he would rather have had a visit from Maddie.

Jody looked around. The sea looked very gray today,
beneath a heavy, overcast sky, and the air was warm
and humid. She stared out at the horizon and saw a line
of pelicans flapping low above the water. Something

splashed nearby, but when she quickly turned to look, she could see nothing.

"Flying fish," Cam said. "They're really jumping. One of 'em slapped me in the face a little while ago — wham! What a way to start the day."

Jody giggled. "Have you seen any dolphins?"

Cam widened his green eyes at her. "Would I see a dolphin and not tell you?"

"I don't know." Jody felt embarrassed.

"Of course I wouldn't," he said easily. He winked. "Don't worry, you'll hear from me if I spot so much as a single fin of any . . .what are they called again?" he asked teasingly. "Oh, yeah — cetaceans."

"Thanks," Jody replied.

"Don't mention it." He took a careful sip of the coffee and sighed with pleasure. "Hey, Jody — if there're any biscuits for breakfast, could you ask someone to bring me one?"

She nodded. The mention of breakfast reminded her that she was hungry — and delicious smells were rising from the galley. After a final, wistful gaze out to sea, Jody went below to eat.

June 24 — after breakfast.

I almost wish I'd let Dr. Taylor put the transmitter into Apollo. Hermes didn't seem to mind it, and Dr. Taylor said it will drop out, anyway, in a few weeks. I would feel happier if I knew where Apollo was.

But that's silly. Apollo is at home in the ocean, whether or not I know where he is. Probably he has gone back to his group, or joined up with a new one. Dolphins are social animals, but Mom says they belong to different groups at different times; they aren't members of the same pod all their lives, like whales.

But I can't stop thinking that Apollo was lonely. I wish I could know that he was all right, after all.

The soft sound of something bumping the hull of the boat made Jody pause and look up. It hadn't sounded like the slap of a wave. As she strained her ears, she was rewarded with the faint but unmistakable sound of a dolphin's whistle.

Her heart gave a thump. She dropped her pencil, jumped out of her bunk, and hurried out on deck, with only one thought in her mind. She hardly noticed that someone called out to her as she raced past.

Up in the open air, Jody saw the familiar dolphin shape in the water right away. She scanned the waves searching for the rest of the group. But this dolphin was alone.

"Apollo?" Jody clutched the rail and leaned out over the side. The wind pushed back her hair and stroked her cheeks.

Below, the dolphin rose up, whistling. It seemed a familiar sound, or was she kidding herself? Yet it was certainly doing its best to attract her attention, Jody thought. His interest in her had to be more than just curiosity. She was *almost* sure it was Apollo.

Then the dolphin turned slightly and leaped up, presenting its right side to her. There was the curving, harp-shaped mark she remembered! It *was* Apollo — without any doubt.

Jody felt she would burst with happiness and excitement! She wanted to run and tell everyone the good news, but she didn't want to leave her newfound friend even for a minute. Luckily, her mother turned up within a few moments, looking puzzled.

"What's going on? The way you raced out, I thought it must be . . ." Her voice trailed off as she saw the dolphin beside the boat. She sighed and shook her head. "I should have known! You and dolphins . . ." Then she looked even more puzzled. "But how on earth did you know? Have you developed psychic powers all of a sudden?"

Jody laughed and shook her head. "I heard something — a little bump against the side of the boat — and I thought I'd come out to check. But oh, Mom, don't you see? It's *Apollo*! He's come back!"

Gina raised her eyebrows, looking skeptical. "Sure that's not just wishful thinking? One bottle-nosed dolphin looks a lot like any other."

Jody pointed at the leaping, racing animal beside the boat. "But look at him! He's excited to see me again. A strange dolphin wouldn't be acting like that, would he?"

Gina thought about it. She walked closer to the side,

grasped the metal railing, and leaned over. For a long minute she gazed into the water and listened.

When she turned back to her daughter, her face was thoughtful. "You're right," she said. "He *is* excited. Those noises he's making . . . well, I wouldn't want to swear to it, I'd really want to be able to listen to the tape again and not rely on my memory, but it does remind me . . ."

"Remind you of what?" Jody demanded, ready to burst with impatience.

"A few years ago I did some work with a couple of captive dolphins known as George and Martha," her mother explained. "Martha was sent away for a while, and George was very unhappy without her. She was brought back, but before George had seen her, before she was returned to the tank, he began this excited vocalizing. It was as if somehow he already knew she had returned." Gina smiled at Jody. "Maybe Apollo's just happy to see you," she said lightly.

Jody frowned. Apollo might be happy to see her, but that wasn't the whole story. She remembered the way the other dolphins had bumped against the boat . . . and she had an idea. "Do dolphins have a good sense of smell?" she asked.

"No," Gina replied, sounding surprised. "They probably can't smell at all. Certainly not the way land animals do."

"Oh," said Jody, disappointed. She had thought about the way dogs know if other dogs have been nearby, and she had wondered if Apollo could possibly have picked up some traces that would tell him other dolphins — maybe his friends? — had been around *Dolphin Dreamer* recently. But now she realized that smelling anything underwater was pretty unlikely.

But Gina went on. "They certainly have a sense of taste, and that probably makes up for the lack of smell. Studies have shown that they can sense even very tiny amounts of chemicals in water, and tell the difference between them."

Jody remembered that the dolphins' skin produced an oil to help them glide through the water. She wondered if any of that oil might still be on the side of the boat where the other dolphins had bumped it the day before. Was it possible that Apollo could taste the oil and recognize that it came from one of his friends? He might be desperately asking her where they'd gone . . . if only she could tell him.

"Jody? What's on your mind?" Gina asked, looking puzzled.

Jody was just about to explain when she had a brilliant idea. She caught her breath. "Mom, where's Dr. Taylor?"

"I don't know," her mother replied, looking even more puzzled. "Probably in his cabin. Why? Jody, what's going on?"

"I've got to talk to him. It's really important!" Jody cried. Then she began to scramble down the hatch. She didn't want to waste any more time. It was important to act quickly, before Apollo left again. She had to find out if her idea would work.

Jody found Dr. Jefferson Taylor relaxing in the main cabin, sipping from a tall glass of iced tea while he paged through a magazine for coin collectors. He wore a faded navy-blue T-shirt, which was stretched a little too tightly across his bulging middle, and his baggy shorts revealed hairy, knobby knees.

"Dr. Taylor," she cried excitedly. "I want to talk to you!"

"You do? Why?" Dr. Taylor clutched his magazine and peered nervously over it, as if expecting trouble.

Jody took a deep breath. "I wanted to ask if you could still track down that group of dolphins."

Dr. Taylor looked surprised at Jody's interest after her earlier disapproval. "The one I tagged yesterday? Yes, of course," he replied. "They can't possibly have traveled out of range yet. In fact, I was just about to check their whereabouts." He laid the magazine aside and stood up.

"*Great!*" Jody cried. She thought quickly. "Dr. Taylor, do you think, when you use your equipment to track them down, you could mark their position on the navigation chart? Then Harry could sail there. You'd have to keep tracking, since dolphins don't stay in one spot for long. But we could — "

"Jody, what are you trying to set up?" It was her father's voice. Jody turned to see both her parents staring at her in some bewilderment. Brittany was standing there, too, her face hard and malicious.

"Isn't it obvious?" Brittany spoke up, before Jody had a chance to answer. "She thinks this is *her* expedition. You guys should hear the junk she tells me about how much she knows, how Dolphin Universe was all her idea, and about all the work she's done to make it happen. She thinks she knows everything. Now she's decided that she's the boss! My dad won't go where I want, but if *Jody* asks him to change course, he'll hop right to it."

Jody was stunned by the hate-filled words pouring out of Brittany. Surely her parents couldn't believe what Brittany was saying. She looked desperately at their faces as they listened.

Gina turned to her daughter, her expression serious. "Okay, Brittany, let's hear Jody's side of the story. Well, Jody?"

"It's not true," Jody said hotly.

"Then maybe you should tell us exactly what did happen," said Craig gently. His normally easygoing face was unusually serious.

Jody felt close to tears. Everything was going horribly wrong. Nobody understood her. "I'm not trying to run things myself, honest," she said in a choked voice. "But I had this idea . . . and, well, I just wanted to know if what I thought of doing was *possible* before I asked you about it. But I *was* going to ask, just as soon as I worked it out." Her voice trailed away. She felt like a burst balloon.

"Well, why don't you tell us all now?" said Craig. He still looked serious, but it was clear he wasn't angry at her.

Everyone crowded around the table to listen — except Brittany, who hung back, trying to look as if she wasn't interested.

Jody explained her theory that Apollo might have "tasted" the presence of the other dolphins, and that was why he'd been so excited to find their boat again. Then she told them her idea: that they should track down the dolphin group and lead Apollo to them. She looked anxiously at her parents to see what they thought.

"You know," said Craig gently, "if Apollo has been separated from his group, chances are he'll soon find them again. Dolphins are much better at tracking things in the ocean than we humans are, even with our fancy equipment. And Poseidon and Company may not have anything to do with your Apollo."

"I know, I thought of that," Jody said quickly. "But even if they weren't his group to begin with, you did say that dolphins migrate to different groups sometimes. Maybe something happened to his old group and he needs a new one. I'm sure he doesn't want to be all alone. I want to give him a chance to meet some other dolphins."

Her parents exchanged a glance.

Jody held her breath.

Then Craig smiled. "Well, why not? Maybe it will turn out to be a wild-dolphin chase — but that's what we're here for, to follow wild dolphins. And it will give Dr. Taylor a chance to use his equipment."

Dr. Taylor brightened up at that. "Certainly, and I'll be happy to demonstrate it to you," he said.

"Yes, I'm sure you would," Craig said hastily. "But we might be a little busy for a long and scientific explanation."

Jody saw her mother's mouth twitch with amusement, and she guessed she was thinking about the long and boring message for TV that Dr. Taylor had recorded a few days earlier.

"All right, then," said Craig. "Let's get started. If you can locate the dolphin, Dr. Taylor, Harry and I can plot a new course."

As everyone rose from the table, Craig stopped and wagged his finger at Jody. "I like it when my kids have brilliant ideas," he said. "But, in the future, would you please run them by me or your mother before involving anybody else?"

"I will," Jody agreed. She tried to sound meek, but somehow a grin insisted on spreading across her face. Her dad thought it was a brilliant idea!

However, a few minutes later, as she hung over the side of the boat and watched Apollo keeping pace with them, she couldn't help thinking of all the many things that could go wrong with her plan. Apollo might lose interest in following them at any minute. Or they might not be able to catch up to the dolphins, even by sailing all day. Dolphins could speed through the water much faster than *Dolphin Dreamer*. They might keep them traveling in circles until Harry got fed up and refused to continue. Or, if Apollo didn't abandon them and they did find the other dolphins, maybe Poseidon and the others wouldn't like Apollo. They might even drive him away. One theory that Jody had read about lone dolphins who made friends with people was that they were outcasts from their groups.

But, like her mother, Jody believed it was best to think positive. And, since they might be sailing for hours yet, it made sense to try not to worry.

That afternoon, Jody sat on the foredeck, watching Apollo. He seemed to be having a great time, bow-riding. He had disappeared occasionally as they traveled, but never for very long. Jody couldn't help feeling that Apollo sensed there was a special reason to stay with *Dolphin Dreamer* and that he shared the excitement that kept bubbling up inside her.

Jody gazed out to sea. The clouds had burned away and the sky was a hard, clear blue overhead. Freshening winds blew them along rapidly — by good luck, in exactly the direction they wanted to go.

Suddenly, Jody froze, clutching the rail hard with excitement. Was that a dorsal fin rising above the waves? Was that another dolphin out there? Yes, it was! And another . . . and another! She gave a yell of triumph and called, "Dolphins off the starboard bow!"

She glanced down at the lower deck and saw that her parents were ready with the camera, and Harry was bringing the boat about, slowing their speed as they approached the dolphins. She looked back down at Apollo — and caught her breath. He'd disappeared.

Then, as Jody searched the water with anxious eyes, she saw him. Apollo was swimming beneath the water, his body like a sleek, gray bullet, heading straight for the other dolphins. She sighed with relief. Of course,

Apollo must have sensed the other dolphins, must have heard their songs, way before she saw them.

The others — Poseidon, Triton, Artemis, Hermes, Castor, and Pollux — formed a tight group and hovered in a mass in the water, unmoving as they waited for Apollo. They didn't look very friendly, and Jody felt a clutch of anxiety. Had she done the right thing? Was Apollo going to be all right?

All of a sudden, as if Apollo had crossed some invisible line in the water, the herd stopped waiting, and charged at him. Big Poseidon was in the lead, and Jody saw him hit Apollo broadside. She saw the impact make Apollo spin away, and she covered her mouth in horror. Poor Apollo! What had she done?

But Apollo recovered quickly and charged back through the water at Poseidon, slamming against the bigger dolphin. Then, twisting away, Apollo swam rapidly to the center of the group, and suddenly they were all slamming against one another, spinning, diving down, and leaping up in the air.

Jody breathed out with relief as she finally understood. They were playing! Now, as they leaped and dived, together and apart, it was impossible to mistake this behavior for anything other than having fun!

Apollo wasn't on his own anymore.

June 24 — continued.

Apollo is back where he belongs — with his friends. Maybe he'd always known where they were; probably he would have found his way back to them in another day or two, without the help of Dolphin Dreamer. *But I'm glad we were there to see the reunion. It was a wonderful sight to see.*

And to think that this is only the beginning of our great adventure!

Dolphin Diaries™

TOUCHING THE WAVES

1

June 25 — after breakfast.

Apollo and the other dolphins stayed around Dolphin
Dreamer with us all through the night, and now it looks
like they are headed for Key West, too! I can't help feeling that Apollo doesn't want to say good-bye any more
than I do. Maybe he is hoping, just like me, that we'll get
another chance to swim together.

Dr. Taylor calls this "fantasy," but I know there is a special bond between me and Apollo. After all, he can't explain why else this group of dolphins should be traveling

so closely with Dolphin Dreamer, *and even he has to admit that dolphins are very intelligent. He just muttered
something about "coincidence." But what does he know?
He was never in the water with Apollo; never touched
him, never gazed into his eyes, never felt that magical,
peaceful feeling. . . . It's hard to find the right words for
how being with Apollo makes me feel. It's so special. . . .*

Jody McGrath sighed dreamily and closed her diary,
thinking about the magical events of the past few
days. Barely a week ago she, her family, and the rest of
the crew of *Dolphin Dreamer* had sailed out of Fort
Lauderdale, Florida, to embark on an international research project on dolphins. Since then, the dolphin she'd
named Apollo had saved her life, and now he and his
friends were swimming alongside the boat like a guard of
honor.

She was suddenly eager to see him again. Stowing diary and pen safely away, she rolled off her bunk and left
the cabin.

Jody found her parents with their assistant, Maddie,
at one of the computers in the main cabin, going over

some data. Dr. Jefferson Taylor seemed to be working hard on his own laptop, but as she walked past, Jody saw the bright colors of a deck of playing cards laid out on his screen and realized he was just playing a game of solitaire!

She smiled to herself. Dolphin Universe had been Craig and Gina McGrath's idea, but they had found it difficult to raise enough money for the project. Then PetroCo, a large oil company, had offered to provide the rest of the money needed to make Dolphin Universe possible — but only if one of their own scientists, Dr. Jefferson Taylor, was added to the crew. So far, however, no one had worked out what use Dr. Taylor was going to be!

Jody walked through the main cabin without disturbing anyone, just exchanging a quick smile with her mother. She poked her head into the galley, where Mei Lin, the boat's cook and engineer, was washing the dishes from breakfast. "Are there any of those yummy rolls left?" she asked.

Mei Lin smiled. "For you, Jody, I think I can find one."

"Thanks!" Jody bit gratefully into the sweet, soft

dough. She was still eating as she swung up through the hatch and out onto the deck.

Harry Pierce, the boat's captain, was at the helm, while his second mate, the handsome Cameron Tucker, was checking the sails. Jody's younger brothers, twins Sean and Jimmy, were close at hand, listening attentively while Harry explained something about wind direction and speed. Brittany, Harry's daughter, was sitting nearby, but she had her back to the others as she stared out to sea with a frown on her face.

Dolphin Dreamer was flying along. Jody gazed up at the cloudless blue sky and breathed in the salty air. It was going to be another blazingly hot day, but for the moment at least, the winds were strong. She heard Cam say that at this rate they'd make Key West in under two hours.

"Thank goodness!" said Brittany loudly. "I can't wait to get to Key West."

"Oh? Is Key West a favorite place, Britt?" Sounding interested, Cam turned his sparkling green eyes in her direction.

Brittany tossed her head, sending her long hair flying. "I prefer Miami or Palm Beach, actually," she said loudly. "But anywhere with shops and people and things to do has got to be better than being stuck on this boat in the middle of nowhere!"

Jody saw Harry Pierce wince at his daughter's words. She felt sorry for him. Brittany had been a last-minute, and most unwilling, addition to the crew of *Dolphin Dreamer*. Telling Brittany that her father would be taking her to the Bahamas for her summer vacation, her mother had dropped Brittany off on the day they were to sail, and then left the country! As there was no one else who could look after her, Brittany had been forced to come along. Harry was trying his best — they all were — to make Brittany feel welcome, but Jody had the feeling that nothing anyone could do would be good enough for her.

Jody climbed up to the forward deck and looked over the side. Her heart beat faster as she saw the dolphins racing along with the boat.

There were the seven wild bottle-nosed dolphins: Apollo, Artemis, Poseidon, Hermes, Triton, Castor, and Pollux. They were leaping through the water, pushing and jostling one another for the best position, "bow-riding" one after another on the wave created by the forward movement of the boat. Dolphins loved to do this with boats of all sizes. Jody's dad had told her that dolphins had even been spotted riding the wave created by the head of a large whale.

Jody felt a big smile break out across her face as she watched them. Her spirits lifted as effortlessly as the dolphins leaped and dived. It was almost impossible not to feel happy in the presence of these beautiful creatures. The bad atmosphere caused by Brittany seemed to blow away like sea foam in the wind.

Eventually, the dolphins grew tired of their sport with the boat and swam off, disappearing into the blue distance. Jody felt a pang as she watched them swim away, but somehow she felt certain this was not the last she'd see of them.

Cam, Craig, and Gina got to work taking down and stowing the sails as the buildings on the shores of Key West came into sight, and Harry switched on the engine.

Moments later Mei Lin appeared on deck. "Harry, I don't like the sound of that motor," she said, frowning slightly.

Jody couldn't hear anything unusual in the noisy drone, but she saw Harry listen intently and then nod slowly.

"Something's wrong," he agreed. "Luckily, for the next two weeks we won't have anything else to do, so we've got all the time we need to —"

"Nothing else to do!" Brittany whirled around to glare at her father. "What about taking me shopping, and sight-seeing? You *promised*."

Harry looked uncomfortable. He cleared his throat. "Of course I will, love."

"Don't worry. I was fixing engines single-handedly long before I met your father," Mei Lin said to Brittany, trying to lighten the mood. "I don't need him. I'll be glad for you to take him out of my hair!"

"Have a little more respect for your captain," Harry said with a mock scowl before turning back to his daughter. "There, you see? I can take a couple of days off. We'll do whatever you want." He smiled hopefully.

But Brittany's furious scowl did not relax. "A couple of days?" she repeated. "Out of two whole weeks? And we have to stay on the boat the *whole* of the rest of the time? What am I supposed to do with myself? Can't we go to a hotel?"

"Of course not," Harry replied, frowning himself now. "This is where I live, so it's where you live while you're with me."

Brittany turned and pointed a finger at Jody. "But *she* isn't going to stay on the boat! I know, because I heard her mother telling her to pack!"

Jody shook her head. Brittany really was spoiled and rude beyond belief! "If you'd bothered to listen, you'd know that we're not going off on a vacation to a hotel," she told the other girl. "We're going to visit CETA, on Cedar Key."

Brittany scowled. "See-ta," she repeated. "What's that?"

"C-E-T-A," Jody spelled out. She paused to make sure she remembered the name exactly and then went on. "It stands for 'Cetaceans as Educational and Therapeutic Associates.' Cetaceans are dolphins," she added, seeing the blank expression on Brittany's face.

Brittany made a face. "I might have known, dolphins again!" she groaned. "But you still haven't told me what it is."

"It's a special center for disabled children," Jody explained. "I think the kids get to swim with dolphins, and it helps them, somehow. I don't really know much more about it — that's what we're here to find out." She began to feel excited again, forgetting her irritation with Brittany as she thought of the days ahead. "It's run by an old friend of my mom's. Her name is Alice Rozakis, and her husband, Jerry, is a psychologist who specializes in helping children. And they've got a daughter my age named Lauren. Gosh, it must be so great for her, to live in a place like that!"

"Only if she likes dolphins," Brittany muttered.

Jody knew that Brittany had no interest in dolphins, so she could hardly believe her ears when the other girl turned to her father and declared, "I want to go to . . . er . . . CETA as well."

Harry frowned. "Brittany, you can't just invite your-self —"

Another voice interrupted him. "We'd love to have Brittany join us, Harry."

Jody turned in surprise at her father's voice. Craig and Gina had come out on deck and must have heard the conversation.

"I'll just give Alice a call on the cell phone, to make sure there's room for one more," added Gina, moving briskly toward the hatch.

Jody turned back to Brittany. "But — but you don't even like dolphins!" she protested. She'd had to put up with the bad-tempered girl for long enough and was looking forward to a break. "You'd enjoy yourself much more here in Key West — your dad said he'll take you out."

Brittany shrugged her shoulders moodily. "Yeah, for two whole days. If I have to spend the rest of the time on this boat I'll go crazy," she said in a low voice. "Any-way, there's got to be more to do than just look at dol-phins on Cedar Key."

Gina poked her head out of the hatch. "Alice says the

more the merrier! Plenty of room in her big minivan, and it'll be like a slumber party in Lauren's bedroom. Lauren's looking forward to it."

Jody's heart sank. Desperately, she tried again to change Brittany's mind. "But we won't have time for sight-seeing — it'll be dolphins, dolphins, dolphins all the time. And you'll be stuck if you come with us — you won't get to do anything fun with your dad!"

"Of course she will," said Gina, giving Jody a warning look. "Harry, Alice says there's an anchorage by their house on Cedar Key, so after you've finished your repairs and so on, you can join us there. And of course we can bring Brittany back here anytime. Alice says they come down to Key West every few days to shop — they're only about twenty miles up the highway."

Harry nodded. "All right. That's very kind. . . . Thank you," he said quietly, looking from Gina to Craig before nodding at his daughter. "Okay, Brittany, run and pack a few things if you're going."

A triumphant smile spread across Brittany's face. She hurried below without another word.

"Don't bother to say thank you," Jody muttered. She stared at the rows of moored boats they were chugging past. She felt as if a heavy weight had settled on her shoulders.

Sean and Jimmy were the first off the boat once it docked, challenging each other to races and acting like puppies let out of a cage.

Dr. Taylor was the next to leave. He wasn't going to Cedar Key. He'd made his own arrangements to visit some other research projects in the Florida Keys. "I will, of course, supply you with detailed reports, so you won't miss anything," he told Jody's parents as he left.

"Thank you. I'm sure that will be very useful to the project," said Gina politely.

They watched from the deck, waving, as Dr. Taylor drove away in a rental car.

Craig McGrath gave a gusty sigh. "Whew, I'm looking forward to a vacation from that guy!"

Jody was also rather relieved to have a break from Dr. Taylor's rather stuffy presence. If only she could have a break from Brittany, too!

Gina McGrath shook her head, smiling. "He's harmless enough," she said. "And he probably feels the same way about us!" She picked up her bag. "Come on, we might as well get going — Alice said she'd meet us in the parking lot, by the flagpole."

Jody shrugged on her backpack. She'd packed lightly, just a few clothes, her diary, and the book she was reading. Since Cedar Key was not far from Key West, they could easily return to *Dolphin Dreamer* whenever they liked.

As she followed her parents and Maddie along the jetty, Jody found her legs were a bit wobbly. Solid ground felt strange beneath her feet after a few days at sea.

"Gina! Over here!"

The call came from a tall, fair-haired woman waving her arms vigorously above her head.

Gina McGrath broke into a smile and rushed forward. "Alice!" The two women hugged each other warmly.

"You remember Craig, of course," Gina said, stepping back with a smile.

"I think the last time we met was at your wedding,"

said the tall woman, shaking Craig's hand. Her face was tanned and friendly and her smile was warm.

"This is our daughter, Jody, and our two sons, Sean and Jimmy," Gina went on. "Brittany Pierce, the daughter of our captain. And this is Maddie, our invaluable assistant — I think you've exchanged a few e-mails with her already!"

They all smiled and nodded at one another, and then Alice Rozakis led them to her vehicle where a tall, serious-looking girl with her brown hair tied back in a long braid was waiting. "This is my daughter, Lauren," she said. Lauren smiled and gave a brief wave at the others.

"Now let's get out of this heat and on our way!" Alice suggested, linking an arm through Gina's.

Jody'd hoped to talk to Lauren — she had about a million questions to ask her — but somehow, as they all piled in, Brittany managed to grab the seat next to Lauren, and Jody had to squash in with her brothers. She tried not to mind as she watched Brittany chatting away with Lauren, but she couldn't help feeling left out.

Instead of asking Lauren about CETA, as Jody would have done, Brittany quizzed her about her favorite movies, TV shows, and pop groups. They seemed to like all the same ones.

Jody gazed out of the window at the ocean, which glittered in the sun on either side of Highway 1. Even now, she seemed to feel its movement beneath her. Soon they left the highway for the entrance to CETA, and Jody sat up, alert.

The center turned out to be a group of low, white-washed buildings with red-tiled roofs in the Spanish style. The Rozakis family home was right next door to the CETA office, and they shared a big, walled court-yard facing out to sea.

As she showed them around, Alice explained that the center had been built around a natural lagoon. This had been fenced off from the open sea to create a large "sea pen" for the resident dolphins. Connected to this big "pen" by canals that could be left open or fenced off, were two large pools, one of them very shallow. This was for the benefit of children who couldn't swim or weren't comfortable in deep water. The bigger pool had a wooden dock projecting out into it.

A short, dark-bearded man in swimming trunks was

standing on the dock with a slim young woman and a little boy who also wore trunks and a life jacket.

"That's my dad," Lauren said proudly.

"Jerry's working right now," Alice explained. "He's promised to join us as soon as he can. Let me just pop into the office and see if there are any messages."

Everyone followed her into the office, which was an airy, friendly space with bright yellow walls, decorated with children's colorful drawings. A young woman with long, shining black hair was seated at one of the two desks, typing something into a computer. She looked up with a welcoming smile.

Alice briefly introduced them. "This is Kim Lo, Jerry's assistant. She keeps everything organized for us. Any messages?" she asked.

"Six e-mails and two phone calls wanting information about the program," Kim replied. "All routine, don't worry — I can deal with them."

"Thank you," said Alice warmly. "I'm just going to get our guests settled, but give me a yell if you need anything."

Once inside the house, Craig and Gina went with Alice.

Lauren showed Sean and Jimmy to a twin-bedded guest room, then took Jody and Brittany to her own bedroom. "You guys can have the twin beds," she said, pointing. "There's an air mattress for me — don't worry, it's really comfortable."

Jody was interested to see that on one of Lauren's bedroom walls was the same poster of leaping dolphins that she had at home.

But before she could comment on it, Brittany called out, "Hey, Lauren, could I use your computer to check my e-mail?"

"Sure," said Lauren. "But maybe later? I wanted to introduce you to —"

"Please?" Brittany interrupted, smiling persuasively. "I'm expecting to hear from my mother — I really can't wait!"

Lauren shrugged. "Okay." She looked at Jody. "How about you? Want to come meet the teachers?"

Jody thought she'd rather meet the dolphins, but she

wanted to be polite, so she nodded. "But shouldn't we wait for Mom and Dad, and Maddie?"

"Oh, my folks'll give 'em the grand tour after they've finished gossiping and drinking coffee. Why should we wait? Come and get introduced!" Lauren's gray eyes gleamed with excitement.

"Okay." Jody wondered what the big deal was about the teachers. Could Lauren have a crush on one of them? "How many teachers are there?" she asked, gazing at Lauren's long, brown braid as she followed her through the house.

"Just four," Lauren replied. "We'd like to have more, but well, it takes a very special type to relate well to the kids who come here for help, and not everyone can do it."

Instead of turning toward the buildings when they came out of the house, Lauren walked toward the lagoon. Jody immediately became more interested: Maybe the teachers were in the water with the dolphins and the children?

Yet she couldn't see anyone as they drew near. The figures who had been standing on the dock were now gone, the shallow pool was empty, and she couldn't see anyone but Lauren and herself in the whole area.

Lauren led the way onto a wooden dock, which curved along beside the fence that separated the lagoon from the open sea. She gazed out at the blue-green water for a moment, and then she whistled.

Jody looked at Lauren, impressed. The whistle was very much like a sound made by dolphins.

Seconds later, a sleek gray form came shooting through the water toward them, the familiar curved dorsal fin slicing through the surface.

Jody laughed with delight. "Oh, you teaser," she said to Lauren. "Making me think I was going to meet some boring old teachers . . ."

"But this *is* one of the CETA teachers," said Lauren, a look of utter innocence on her serious face. "The dolphins are the teachers here, because they're the ones who help the kids to learn. My dad thinks of himself as just an assistant — he'll tell you that."

The dolphin poked his head up out of the water and clacked and whistled at Lauren. Then he turned his head to examine Jody with a bright, intelligent eye.

"This is Nick," said Lauren. "See that little notch on his fin? That'll help you to recognize him."

Another bottle-nosed dolphin popped up beside Nick, whistling.

"Hi, Nora," Lauren said. She whistled back, setting off a chorus of whistles from the two dolphins. "Nick, Nora, meet Jody. Can you whistle, Jody?" They like it when you do."

It was hard to stop smiling at the enchanting crea-

Two of CETA's teachers — Nick and Nora!

tures long enough to pucker up, but Jody did her best. She was rewarded with a stream of chattering clicks and whistles from both Nick and Nora, who rose out of the water to nod their heads, as if in approval.

"I have a recorder," Jody told Lauren. "The dolphins we've met at sea seemed to love me playing it to them. I wish I hadn't left it on the boat."

Lauren nodded. "The dolphins love music," she said. "When Dad sits out in the courtyard playing his guitar, they all come into the shallow pool to listen! You could pick up your recorder later." She looked around. "Maxi's over there, so Rosie must be nearby. Rosie is Maxi's daughter."

They walked farther along the dock to meet the other two dolphins.

Maxi was the biggest and, Lauren said, the oldest of the CETA dolphins. She seemed uninterested in her visitors, or maybe she'd just had a hard day. She swam slowly away as Rosie came speeding up to check them out. Rosie was a slim, sleek young thing with a knot of scar tissue over one eye.

"What happened?" Jody asked, pointing.

"Fish hook," Lauren said solemnly. "The vet said if it had gone in one inch nearer, she'd have lost the eye."

Jody shuddered. "How awful!"

But the accident was obviously long forgotten by Rosie, who leaped straight out of the water when the girls drew near, showering them with water.

Jody gave a shriek and then laughed. Like an echo, Rosie made a sound very much like human laughter.

"Rosie's our wild girl," said Lauren affectionately. "But only if you can take it. Put somebody shy or scared in the pool with her and she'll be as sweet as pie."

"She's your favorite, isn't she?" Jody guessed.

Lauren hesitated, then nodded. "I love them all," she said. "But I guess I do love Rosie the best. I've known her since she was a baby. She's only five now — that's a young teenager, Mom says."

Jody recognized a kindred spirit in Lauren. Here was someone else who knew the joys of having a dolphin for a friend. She grinned, suddenly sure that the next two weeks on Cedar Key were going to be absolutely wonderful.

2

Jody spent the rest of the afternoon being shown around by Lauren. Later, they were joined by Brittany and the twins. They didn't meet Lauren's father, Dr. Jerry Rozakis, until he appeared at the dinner table, apologizing for keeping everyone waiting.

"Call me Jerry," Dr. Rozakis said as he shook Jody's hand. "Everybody does." He was a short, wiry man with a head of black curls and piercing blue eyes. Although he was lively and enthusiastic, and obviously pleased to have guests, Jody thought he looked tired.

They were just finishing big bowls of fiery chili

served with tortillas and salad, when Bud, a tall, lanky young man who helped with the care of the dolphins, came in.

"Hey, Jerry? Sorry to bother you," he said, "but there's something going on down at the sea gates. They won't come in to be fed." Bud waved his big hands around. "I don't know what to do. . . . I know I'm not supposed to leave till they've had their dinner, but I don't want to be late for my date."

Jerry sighed and put his napkin on the table. "That's okay, you run along, Bud. I'll make sure they're fed."

"Thanks, Jerry. Appreciate it!" Bud said, and hurried out of the door.

Jody saw that Alice didn't look pleased. "Really, Jerry, you're too easygoing. We pay him to do a job — he knew the hours when he took it," she said disapprovingly.

"I don't mind, honey," Jerry replied, rubbing his face wearily as he spoke. "You know I like to check on them every night myself."

"Is there a problem?" Gina asked, sounding concerned.

"Only with our assistant," said Alice, managing a smile. "The dolphins are probably not responding because they're too interested in something on the other side of the fence. Wild dolphins, most likely," she explained. "They stop by to have a chat with ours from time to time. Our dolphins get very excited. Well, they're social creatures. But after a while they'll remember it's feeding time. There wouldn't be a problem if Bud wasn't in such a hurry."

Wild dolphins! Jody caught her breath.

"We've been swimming with wild dolphins," Sean said proudly.

"Can we go and look?" Lauren was eager, watching her mother for permission.

Alice nodded. "If you've finished your dinner," she replied.

"Come on Jody, Brittany," Lauren said. She looked at her mother. "We can feed them, then Dad can just relax."

"He can try," said Alice with a short laugh. She smiled at her daughter. "Thank you, Lauren. That would be helpful."

The twins, too, were scrambling out of their seats. Jody expected Brittany to make a scornful comment about dolphins. She never hesitated to sneer at Jody's interest, but she must have decided it was worth being nice to Lauren, because she followed without a word.

Outside, night had fallen. Jody couldn't see any of the dolphins in the dark water.

"Where are they?" Jimmy demanded.

"Shh. Listen," Lauren whispered.

The sound of distant creaks, clicks, and whistles carried on the breeze over the water.

Jody's heart began to pound. The hairs on the back of her neck lifted at the sound of one particular, strangely familiar, whistle. "Apollo," she whispered.

"What?" Brittany snapped. "How do you know? You can't even see them! It could be any dolphin!"

But Jody was sure. "It's him. That was his signature whistle — I recognize it!"

"As if you could recognize a whistle!" Brittany said scornfully.

"Every dolphin makes a special whistle, which might be like a human's name," Lauren said, gently backing up Jody. "It's called a 'signature' whistle because it seems to be the way dolphins identify themselves. I've learned to tell the difference between the sounds our dolphins make — there! That was Rosie!"

"This is boring," Jimmy complained. "I can't see a thing! I thought we were going to get to feed the dolphins."

"Yes, we are," Lauren said. "They might be ready to come now." She walked over to the side of the water where two big white buckets full of fish had been left, along with a large whistle hanging on a thick cord. She picked this up and blew a long blast on it.

After a long moment of silence, two dark, snub-nosed shapes popped up from the water, practically at Lauren's feet. Everyone except Lauren jumped.

"They're so fast and quiet," Brittany said. "I didn't even hear them coming."

She sounded nervous rather than admiring, Jody thought.

"Yeah, aren't they great?" Lauren replied. As she spoke, Lauren tossed two fish out. "Here, you want to feed them?" she asked, turning to Brittany.

Brittany backed away. "No thanks. I don't want to get my hands all smelly."

"I do!" Sean and Jimmy spoke at once, and jostled each other to get at the fish.

"Take it easy," Lauren said, laughing. "Even dolphins don't fight over dead fish! There's plenty to go around."

"But only two dolphins," Sean noted. "Which ones are these?"

"Nick and Nora," Lauren replied. "They're the greediest. Maxi and Rosie will be here in a minute."

Sure enough, seconds later, another dolphin glided up to be fed. Jody identified her by her size as Maxi. "I guess Rosie must still be gossiping with Apollo," she said.

Brittany snorted. "That is so babyish — as if animals could talk!"

"My mom thinks they do," Lauren said calmly, still flinging fish into the gaping mouths below her. "Maybe they don't use words, like us, but they do tell each other things. Mom worked on a study about it years ago."

"Oh," Brittany said, sounding surprised. "So what are they telling each other now?"

Lauren shrugged. "I wish I knew. Mom says maybe the wild dolphins come to find out if the dolphins behind the fence are okay, to find out if they're mistreated, or prisoners. If that's true, I hope ours are telling the wild ones that they're happy here."

"But they *are* prisoners here, aren't they?" Brittany challenged. "You've got them trapped behind that fence."

Jody was eager to hear Lauren's reply. She'd wondered uneasily about this herself.

"No," said Lauren. "They don't have to stay here if they don't want to. There's a gate in that fence — the sea gate. We open it every weekend and they can go out if they want. But so far, they've always come back. They must like it here."

Jody gazed into the distance at the dark sea, where Apollo and his friends were on the other side of the fence. Although she couldn't see it now, she recalled that the fence rose only a couple of yards above the surface of the water. A dolphin could easily jump that high. That meant that the CETA dolphins could escape out to sea at anytime, whether the sea gates were open or not. They must stay because they liked it here, as Lauren said.

"Hmm, so they're kind of like your pets," Brittany said. "I had a cat called Hazel who used to go off wandering for hours — sometimes all day. But she always came back at dinnertime. Until —" She broke off.

"What happened?" Lauren asked gently.

Brittany shrugged. "We never found out. My mother said she probably found a new home she liked better. . . . But I think she must have died. She probably got hit by a car. . . ." Brittany's voice sounded flat and sad.

How awful, Jody thought, feeling sorry for the poor lost cat. She was surprised to find that she also felt sorry for Brittany.

"Gosh, you must miss her," said Lauren warmly.

Brittany nodded a little stiffly, but let Lauren put a comforting arm around her.

They carried on feeding the dolphins together,

Lauren still fussing around Brittany. But it was clear from the way that Brittany ignored Jody that she wanted no sympathy from her.

When feeding time was over, Jody left Brittany and Lauren to it and, feeling a little lonely, went to rejoin the others inside the house.

June 26 — after breakfast.

Lauren is taking tennis lessons this summer, and her mom arranged for me, Sean, and Jimmy to have lessons this week, too. Of course, she didn't know Brittany would be with us . . . I earned lots of brownie points by saying Brittany could take my place and I would stay here. The truth is, I'd much rather stay here and learn how "dolphin-assisted therapy" works, instead of standing in the hot sun trying to hit a ball over a net.

Even so, I didn't much like being left behind. I got a funny feeling in my stomach, watching Lauren and Brittany go off for their first lesson together, a few minutes ago. They were giggling about something, and hardly seemed to notice when I said good-bye. It really hurt!

I like Lauren, and I think she likes me. We both love dolphins more than anything, and I'm sure we'd be better friends if Brittany wasn't here.

But Brittany is making a real effort to get all of Lauren's attention. She doesn't let on to Lauren that, really, she couldn't care less about dolphins — she just changes the subject — to things I don't know much about, like pop music, fashion, and some TV shows they both love which I've never seen. Plus, she's got Lauren feeling sorry for her, and pretends to be this sweet, misunderstood girl that everybody else is mean to (especially me!).

Well, I am not going to stoop to Brittany's level. I won't say anything bad about her to Lauren — but I can write down how I really feel here, where no one else will see it.

The working day at CETA was about to begin. Craig and Gina had decided that, with the parents' permission, they would make a video record of each session, to become part of the Dolphin Universe database.

As they set up their equipment, Jerry Rozakis filled them in. "Our first patient of the day is named Heather. She's four, and has Down's syndrome." He bent down to stroke Maxi, who was lying quietly in the shallow pool, then went on seriously, "Long ago, it was assumed that people born with Down's could never learn anything. But we know now that's not true. Some people are more severely handicapped than others, but you never really know how much someone can achieve unless you give them their best chance. Children like Heather need help in paying attention so they can begin to learn. And a good way to get someone's attention is to connect learning with something fun."

"Dolphins?" Jody guessed.

Jerry grinned. "Right. A grown-up like me is boring, but a dolphin is fun. So guess who's the best teacher here?"

Jody grinned back. "Maxi!" She liked Lauren's dad, and she bet he was a great teacher, whatever he said.

Jerry gazed out at the deeper water, where the other three dolphins dipped in and out of view. "Rosie, Nick, Nora . . . they're all wonderful teachers, too," he went on. "We try to match the personalities of the children to those of the dolphins. Maxi is the most 'motherly' — older than the others; the most patient. She's the best choice for younger or more timid children. Rowdier children might get on better with Rosie or Nick. And sometimes one of the dolphins will just take a special liking to a particular child. Dolphins know who they like —" He broke off as the door to the office opened.

His assistant, Kim, came out with a man and a woman who were holding the hands of a little girl in a red swimsuit and a bright orange life jacket. They were all smiling broadly.

"Guess what, Jerry," called the woman, who seemed to be the child's mother. "Heather got herself dressed this morning — she put on her swimsuit all by herself!"

"Wow, that's great!" Jerry crouched down to talk to the little girl. "Is that right, Heather? No help from anybody?"

"No help," Heather replied proudly. "I do it all by myself!"

"Well, you'll have to tell Maxi about it — I'm sure she'll be pleased with you," Jerry said.

Heather clapped her hands excitedly. "Want see Maxi! Want go in water!"

From the pool came a string of clicking sounds that

seemed to say Maxi was as eager for this meeting as Heather was.

"Soon," Jerry promised. "First, we're going to sit on the side of the pool, and you and Maxi are going to play a game with me, okay?"

Heather nodded, and sat down obediently.

Jerry showed her a box of brightly colored plastic toys. "Find the blue ball," he said.

The little girl plunged her hand into the box and grabbed a blue ring.

"No, listen to *both* words, Heather: blue . . . ball." Jerry spoke slowly and clearly.

This time, Heather paused, and looked carefully before pulling out the correct toy.

"Yes! Very good, Heather!" Jerry smiled as he praised, and offered a reward. "Would you like to throw the blue ball to Maxi?"

"Yes!" Heather beamed with delight. She drew her arm back and threw the ball. A moment later, Maxi returned it to her, which caused Heather to laugh and clap her hands.

Maxi at work!

"Okay, Heather, now I want you to find a red block," said Jerry.

The little girl found it the first time.

The simple lesson went on for about ten minutes, and then Heather was allowed to slip into the pool along with Jerry, to play with Maxi. Although this was her reward for paying attention and doing well, the lesson wasn't over. Kim tossed different colored rings into the water, then Maxi fetched them, one at a time, and returned them to Heather, who had to name the color for Jerry. She got them right every time, without pausing or struggling.

Jody watched, fascinated. She knew that some people — even her scientist mother — scoffed at people who made unscientific claims for dolphins having special powers. But it seemed that there was something almost magical between this little girl and Maxi.

When Heather's time was up, Jerry rejoined the McGraths while Kim went to fetch the next patient from the office.

Jerry explained that ten-year-old Bobby Fox was severely mentally retarded. He couldn't even speak, and the doctors and teachers who had tested him didn't know how much he could understand.

"His parents had nearly given up hope of ever reaching him," said Jerry in a low voice. "But in the weeks that he's been coming here, we've seen a great improvement. It won't mean as much to you since you didn't see him a month ago, but we think of him as one of our great successes."

A few minutes later, Kim returned with a dark-haired woman wearing a long blue dress, and a short, dark-haired boy in swimming trunks and a life jacket. He dashed toward the deeper pool, where Jody had noticed Nora swimming by herself. The woman cried out and tried to grab him, but he was already out of her reach.

"Bobby, stop!" Jerry spoke loudly and firmly, and the boy froze at the edge of the pool.

Nora poked her nose up out of the water and made a sound like a creaking hinge.

At this, the boy began to make a clicking sound.

Jody caught her breath in surprise. Jerry had said that Bobby couldn't speak, but here he was trying his best to talk — with a dolphin!

The first part of Bobby's session took place on the dock overlooking the deeper pool. Jerry used the same box of toys, and asked the same sort of questions that he had asked of Heather. But what the four-year-old had found easy was a great struggle for this ten-year-old.

Jody could see that Bobby had trouble understanding even simple ideas such as "bigger" and "smaller." It was very hard for him to sort bricks by color and size. But he tried. He made noises of frustration and anger, but he did not give up. Jody saw that he was so eager for a chance to join Nora in the water that he would do his best to do what he was asked.

After ten minutes of this hard work, Bobby was allowed to get into the water with Nora. She swam right up to him, and Bobby stroked her gently, gazing at her lovingly. Jody felt a lump in her throat as she remembered Apollo. She knew just how Bobby felt.

3

Alice returned with Lauren, Brittany, Sean, and Jimmy at noon, when everyone stopped work for a quick lunch of sandwiches and salad.

"So what do you think of CETA so far?" Alice asked Gina and Craig as they gathered in the big kitchen to eat.

"It's very impressive," Craig replied. "I do have some questions, though."

"Fire away," said Jerry, biting into a cheese and tomato sandwich.

"Well, I understand the theory behind it," Craig began slowly. "And it's clear from what we've seen this morning that dolphin-assisted therapy really does work for the children, but what's going to happen after they leave? They're making progress while working with the dolphins, but there won't be any dolphins to help them out at home."

Jerry put down his sandwich and scratched his beard. "That's true. There is a limit to what we can do here. It wouldn't be practical for children to keep coming to us day after day, for years on end. We aren't aiming to replace other kinds of schools or therapies. But we hope that the experience of learning with dolphins for a little while will have a lasting effect. The idea is to 'jump-start' the child, give them an extra boost that will get them going."

Gina paused with her fork above her salad. "And does that work?" she asked.

"Yes, for many people," Jerry replied. "Sometimes it's enough for the kids to realize that they *can* learn — a breakthrough can lead to real progress that will continue long after they leave us."

"Did you meet Heather?" Alice asked from across the table.

Craig, Gina, Jody, and Maddie all nodded.

"Heather's a good example," Jerry said enthusiastically. "When her parents said she'd dressed herself this morning, I thought, *yes*! Her excitement about the dolphins has carried over into her daily life — she's just generally more alert. And that has lasting effect — it nearly always does. The more she learns to do, the more self-confidence that will give her, and the more she will try to do."

"I could see that Heather really loved being with Maxi," Jody said.

Her mother nodded. "The dolphins certainly kept the children's attention — which, as you said earlier, is the first step in getting someone to learn anything."

"I think you've convinced us all that dolphins are great teachers," Craig added.

"Oh, they're more than that," Alice told them. "They also play a great role as healers."

Jody leaned forward, even more curious now. But she saw that her mother was looking skeptical.

Gina shook her head. "Oh, Alice. You're not talking about all those people who go swimming with dolphins and claim they've been cured of their illnesses, are you?"

Alice gave her old friend a level look across the table. "Yes, Gina, I am."

"But that's just an emotional reaction," Gina protested. "It's not something you can measure, or prove. We're scientists, Alice — we have to look at the facts, not just listen to people's stories."

Craig cleared his throat. "Um, but, Gina, you know that, as a psychologist, Jerry does have to listen to people's stories, and be concerned with their emotions."

Jody recognized her father's peace-making tone, and so, it seemed, did Alice and Gina, because they both burst out laughing.

"We're having a friendly discussion here, darling," Gina told her husband. "You know that I always try to keep an open mind."

"Anyway," Alice continued, "I was just about to explain that my interest as a scientist is in trying to prove that dolphins *can* have a measurable effect on making people feel better." She paused for a sip of iced tea.

"Alice is studying the effect of sound vibrations on brain waves," Jerry added. "There have already been studies on the effect of sounds we hear, like music, on our emotions, but even sounds we can't hear — ultrasound — can affect us."

"Ultrasound?" Brittany suddenly spoke up from the far end of the table where she'd been talking about tennis with Lauren. "That's something they do in hospitals. My aunt had an ultrasound scan when she was pregnant, to make sure her baby was okay. What does that have to do with dolphins?"

"Ultrasound is the term used for sonic vibrations, or sounds, that we humans can't hear," Alice explained.

"But dolphins can," Jody guessed. She remembered her dad explaining to her, Jimmy, and Sean how important sound was to dolphins; that they find their way around using sound rather than sight.

"Yes," Alice agreed. "Dolphins can hear and make sounds in the ultrasonic range. The sort of ultrasound scan Brittany mentioned can give us information about things we can't see, and dolphins probably use their ultrasound in the same way. Some doctors have suggested

208

ultrasound could be used for healing. It might be used instead of surgery, to destroy a tumor, for example."

Jody was so fascinated she forgot to eat. "Could dolphins do that?" she blurted out.

"Oh, no," Alice said quickly, shaking her head. "I wasn't suggesting that! The ultrasound frequencies used in medicine are much, much higher than anything a dolphin could produce. But there's no doubt that the experience of spending time with dolphins has made many people feel better."

"Feeling loved and accepted makes people feel better about themselves," Jerry added. "People who have pets — or companion animals, as they're sometimes called — are usually healthier and happier than people who live alone."

"And that's not just an animal-lover's opinion," Alice said with a teasing smile at Gina. "There have been scientific studies to prove it!"

"Oops!" exclaimed Jerry with a look at his watch. "I hate to eat and run, but I have to look at some paperwork before the next patient arrives." He got up. "I'll see you all later."

209

Alice rose and began to clear the table. "I'll get these washed, and then —"

"I'll do it, Mom," Lauren said.

"I'll help you," said Jody.

"That's okay, Jody," said Brittany, starting to help Lauren stack plates. "You run along with your folks and study those dolphins — Lauren and I can manage just fine without you." Her tone was poisonously sweet.

Jody's heart sank.

But Lauren smiled at her. "Up to you," she said, "but I thought we could all go swimming when our food's digested."

"Great," said Jody. It seemed that Brittany hadn't managed to turn Lauren against her, after all. "I love swimming."

"Okay then, clearing up won't take long between the three of us," said Lauren, throwing Jody a dishcloth.

Brittany sulked for a few seconds, then decided to make the best of it. "My mom and I have our own swimming pool at home in West Palm Beach," she bragged.

Lauren laughed. "So do we — and ours has dolphins in it!" She turned away to scrape leftovers off a plate.

"Oh. We're going to swim *with* the dolphins?" Brittany's voice suddenly sounded wary.

"Uh-huh, it'll be the best swim you've ever had," Lauren replied.

But Jody could see from Brittany's face that she wasn't convinced. A few days earlier, Brittany had refused the chance to join the McGraths in the sea to swim with a wild dolphin, and Jody had guessed she was afraid. But whatever Brittany might imagine about wild dolphins, surely she could see that the dolphins at CETA were completely safe!

"I thought the dolphins had to work with your father." Brittany said edgily.

Lauren finished stacking the last of the plates in the dishwasher. "He'll have one in the pool, but the others will be in the sea pen — the lagoon. That's where we're going to swim," she explained.

Jody waited to see if Brittany would come up with some excuse not to swim, but an hour later, Brittany had changed into her swimsuit and accompanied them outside.

Gina had asked Jody to take the twins along and, as usual, they had to be first into the water, giving their war cries as they raced each other. Laughing, Lauren dived in right behind them.

Brittany hesitated on the edge of the water, gazing nervously out at the three dolphins swimming so close to Lauren and the boys. When she saw Jody watching, her expression changed. "What are you staring at?" she demanded angrily.

"Nothing. I just thought . . ." Jody hesitated, feeling awkward.

"You just watch out for your kid brothers, not me," Brittany snapped. With that, she took a deep breath, and dived in.

Shrugging, Jody dived in, too, and swam after the others.

Sean and Jimmy were stroking the dolphins and bombarding Lauren with questions. "What's this one's name? Do they know any tricks? Can we play with them? Will they give us rides?"

"Take it easy," said Lauren, shaking her head against the twins' rapid-fire questions. "Get to know them first — let them get to know you, and then they'll play with you." She pointed to the dolphin Jimmy was stroking. "That one's Rosie. The one behind you is her mother, Maxi. And here comes Nora! Whoops!" She giggled as Nora butted her affectionately.

Jody swam over to join them. She stroked each dolphin in turn, marveling at the wonderfully soft, smooth skin beneath her fingers.

"Sean, don't do that," Lauren said warningly.

"What?" asked Sean in surprise.

Jody turned quickly to see what the twins were up to. Sean was just treading water, but his identical brother had his hand over Rosie's blowhole. "Jimmy, don't!" she said sharply.

"I just want to feel —" His explanation was cut short as Rosie decided she'd had enough and submerged abruptly, slapping her tail to make a small wave that splashed over Jimmy.

He came up sputtering. "Hey! That's not nice!"

"How would you like it if somebody put their hand over your nose and mouth?" Lauren demanded. "You were stopping her from breathing, and *that*'s not nice."

Swimming with Lauren and the twins

"You should know better than that," Jody added.

Jimmy scowled. He looked away from their accusing stares, and noticed Brittany, far away from them, looking miserable at the side of the pool.

"Hey look, the dolphins don't like Brittany!" Jimmy declared.

"Don't be silly, Jimmy," Jody said warningly. A quick glance assured her that Brittany hadn't heard. "Leave her alone," she ordered.

"Yeah, that's what the dolphins are doing," Sean chipped in, deciding to back up his brother. "They're leaving her alone! They won't go near her! Wonder why?"

"Maybe she smells bad," Jimmy said, smirking.

"Jimmy, you watch your mouth!" Jody said sharply. But he had a point, she realized. All three dolphins had approached her and the boys, but none had gone near Brittany.

"Okay, okay, sorry." Jimmy shrugged. "But I'm not making it up — you can see they don't like her."

"It's the other way around," Lauren said quietly.

"Huh?" Jimmy stared at her.

Lauren glanced over at Brittany, who straightened up in the water at her look, forced a smile, gave a little wave, and finally began to swim toward her. "All dolphins are good at reading body language, and the CETA dolphins have to be especially good at knowing what people want," Lauren explained. "We couldn't possibly have a dolphin here who might frighten a child. They can tell when people are afraid of them. They won't go near anyone who doesn't want them to."

"You mean Brittany's scared of the dolphins?" Sean didn't speak loudly, but Brittany was too close not to hear him.

Jody saw her flush.

Jimmy couldn't let it alone. "Brittany's a scaredy-cat!"

"I am not," Brittany said angrily.

"Scaredy-cat, scaredy-cat!" Both boys started in.

"Come on, let's get away from these little monsters," Lauren said to Brittany. "I'll race you to the dock."

But Lauren's attempt to distract the other girl failed. Brittany thrust her face close to Jody's. "Did you tell them I was scared?" she demanded.

Jody drew away. "No, of course not," she replied hotly.

"But you think I am, don't you?" Brittany spat, glaring furiously. "Well, I'm not. Just because I'm not crazy about dolphins doesn't mean I'm scared of them. They're tame animals. I know they don't hurt people."

"I know," Jody said, trying to calm her. "The boys are just teasing."

"Nobody thinks you're scared," Lauren said.

"Then why won't the dolphins come to me?" Brittany demanded.

"Um . . ." Lauren bit her lip. "Maybe you're giving off the wrong signals."

"What signals?" Brittany looked baffled.

"Why don't we leave it for another time?" Lauren suggested.

But Brittany persisted. "No!" she said. "I don't happen to think that touching a dolphin is such a big deal, but I'm not letting those kids say I'm scared! Show me how to get a dolphin to come to me," she demanded. Then she must have realized how bossy she sounded, because she added, "Please?" in a desperate little voice as she gazed at Lauren.

Lauren gave in and nodded. "Okay, the main thing is

to be relaxed," she explained. "They're attracted to people who are playful and interested in them. If you try to mimic them in the way you move — pretend you're a dolphin — they'll probably be interested, and come closer. Watch me." Lauren flipped over in the water. She began to wriggle and glide, using her whole body to propel herself through he water.

Jody grinned as she watched, remembering her own clumsy attempts to mimic the graceful, powerful movements of a dolphin.

Lauren's demonstration was cut short by Rosie, who rolled through the water to rub herself against the girl. The two of them swam together in harmony for a few moments as Jody and Brittany watched.

"Wow," Brittany murmured.

Surprised, Jody realized that even Brittany was impressed by the beauty of the sight, and the obvious affection between Lauren and Rosie.

Then, wrapping her arms around the dolphin, Lauren surfaced. She gave a low whistle, and rubbed her face against the side of Rosie's head. She seemed to be whispering something. Jody wondered if Lauren was telling Rosie to make friends with Brittany. Then a small sound made her look around.

Another dolphin, Maxi, had approached Brittany. She was only inches away, lying sideways, watching the girl with one eye.

Jody held her breath as she waited to see what would happen next.

Brittany was very still. But she didn't look frightened.

The dolphin began to move. She swam in a slow, close circle around Brittany, then dived lower in the water, pointing her beak at the girl's body and making a stream of distinct clicking sounds. After a while, Maxi surfaced and rolled onto her back, showing her belly.

For a moment, Brittany didn't move.

Jody bit her lip, willing her to respond.

Finally, slowly, cautiously, Brittany stretched out one arm. Her hand came to rest on the dolphin's underside. She began to stroke Maxi, gently at first, and then more firmly. A look of wonder spread over her face, and she began to smile. "You like that, do you?" she murmured. She seemed to have forgotten everyone else, as if she and Maxi were alone together. And, for once, she looked relaxed, almost happy.

June 26 — bedtime.
Brittany was a lot easier to be around this evening. For once, she didn't jump on everything I said, or make me feel left out by hogging Lauren's attention the whole time. Could this be due to what happened with Maxi? Who would have thought a dolphin could cure bad temper!

Kim came over and watched us while we were swimming, and later I heard her talking to Mom. She thought Brittany must be an orphan or something. She said Brittany was such a "sad girl," and that she had noticed Maxi "mothering" her. She said watching them together made her think of someone else Maxi had helped: a little girl whose father had died in a car crash.

I wonder . . . maybe Brittany does feel her mother has abandoned her . . . and Maxi is helping. . . .

4

The next morning Alice announced that she had borrowed four bicycles so that Lauren could take their visitors on a tour of Cedar Key. "And I've packed you a picnic, so you won't have to hurry back for lunch," she added, smiling.

Sean and Jimmy were thrilled. Living on a boat, they had missed their bikes. Now, they couldn't even wait to finish breakfast before rushing out to inspect the borrowed wheels.

Jody felt torn. She was fascinated by the work being done at CETA and wanted to see more of it. But it would be fun to explore the island, too. She looked over at the others. Her heart sank as she saw the now familiar stormy expression on Brittany's face. Her good mood hadn't lasted very long!

"It'll be too hot to go out on bikes," Brittany groaned. She looked from Lauren to Gina for agreement.

"Not if you go out right now," Gina said. "This is the coolest part of the day."

Brittany stared down at the toast on her plate. "I'd rather go swimming," she said stubbornly.

"Take your suits," Alice suggested. "Lauren, you could take them to Sea Horse Bay."

"Sea Horse Bay?" Jody repeated, her attention caught by the name.

"It's a really cool place," Lauren told her. "You can see pygmy sea horses floating in the shallows. They're wonderful! And we can swim off the edge of the sandbank, where it's a little deeper."

"Just be careful of the current," Alice warned. "Because the water isn't deep, people tend to think it's safe, but the current is very strong, so you do have to pay attention."

"I know all that, Mom," Lauren said, in a put-upon tone.

"Well, our guests don't," her mother pointed out. "Make sure Sean and Jimmy understand. Enjoy yourselves!"

Brittany looked sulky, but she didn't say anything. Jody thought she must have realized that if she complained she'd get left behind on her own.

"Do you know anything about the Florida Keys?" Lauren asked as they got ready to set off, rubbing themselves with sunscreen and mosquito repellent.

"I know! Key is another word for island," Sean offered.

Lauren nodded. "They are islands, but most of them, including this one, are joined together by a hundred-mile stretch of highway — Highway 1. But we're not going on the highway. We can get around Cedar Key on local roads and trails. That'll be more fun, and it'll give us a chance to see more wildlife."

"Oh, boy, I hope we see some alligators," Jimmy said excitedly.

Jody shuddered. "I hope we don't."

Brittany smiled unpleasantly. "Don't tell me Jody is scared of something?"

Jody could feel her face going red. "I'm not scared — I just don't like them much," she insisted. "Or rattlesnakes, or water moccasins."

"I'm not crazy about them, either," Lauren said. She finished fastening the bag containing their picnic onto her bicycle and wheeled it into position on the driveway. "Come on, let's head for Sea Horse Bay!"

Jody's heart lifted as they pedaled away. It was sunny and warm, already shaping up to be another blazingly hot day, but Jody had spent her whole life in Florida, and was too used to the climate to mind the heat. Patches of trees — Lauren had said that they were known here as "hammocks" — provided intervals of shade as they traveled, rolling along the quiet trails that crisscrossed the little island.

"When are we going to stop?" Brittany asked after a while. "I'm dying of thirst!"

Jody was starting to feel tired and thirsty, too, but she didn't want to complain, especially since her little brothers were still going strong.

"Lauren glanced back over her shoulder. "Nearly there!" she promised. "It'll be worth it!"

A few minutes later Lauren came to a halt, jumping off her bike in the shade of a mangrove hammock. She pointed to where the trees ended. A clean, empty, sandy beach gleamed in the sun. "Sea Horse Bay," she said, sounding a little breathless.

Jody forgot her thirst and gazed out at the blue, shallow water of the sandbank. She smiled. "It's beautiful." And then her eyes went beyond, to the deeper water. She couldn't help searching for signs of dolphins wherever she went. But she saw none here.

"Water, water," gasped Jimmy. He dropped to his hands and knees and began to drag himself across the ground. Seconds later, Sean was rolling on the sand, clutching his throat.

Lauren handed Brittany and Jody soft drinks out of her saddlebag, then took one for herself. She ignored Sean and Jimmy until they jumped up, indignant.

"Hey, what about us? Don't we get drinks?" Jimmy demanded.

The calm before the storm . . .

"Sure, all you have to do is ask." Smiling sweetly, Lauren took two more cans out for them.

For the next minute the silence was broken only by thirsty gulping sounds.

Jody finished her drink and stowed the empty can away in her knapsack. She breathed in deeply, enjoying the salty tang of the air and the peaceful surroundings, and then she noticed that they were not the only people on the beach. At the other end of the bay, a dark-haired woman in a long white dress was walking along with a little boy who looked about five years old.

Suddenly, the boy veered away from the woman and splashed into the water. The woman called to him, but Jody couldn't hear her words. The boy didn't look around or respond in any way to her call. He just kept walking through the water.

The woman stopped and hiked up her long, gauzy dress. Balancing on one leg, she tugged off one sandal and called again. This time, her voice carried across the beach. "Wait, Hal! Stop right there!"

The boy must have heard her, too, but he didn't stop.

He didn't even pause. He kept on walking through the water. But the water was only up to his ankles.

The woman must have realized he was in no danger, too. She looked at the sandal in her hand, not bothering to take off the other one and run after him. "Hal! Come back here!" she called. But she no longer sounded urgent, and didn't seem to expect a response.

"That's a very bad little boy," said Brittany, sounding amused.

Jody kept watching. Something was making her uneasy. There was something wrong, but she couldn't put her finger on it . . . until she realized it was the darkening shade of blue in the water where the little boy was headed. Maybe, with her dark glasses on, the woman couldn't see where the line of darker blue water marked the point where the sandbank ended, Jody thought.

Urgently, she turned to Lauren. "It looks to me as if the sandbank ends just there," she said, pointing. "That little boy is walking toward much deeper water!"

Lauren gasped. "You're right, Jody," she said. "We have to stop him, before he goes too far!"

There was no time to think about it. Jody grabbed her bike and pushed off, pedaling as hard as she could.

Too late! The little boy reached the end of the sandbank. His arms flew up as he slipped, dropping out of sight beneath the water.

The woman on the beach screamed and started to run, but then she stumbled on her single sandal, falling to the ground.

Jody went flying past the woman, straight into the shallow water. Then she leaped off the bike, letting it fall, and plunged into the deeper water.

She looked around wildly for some sign of the little boy and saw his bright blue T-shirt. He was facedown in the water. Her stomach lurched with fear, but she grabbed the cloth of the shirt and pulled the boy to her.

As she lifted him out of the water she was relieved to hear him give a deep, choking cough. "Are you okay?" she demanded.

The boy's eyes were shut tight against the salt water. He sputtered and spat, and then wriggled in her grasp. His feet were on the seabed now, but the waves lapped at his chin. Jody was afraid to let him go, fearful that he would slip under again, or that the current might pull him away.

"Hang on to me," she told him. "We're just going back onto the sandbank — then I'll let you go."

He didn't resist her efforts to pull him into the shallower water, but he didn't help, either. Jody remembered how he had seemed to ignore the woman's calls, and wondered if he was deaf.

"Is my son all right?" cried the woman as she took hold of the boy, hauling him onto dry land. Her voice wobbled as she said, "Thank goodness you were there — how can I ever thank you?"

"I think he's okay," Jody told her. "Just a little —" She stopped. She was going to say "frightened" but as she looked at the boy, she realized that was wrong. Apart from being soaking wet, he looked unaffected by his near-drowning experience, even struggling against his mother's attempt to hug him. He pulled against her, gazing out to sea.

Jody went to fetch her abandoned bicycle, hoping the salt water hadn't damaged the gears. By the time she got it back to the beach, she found Lauren, Brittany, Sean, and Jimmy clustered around the woman and the little boy, offering them towels, food, and drink. Sean even pulled off his own T-shirt and offered it to the boy.

The woman accepted a towel to dry her son. While she rubbed him he stood like a statue, his face blank and expressionless.

"What's your name?" the woman asked Jody. "Where do you live?"

Jody introduced herself and the others. "Lauren lives here on Cedar Key with her parents. We're just visiting," she explained.

The woman nodded and smiled at each of them in turn. "I'm Janet Davis. This is my son, Hal. We're visiting, too. . . . We came up from Key West for the day. It seemed so safe and quiet. Hal has a thing about the sea, he really loves it. I didn't want him to go in the water, but I could see how shallow it was . . . or I thought I could. . . . I thought he was safe." She bit her lip and gently stroked her son's wet brown hair.

"You should teach him how to swim, then he would

be safer," Jody said. She felt a little awkward, giving advice to an adult, but it seemed so obvious.

"Yes, of course, but it's very difficult. . . ." Janet Davis's voice trailed off.

Hal pulled away, heading for the water again. His mother held him firmly. "No, Hal. Not now. Stay with me."

Lauren was staring intently at the boy. Then she raised her calm eyes and asked his mother, "Is Hal autistic?"

Janet Davis raised her eyebrows in surprise. "Why, yes, he is. But how did you know?"

"My father is a psychologist," Lauren explained. "Autism is one of his special interests. I've seen a lot of the children he's helped."

"Really!" Not taking her eyes from Lauren's face, Janet caught her son firmly as he tried to move away again. "What's your father's name?"

"Dr. Jerry Rozakis," Lauren replied.

"Maybe I should talk to him," the woman said eagerly. "We've seen other specialists, of course — all over the world."

"You should talk to my dad," Lauren agreed. She

232

went on proudly, "He's had wonderful results helping autistic children with dolphin-assisted therapy."

Suddenly, something seemed to shut down in the woman's face. She had been so interested, but now she looked wary.

"It's really good," Jody jumped in, eager to recapture Janet Davis's interest. "I've seen the way the kids respond to the dolphins — it really makes a big difference. The center is called CETA — that stands for Cetaceans as Educational and Therapeutic Associates. Lauren's dad says the dolphins are the teachers, and it's really true!"

But it was no good. Jody had the feeling that no matter what she said, it wouldn't register. Janet Davis had withdrawn from the conversation. For some reason, she just didn't like the idea of dolphin-assisted therapy. The warmth had gone.

The woman's expression was remote, almost chilly, as she handed Lauren back her towel. "Thank you very much for everything. I am very grateful for your help."

Jimmy had been trying to catch the little boy's attention by making silly faces, without success.

Now Sean leaned in close. "Hey, want to come look at our bikes? I'll give you a ride."

The little boy stared blankly out to sea. His mother pulled him closer to her and began to move away. "I think we'd better leave now."

"Please, let Jerry Rozakis explain what he does," Jody insisted. "While you're here, you really ought to come and visit CETA, and see for yourself. It might help." She was starting to feel a little desperate.

But it was no good.

"I'll think about what you've said," Janet Davis said, her voice now icy. "Come, Hal. We're going."

Janet Davis and her son walked away along the beach without looking back.

5

June 27 — bedtime.

One of the things that is so great about CETA is that the dolphins really are free. Dolphins in captivity aren't as healthy as wild dolphins, and they don't live as long. Even when they are kept in large pens and have lots of company, they suffer more from stress and diseases.

Alice and Jerry do their best to keep the CETA dolphins healthy and happy. Once a week they open the sea gate, and the dolphins can go out into the open sea if they want.

Alice talked about a scientist called John Lilly, who

came up with the idea that people and dolphins could work together as equals. Instead of thinking they "own" dolphins, keeping them like slaves for their entire lives, buying and selling them, people who work with dolphins should treat them fairly and let them go after they've finished their "term of service."

I can't wait to see what happens tomorrow. It's Sunday, and the sea gate will be opened. I wonder if the CETA dolphins will go out and play with Apollo and his gang?!

It was Sunday morning and Jody had been too excited to eat much breakfast. "Can we go out and watch the dolphins as the sea gates are opened?" she asked, the minute she'd shoveled down some cornflakes in record time.

"I'm afraid they'll go too far out in the lagoon for you to see very much," Alice began. "Unless . . ." She broke off uncertainly.

"Oh, Mom, can we go out in *Princess?*" Lauren asked eagerly.

Alice looked at Jody's parents. "Jerry and I have too much paperwork to get through today, but . . . would either of you feel comfortable handling a small speed-boat?"

Craig's eyebrows lifted, his eyes gleamed, and he rubbed his hands together briskly. "Lead me to it!"

"I think you can trust him with your boat," Gina said, laughing. "At least, with Lauren and Jody along to keep him under control."

"You're not going?" Alice asked Gina.

Gina shook her head. "Maddie and I need to edit some of the video footage we shot during the week."

"Not much of a day of rest," Craig commented.

"It never is around here, except for the dolphins," Alice said as she walked over to the storeroom. The dolphins' food supply was kept there, and it also housed a control panel for all the outside lights and the under-water gates.

"Dad never gets any time off," Lauren told Jody. "Even when there aren't any patients, there's always some work that has to be done."

The dolphins seemed to know what day it was, because they were waiting by the sea gates. Jody saw a little ripple go through the water as there was a motorized hum and then, with a clanking sound, the underwater gates swung open.

Rosie shot through first, followed closely by her mother. Jody thought she caught a glimpse of Nick and Nora deep beneath the water, but she couldn't be sure. She raised her eyes to stare out at the calm waters of the lagoon, searching for some sign of the wild dolphins, but nothing showed above the surface.

"We'll see them better from *Princess.*" Lauren spoke as if she'd read Jody's mind. "I'm so glad your dad is going to take us! I'll go get Brittany!"

Jody's heart sank. She turned to her father. "Should I go get the twins?"

"You can tell them what we're doing, but I doubt you'll tempt them away from those bicycles," Craig said with a grin.

As Craig had predicted, Sean and Jimmy weren't interested. Their plans for the day involved bicycles, exploring, and snake hunting. The boys had been strictly forbidden to try to catch or touch any snakes, but Sean kept a careful, constantly updated list of every snake he spotted.

On her way back, Jody met Lauren by herself. "Brittany wanted to do something on the computer," she said with a shrug.

Jody nodded, trying not to show how relieved she was. She couldn't tell if Lauren was disappointed, but for herself she was glad to have a break from Brittany's moods, and the chance to spend time with Lauren on her own.

Princess was a small, rather elderly powerboat that was berthed in the lagoon on the other side of the sea pen. Lauren led the way along a narrow, winding path at the back of the house. They jumped in and Craig swiftly got the boat moving, heading out to sea.

"There they are!" Lauren was the first to spot the group of dolphins.

Craig powered down, and then, as they drew close to the dolphins, cut the engine. They floated in silence. Jody leaned over the side, trying to count the constantly moving group of sleek, shining gray animals. Three . . . four . . . six . . . eight?

"There's Rosie," Lauren cried. "See the scar above her eye? Who's that with her? Is it one of the wild dolphins?"

As Lauren spoke, Rosie and the other dolphin leaped high into the air, passing so close to the side of the boat that Jody felt the spray on her face. She blinked and looked again. Was that a faint, harp-shaped marking on his jaw? She decided that it was. "I think that's Apollo!" she cried, thrilled.

It seemed the dolphins were excited, too. Jody had never seen them leap so high, or so often. They were chasing one another through water and air, bumping their bodies together, leaping over and under each other in some complicated pattern.

"It's almost like they're dancing," Lauren said. "Oh, look, there's Nick! But that's not Nora he's with . . . that's another one of the wild dolphins."

Jody shielded her eyes from the sun. "I think that's Poseidon. He's the biggest of this group. That little one over there is Triton. There's Hermes! And I think that one is Artemis, although it could be Castor or Pollux."

"Oh, they all have names from Greek mythology," Lauren noted. "Cool! Whose idea was that?"

Jody felt herself blushing. "Mine, I guess. I named

Apollo first, so when we met the rest of his group, it seemed like a good idea."

They spent nearly an hour watching from *Princess* as the dolphins played. Jody longed to get into the water and swim with them, but her father vetoed that suggestion. All too soon, it seemed to her, he said it was time to go back.

Craig gazed out at the dolphins, who were now swimming farther away from the boat, and from the lagoon itself. They seemed to be headed for the open sea. He frowned. "I'd suggest following them, but we might run out of fuel. I hope CETA isn't about to lose its entire nonhuman staff," he added uneasily.

"Oh, they'll come back for their next meal," Lauren said confidently. "They always do."

Maxi had returned by midday, and Lauren and Jody helped Alice to feed her.

"Won't the others be hungry?" Jody felt worried. She knew that dolphins needed to eat a lot.

Alice raised her eyes to stare out at the lagoon. There was a line between her eyes, but she made an effort to smile at the girls. "They don't have to be. As the saying goes, there's plenty more fish in the sea!"

"Probably they'll feed with the wild dolphins," Jody guessed. Then she frowned. "But why did Maxi come back?"

"Maxi has spent nearly her whole life in captivity, a lot longer than the others," Alice explained. "You could say she's lost her hunting instincts. She relies on us to be fed." She tossed another fish to the waiting dolphin as she spoke.

Jody thought about it. "Then how about her daughter? If Rosie's never been a wild dolphin, how does she know how to hunt?"

"We taught her . . . with the help of Nick and Nora," Alice replied. "We were determined she should be able to fend for herself because someday she may want to go and live free." Alice gestured around at the lagoon. "The dolphins here can keep their hunting instincts because they're still living in the sea, not in a small manmade pool where the concrete walls would bounce sounds right back at them. You know that dolphins use sound to hunt and to get around?" She looked at Jody.

Jody nodded. "It's called echolocation, isn't it?" she said. "Dolphins can find their way around in the ocean, and track down their food by using sound." She tossed Maxi the last of the fish.

"That's right," Alice replied. "Maxi wasn't so fortunate. Before she came to us, she was kept in a big, concrete tank. If she'd tried to use echolocation to find food the way she would in the open sea, the sounds would have bounced off the walls — it wouldn't have worked. She might even have found it painful. So she would have stopped doing it. And you know that if you stop practicing a skill, you lose it. That's what seems to happen with dolphins, and that's why just releasing all captive dolphins into the wild, as some people would like to do, isn't so smart." Alice turned the bucket upside down to show Maxi it was empty. "That's all you get, honey."

Maxi chattered at them, and opened her mouth to show her teeth before sinking below the surface and swimming slowly away.

* * *

By five o'clock there was still no sign of the other dolphins. As everyone gathered in the kitchen, Alice Rozakis couldn't hide her concern.

"They've never stayed out so long," Lauren confided to Jody and Brittany. She tugged at her braid in a worried way.

"Have you got some way of calling them?" Gina asked.

Jerry nodded. "Time to ring the dinner bell," he said. "If that doesn't get them . . . well, then all we can do is wait and hope they'll decide to come back."

They all went outside. Jody hadn't noticed the bell before, and now she wondered how she'd missed it. It was a big, old-fashioned brass bell suspended from a wooden archway, with a rope hanging down.

"It's an old-fashioned school bell," Alice explained. "It was a present from a friend. It's more than a hundred and fifty years old." She grasped hold of the rope and pulled. The loud, clanging sound of the bell tolled out.

"Calling all tardy young scholars — and dolphins," said Craig, shading his eyes against the sun.

Jody peered out at the glittering water of the lagoon and held her breath, wishing for a response.

Alice continued to toll the bell, and they all waited in silence, watching and hoping.

Lauren was the first to see them. "Look, it's a whole group!"

Now Jody also spotted the dark, curving fins poking through the waves. She counted ten. "It must be Apollo and his group *and* your dolphins," she said. "Maybe they've come to say good-bye?"

To everyone's astonishment, all ten dolphins came through the sea gate, into the sea pen, and swam in close to the shore.

"There's Nick and Nora, and Rosie!" Lauren cried out their names with delight.

Jody recognized the wild dolphins as well.

"But why have they all come?" Lauren asked.

"Yours must have told them what a great place CETA is," Craig joked. "They decided they like people, after meeting us, and now they want to know more about us."

"Maybe they've come for the food," Maddie suggested. "They've never heard of anything like it — all the fish you can eat, without the bother of having to catch them yourself!"

Jerry groaned and ran his hand through his curly hair. "They'd eat us out of house and home! We don't have enough fish to feed ten hungry dolphins!"

"I don't think we should even try to feed them." Alice had left the bell and was standing beside her husband, her hand resting on his arm. "Probably they came along out of curiosity, and they'll soon leave. I'm sure ours will wait to be fed."

Sure enough, most of the wild dolphins soon decided they had seen enough of the fenced-in lagoon, and swam away out to sea. Only Apollo remained behind with the four CETA dolphins.

"That's the dolphin we've told you about, Jody's special friend," Craig said. "It was probably his idea to come here in the first place."

"Well, I don't mind giving him a few fish, as a thank-you for bringing our dolphins safely home," Jerry said. He was looking much happier now.

Apollo poked his head out of the water and reared up right in front of Jody.

Rosie and Apollo are off!

She whistled at him, trying as best she could to imitate the sound she remembered, and was thrilled when he whistled back.

Rosie rose out of the water right beside Apollo. She whistled, too.

Then both Rosie and Apollo sank beneath the water and swam away. They were headed for the sea gate.

"Rosie, no!" called Lauren, sounding worried.

"Rosie!" Alice ran for the bell and began to pull the

rope. As it clanged loudly in the air, Nick and Nora became excited, jostling each other at the side of the pen
and making impatient clicking sounds. Maxi joined
them. It was obvious they knew what the bell meant,
and were eager to be fed.

But Rosie did not respond. She and Apollo were
heading for the freedom of the open sea just as fast as
they could go.

6

June 28 — bedtime.
Rosie is still gone.

Lauren's parents went out in Princess *to try to find her. She came right up to the boat once, but nothing they tried would make her follow them back to the center. After a while she swam off with Apollo and they had to give up.*

They decided to leave the sea gate open tonight, just in case Rosie comes back. Jerry was really gloomy. He said maybe it would be better if the other three dolphins decided to swim away tonight and join Apollo's group. Then they'd have to close down CETA and find some less stressful work. I hope he didn't really mean it.

Lauren is really unhappy — she misses Rosie so much — but she is being brave. She said all that really matters is that Rosie is okay, wherever she is.

I can't help feeling guilty. WE brought Apollo here, and if it hadn't been for that, Rosie would never have gone away.

In the morning, there was still no sign of Rosie. Jody rushed outside with Lauren first thing, leaving Brittany still yawning in her bed. They were greeted by creaking calls from Nick and Nora, eager for their breakfast.

Tight-lipped, Jerry went to shut the sea gate. "Bud should be here by now," he muttered.

"I'll feed them, Dad," Lauren volunteered.

"Thanks, sweetheart." Jerry patted his daughter on the shoulder before vanishing into the house.

"I'll help," Jody said, and followed Lauren to the storage room to fill buckets with the last of the fish.

Lauren told her there would be a fresh delivery later in the day, and slipped the thick cord with a whistle on it over her head.

Brittany appeared just as they were lugging the buckets down to the waterside. "Did your dolphin come back?" she asked Lauren.

Wordless, Lauren shook her head. She began to fling fish into the eager, waiting jaws of Nick and Nora. Jody followed her example.

"Hey, Maxi, it's breakfast time," Lauren called.

Jody looked around but could see no sign of the third dolphin. Her heart gave a painful lurch. "Did Maxi leave, too?"

"No, she's over there." Lauren nodded toward the other side of the sea pen. "I don't know what's wrong with her; she's acting like she's not interested."

Now Jody made out the shape of the mother dolphin, swimming listlessly up and down, with her blowhole just above the surface.

"She's missing her daughter," said Brittany, staring intently into the water.

Jody turned to look at her in surprise. Could this be the girl who thought dolphins were boring, dumb animals?

Lauren nodded, tossing more fish to Nick and Nora.

"You're right," she agreed. "Maxi and Rosie have never been apart. And Rosie is still pretty young. In the wild, she'd probably stay with her mother for a couple more years." She frowned unhappily, then turned to Brittany. "It's not going to do her any good not to eat. Do you want to try and tempt her?"

"Me?" Brittany's eyes widened. She hesitated and then slowly nodded. "Okay. I'll try." With a grimace, she picked a fish out of the bucket and crouched down, holding it by the tail over the water.

Nick swam up and grabbed the fish, taking Brittany by surprise. She shrieked and fell back on her heels.

Jody gave a snort of laughter.

Brittany glared at her. "Real funny, Jody! I'm trying to do something nice, here. The least you could do is keep those two greedy-guts out of the way!"

"I'm sorry," Jody said meekly, struggling to keep a straight face.

Lauren pointed to the other side of the pool. "We'll take these two over there. Brittany, why don't you take that bucket down to the dock, and try to feed Maxi from there?"

As Brittany nodded, Lauren blew a short blast on the whistle to get Nick and Nora's attention. They responded quickly, and followed the two girls around to the other side.

"Don't feed them too fast," Lauren advised Jody. "We can drag it out and give Brittany a better chance to coax Maxi."

Jody looked across to the dock. Brittany was now sitting on the edge with her bare feet dangling into the water, and she was saying something in a low, gentle tone. After a few moments, Maxi responded by coming to investigate. She nudged Brittany's feet. With a giggle, the girl pulled her feet out of the water, and Maxi poked her beak out after them.

Quick as a flash, Brittany swung a fish at the dolphin. Her mouth opened for it, and, once she'd had a taste, Maxi regained her appetite enough to gulp down several more. But she didn't eat as much as normal, and once she'd decided she'd had enough, neither Brittany nor Lauren could coax her back for more.

"Never mind," said Alice when they told her about it later. "You did well."

Brittany gives Maxi her lunch

Returning to the house, the girls had washed their hands, and were ready for their own breakfast. The boys had already gone off to play, and Jerry to work, but Alice, Gina, Craig, and Maddie were still sipping cups of coffee at the big round table.

"It's not surprising if Maxi is grieving . . . her appetite will be less than usual, but as long as she doesn't starve herself, she'll be okay," Lauren's mother went on as the girls poured themselves bowls of cereal.

"But will you?" Jody's mother, sipping a cup of coffee, leaned forward to look closely at her friend. "Can you manage with one less dolphin?"

Alice managed a pained smile. "We'll have to, won't we? It'll mean more work for the other dolphins — and Rosie was shaping up to be one of the very best — but, well . . ." She shrugged and stared down into her coffee. "Actually, we've been offered another dolphin from a Sea-Life Center that doesn't really have the space to keep him. We weren't sure that we could afford the price they're asking, and Jerry already has about as much as he can do without having to start training a newcomer, but with Rosie gone, I don't think we have any choice."

"I have an idea," Brittany said suddenly.

They all turned to look at her. She reddened at the attention, but explained her idea. "I could ask my dad to take us out on *Dolphin Dreamer* to look for Rosie. If we found her, maybe we could tempt her with some fish, like I did with Maxi, and she might follow us back to the lagoon. I'm sure once she got close enough to hear her mother she'd want to come back to her." As she finished speaking, Brittany dropped her eyes and stared down at the table.

Jody was too astonished to speak. It was an idea she wished she'd had first. And for Brittany to think about something other than her own problems was amazing!

"That's a great idea, Brittany," Lauren said enthusiastically. She pushed her empty cereal bowl away from her and looked at her mother. "Can we try it?"

They all looked at Gina, who said slowly, "Well, I don't see why not. Knowing Harry, he's probably getting bored with Key West by now and would be happy for a chance to spend the day sailing."

"You could take my car," Alice said to Gina.

Gina smiled warmly at her old friend, then looked at the three girls who were waiting, breathless, for her to speak. "Okay," she said decisively. "Let's do it!"

Maddie and Craig decided they wanted to go along, which meant the twins had to be included, so in the end the expedition proved to be an unexpected reunion of the whole crew — with the exception of Dr. Jefferson Taylor.

Touching the Waves

The sight of *Dolphin Dreamer* brought a smile to Jody's face. As her feet touched the deck for the first time in four days, she felt she had come home again. She filled her lungs with sea air and lifted her face to the blazing sun.

As they sailed out of the marina at Key West, the sound of nautical phrases barked out in Harry's English accent or Cam's drawling Southern tones was like music to her ears. Jody had been too interested in all that was going on at CETA to really miss life on board *Dolphin Dreamer*, but now she realized how great it was to be back.

Looking at Harry's weather-beaten, bearded face, and Cam's rugged good looks, she mentally added: and to have the whole family together again. Even though they weren't actually related, she had come to feel that the *Dolphin Dreamer* crew was part of her family.

In a minute, Jody decided, she would go below to chat with Mei Lin and find out what she'd been up to in Key West. But right now, with the wind ruffling her hair and the sun warm on her bare arms and face, all she wanted to do was lean against the rail and enjoy the wonderful sensation of being where she belonged, at sea again, in the company of her family and friends.

Despite such a promising start, the expedition was not a success. They spotted a group of dolphins once, but they were too far away to be identified. Jody found herself wishing, for once, that Dr. Taylor were on board. He had tagged Hermes, one of the members of Apollo's group, and could have used his equipment to tell them where he was. Chances were that wherever Hermes was to be found, Apollo and Rosie would not be far away.

But the dolphins in the distance did not seem interested in approaching *Dolphin Dreamer*. Harry and Cam enjoyed the challenge of trying to catch up with them, but it proved impossible. The speedy creatures soon disappeared, not to be seen again.

Late in the afternoon they sailed into the lagoon where CETA was located. Standing beside Lauren, Jody strained her eyes for any sign of dolphin activity on this side of the fence.

"Well, it was a good idea," Craig said quietly, resting

his hand on Jody's shoulder. "But I think we might as well accept that it didn't work."

"It was a terrible idea," Brittany snapped from her place on Lauren's other side. "If I'd realized this boat was too slow to catch up to a bunch of dolphins, I would never have suggested it! What a boring, wasted day!"

Jody saw Lauren bite her lip as she looked at Brittany. Then she said in a low voice, "It was a *good* idea. You were trying to help, and I'm glad we got the chance to look for Rosie, thanks to you and your dad. You couldn't have done any more."

Brittany's scowl disappeared as she saw that Lauren meant it. "I really wanted us to find her and bring her back," she said quietly. "So Maxi would cheer up." Then she made a face. "Anyway, I can't wait to get off this boat again. Of all the boring ways to spend time, sailing has got to be the absolute worst!"

Jody winced, hoping that Harry hadn't heard.

Lauren turned to Craig. "Could we get off here instead of sailing all the way back to Key West?" She gazed up at him appealingly.

"You want us to dump you in the lagoon?" Craig pretended to be shocked.

"I'm not getting my clothes wet," Brittany said with a scowl.

Lauren turned to the other girl to explain. "If we sail around past the sea pen to the bay where *Princess* is berthed, we can get off at the dock and walk up to the house."

Craig nodded. "Okay. I'll go and tell Harry."

There was a black limousine with a driver waiting outside the CETA office when Jody, Lauren, and Brittany arrived back.

Jody looked at Lauren in surprise. "Is that for one of the patients?"

Wide-eyed, Lauren shook her head. "Not unless it's a new one!"

They went through the archway into the central courtyard and found Lauren's father talking to a smartly dressed man.

Brittany gave a little gasp, and Jody looked at her in

surprise. Before she could ask her if she knew the man, Jerry had caught sight of them.

"Ah, here's Jody now!" he called out. "She's the one you want to talk to."

"Me!" Jody exclaimed in surprise.

"This is Gavin Davis," Jerry said.

"I'm Hal's father," the man explained, reaching out and grasping Jody's hand tightly. "I'm sorry it's taken me so long to come over here to thank you personally for saving my son."

Jody felt herself blush. "Oh, well, I'm glad I was there. I'm glad I could help."

"So are we," Gavin Davis replied. "More than I can possibly say." He paused, still holding her hand, gray eyes shining with emotion behind gold-rimmed glasses.

Jerry stepped in to introduce him to everyone else. Jody noticed that Brittany seemed completely awe-struck, and couldn't stop staring at Gavin Davis. She wondered why. Although he seemed very friendly and likeable, surely he was a little too old to inspire a crush!

Gavin Davis cleared his throat. "I was just about to

tell Dr. Rozakis, I've been very impressed by what he's shown me today. As you know, my son Hal is autistic. A couple of years ago, my wife and I wondered if swimming with dolphins might help him. We wrote to CETA and one other place in Florida, but both had waiting lists. Then we heard about a place in Mexico where anyone could swim with dolphins, at anytime. We were too impatient to wait, so we decided to try that." He shook his head, his expression turning grave.

"Well, we were horrified by the conditions we found there. The dolphins were kept in tiny little pools, separated from one another, and they were never allowed to rest. Each one was forced to share the pool with dozens of visitors every day. We even saw people teasing and tormenting the poor animals, who couldn't escape." He continued his story in a low, sad voice.

Jody felt sick at the thought.

"No wonder your wife didn't seem so keen when I told her about CETA," Lauren said.

Gavin Davis nodded. "What we saw was so awful, it made us give up the idea of visiting anywhere else that kept captive dolphins. But we did like the idea of introducing him to wild dolphins, so I bought a yacht. We spend most of our vacation time on it," he concluded.

"But Hal can't swim," Jody pointed out. Surely Gavin hadn't forgotten that!

Gavin looked rueful. "Yes, that is a problem. We've tried and tried to teach him, but we just can't get him to concentrate!"

"The dolphins here could teach him," Lauren blurted out, a wide smile on her usually serious face.

"I really do hope so," said Gavin Davis. Turning back to Jerry, he said, "I'm sure you still have a waiting list, but I'm hoping that you'll make an exception, and squeeze us in for a few sessions, as soon as possible. We're staying here in Florida for the next two weeks."

Jody turned eagerly to look at Jerry Rozakis. She felt sure he couldn't refuse.

But the short, bearded psychologist shook his graying head. "I'm sorry, Mr. Davis," he said gruffly. "But it's just not possible."

"Oh, Daddy!" Lauren cried. Jody felt as distressed as her friend sounded.

"I'll happily pay twice your going rate," Gavin Davis said, "Or more. Add a bonus for every session — name your price!"

But Jerry would not back down. "This isn't about money," he explained. "With Rosie missing, the other three dolphins will have heavier schedules than usual. It wouldn't be fair to any of the other patients to cancel their sessions —"

"Oh, no, I'm not asking you to do that," the man insisted. "But maybe, in your spare time, in the evenings, or next weekend," he suggested hopefully.

"Spare time!" Jerry gave an angry, barking laugh. "What's that? I already work practically every hour there is . . . if I'm not with the patients there's paperwork, routine maintenance, making sure everything gets done. Maybe you're going to suggest I should give up eating, or sleeping?"

There was an awkward silence.

"I'm sorry," Jerry began, with a sigh. "It's not your fault. . . ."

"No, no," said Gavin Davis calmly. He sounded thoughtful. "I simply hadn't realized that you ran everything yourself. You could save yourself a lot of stress if you learned to delegate."

"Oh, right!" Jerry exploded. "Who am I supposed to delegate *to*? Kim's a great help, but she's still a trainee, and she's probably going to leave next year and go back for her Ph.D. Bud does most of the maintenance work, but it's really too big a job for just one man. Alice does what she can, but she has her own work. . . ."

"Have you thought about hiring more staff?" Gavin Davis asked in a businesslike way.

Jerry gave a bitter laugh. "Thought about it! Dreamed about it, more like. I just can't afford it."

"You might find that with reorganization the additional staff would pay for themselves," Mr. Davis said. Pushing his glasses up on his nose, he leaned forward to look into Jerry's eyes. "Will you let me do something for you?" he asked. "Consider it my inadequate thanks for Jody's quick thinking. Make time this week — two hours — for a meeting with me and my financial advisor. You won't regret it, you have my word that it will be two hours well spent. You'll answer our questions, and we'll make some suggestions. You don't have to follow them, of course. Just let us try to help. Will you do it?"

For a moment, Jody was sure Jerry was going to refuse. She held her breath, waiting.

Then Jerry shrugged. "Okay. Two hours. But it'll have to be in the evening." He looked a little bemused, as if surprised by his own agreement.

Gavin Davis nodded. "Should we say Wednesday? Eight o'clock?" When this was accepted, he turned to Jody again. "I'd also like to do a little something special for you. Would you enjoy a day out on my yacht?"

Before she could answer, Jody was surprised to hear Brittany's voice, breathless with excitement, saying, "Oh, yes, that would be wonderful! We'd *love* to come!"

The man smiled. "That's great." He winked at Jody. "Feel free to bring along any other friends or family members who'd like to come — there'll be plenty of food for lunch. We'll make it a party! I'll send the motorboat to pick you up tomorrow at eleven."

7

As soon as Gavin Davis had left, Brittany practically exploded with excitement, jumping up and down and squealing. "Oh, I'm so glad I came here! We get to go on Gavin Davis's yacht! This is so exciting! I can't wait until tomorrow!"

The others all stared at her in astonishment.

Brittany giggled. "I can't believe you all, pretending to be so cool about it!"

"Well, I'm not pretending," Lauren replied. "And I'm kind of surprised that *you're* so excited, after what you said about sailing being so boring."

For once, Jody detected an edge of impatience in Lauren's normally friendly manner toward Brittany.

"This is completely different," Brittany said. She rolled her eyes. "Gavin Davis isn't going to have some dinky little sailboat — he's a multimillionaire! Don't you know who he is?"

"It looks like none of us do," said Jerry. "So why don't you tell us?" he suggested.

Brittany took a deep breath. "They call him the 'Biz Whiz,'" she began. "There was a story about him in *People* magazine a few months ago, and he's been on the cover of *Business Week*. My mom says he's a financial genius."

"What does he do?" Jerry asked.

Brittany shrugged. "Well, I don't know, exactly. But it said in *People* magazine that he'd made a fortune by helping to save businesses that were on the brink of disaster. They said that everything he touches turns to gold."

Jody noticed that Jerry had gone rather pale. "I think I want to go inside and sit down," he said in a faint voice. "I can't believe I nearly told him to go away. People pay that man lots and lots of money to sort out their business problems. And he's just offered to help CETA for free!"

June 29 — evening.
Have been invited to spend tomorrow on the Davises' yacht — turns out Mr. Davis is a millionaire and is going to help CETA! Couldn't believe it when Brittany insisted on calling Mom on Dolphin Dreamer to ask her to bring more of her clothes back so she could find something good enough to wear for the occasion! I just know she is going to gush and giggle all over the place. How embarrassing!

It was another typical beautiful hot summer Florida day as Jody and the others waited on the dock of the bay for the promised motorboat. Craig and Gina had decided to stay at CETA to help Bud with some heavy maintenance work that needed to be done, and the twins voted for another day out the bicycles. But besides Lauren and Brittany, Maddie had accepted the invitation. And soon afterward, so had Cam. Jody guessed that he really just wanted the chance to spend more time with Maddie, who was looking especially great in a short orange skirt and midriff top.

After trying and rejecting practically everything in her wardrobe, Brittany was wearing a white sundress, and had gotten Lauren to help pin up her hair.

Jody felt very plain by comparison in shorts and T-shirt, and was glad that Lauren had also chosen to stay casual in her usual cutoff jeans and sleeveless shirt. Brittany had urged Lauren to dress up, but Jody had heard Lauren calmly but firmly declare that she preferred comfort to fashion. Perhaps Lauren had started to realize that she and Brittany didn't really have very much in common, after all.

Soon a motorboat came roaring through the lagoon and pulled up to the dock.

The handsome, black-haired young man at the wheel identified himself as Rob Holdstock, of the yacht *Daisy Mae*. "Gavin apologizes for not coming along, but he wasn't sure how many passengers there would be," he explained. "I thought I might have to make two trips, but I can see that won't be necessary. Can I give you a hand getting on, Miss?" he asked with an admiring look at Maddie.

"That won't be necessary," said Cam jealously. Then, blushing, as Maddie shot him an amused glance, he added, "I mean, there's no need for you to get out; I'll make sure everyone boards safely."

When Gavin Davis had spoken about his "yacht," Jody had imagined something about the size of *Dolphin Dreamer*, a boat that would be perfectly com-

The Daisy Mae

fortable for a family of three plus a small crew to spend their vacations on. The reality took her by surprise. *Daisy Mae* was enormous.

Cam whistled through his teeth as the large, luxurious yacht came into sight, just beyond the lagoon. "Wow," he said, scratching his blond head in amazement.

"It looks like an ocean liner compared to what we're used to," Maddie said.

"It's my idea of what a yacht should be," Brittany sighed, her face glowing with excitement.

Janet and Gavin Davis welcomed them on board, smiling broadly and looking genuinely pleased to see them. Janet wore a gauzy, sea-green dress, but her husband was casually dressed in faded cutoffs and a Miami Dolphins T-shirt.

"Where's little Hal?" Lauren asked.

Janet smoothed her hair back from her face. "He's watching TV," she said with a sigh. "I tried to get him interested in coming out to say hello, but . . ."

"He'll come out once we're moving," Gavin said. "Hal likes it best when the boat is moving," he explained.

"Come on, I'll give you the grand tour," said Janet, including them all in her smile. "Follow me."

Inside, *Daisy Mae* was more like a luxurious hotel than a boat. The cabins were all so large, and so lavishly furnished, that Jody found herself thinking of them as rooms. It was staffed like a hotel, too, with two chefs working in a large, gleaming kitchen. "What would Mei Lin think of this?" she whispered to Maddie, who grinned back.

There was a "grand cabin" and a "small cabin" and even a room devoted to television viewing, furnished with the most up-to-date equipment, its walls lined with videotapes and DVDs.

Hal, absorbed in an episode of *Thomas the Tank Engine*, didn't show any sign of noticing that he had company when Janet led them in.

"Hal, when this one is over, it's time for lunch," Janet said, speaking to her son in a clear voice. "I'll come back to tell you then."

The boy did not move, speak, or interrupt his viewing in any way.

"Did he hear you?" Maddie asked.

"I'm not sure if he notices anything else when he's that absorbed in something," Janet replied. "But I have to keep trying. I'll come back in five minutes and try again, but he's probably going to start screaming when I switch the set off."

Lunch was delicious and lavish. Everything had been laid out on the long table in the grand cabin, and everyone was invited to load up a plate and take it out to eat on deck.

"Wow, these are some picnic plates, huh?" Lauren rolled her eyes and pointed to the gleaming white, gold-edged china.

Jody returned her grin as she began scooping up portions of fresh shrimp, barbecued ribs, potato salad, coleslaw, guacamole, tortilla chips, and garlic bread. Soon her plate was full — though she hadn't sampled half of what was offered. She picked up some silver cutlery and one of the crisp, white linen napkins.

Chairs had been set out under the shade of an

awning on deck, and there was a choice of cold drinks in a cooler.

After she'd eaten all she could, Jody went up for a stroll on the forward deck. Up there, she could feel how swiftly they were moving. As she paused to look over the side, she saw something that made her heart pound faster: a group of dolphins was riding the bow-wave created as *Daisy Mae* cut through the water.

There were five or six of the sleek, gray animals, leaping and diving, bumping against one another play-fully as they jostled for the best position. Her eyes swept over them, searching for distinctive differences. Bottle-nosed dolphins all tended to look very much the same, especially from a distance. Then she caught her breath as she saw the bright blue plastic tag in one dorsal fin.

"Hermes!" she breathed. There could be no doubt about it. There was the plastic dart with the micro-transmitter that Jefferson Taylor had fired into one of Apollo's group.

So where was Apollo? Eagerly, she scanned the leaping dolphins, searching for her special friend. But there were only six dolphins in the water. Mentally, she identified each one, and neither Rosie nor Apollo was among them.

As she frowned and chewed her lip in dismay, Jody was joined at the rail by Janet and Hal, Lauren, and Brittany.

"Oh, that breeze feels great," Lauren exclaimed. Then she caught sight of the dolphins and gasped.

Everyone else seemed to notice the dolphins at the same time, including Hal, who gave a wordless cry and reached out with both hands.

Jody was glad to see his mother had a firm grip on him. She really didn't like the idea of having to test her lifesaving skills in deep water, for real!

"Are those the dolphins you were looking for?" Janet asked.

Lauren had been leaning over the side for a better look. Now she drew back, disappointment plain on her face. "No," she replied flatly. "Rosie's not there."

"Neither is Apollo," Jody told her.

"So you think Rosie might be with Apollo?" Lauren asked.

Jody nodded, gazing sympathetically into Lauren's worried face.

"Here comes another one," Brittany called out. "Look, Lauren, is that Rosie?"

Lauren turned eagerly back to look, shading her eyes against the sun. Almost immediately, she shook her head.

But Jody recognized the solitary dolphin. "It's Apollo!" she cried joyfully.

In response, Apollo reared up out of the water, clicking and chattering urgently.

"It's almost like he's trying to tell you something," said Janet Davis in surprise.

Jody leaned over the side, longing to be closer to Apollo. He was clacking his jaw in a way she hadn't seen before, moving his body back and forth and whistling loudly. "What is it?" she murmured. She could sense his distress.

"It must be about Rosie," Lauren said, giving words to Jody's feeling. "She isn't with him, or with the others. There must be something wrong, and he's come to tell us!"

Now, seeming to give up trying to make Jody understand, Apollo dived underwater again, throwing himself against Poseidon to get the big dolphin's attention.

Gradually, all the dolphins stopped their joyful play and began to swim around Apollo in a tight circle.

Jody and the others watching from the boat could hear a lot of rapid clicking, whistling, and other sounds, as if the dolphins were having a furious discussion. Then, as if they'd all agreed, they suddenly shot off in a group, moving rapidly away.

Hal gave a disappointed cry.

Jody felt exactly the same way. To her surprise, the lead dolphin — it was Apollo — suddenly broke away from the group and raced back to the side of the boat. He rose up out of the water, making another series of loud, sharp clicks, before swimming back to his group.

This time, Jody had no doubt about what he meant.

"What's going on up here?" Gavin Davis's friendly voice sounded behind her.

Jody turned to look at him. "Apollo wants us to follow him," she said. "I think there's something wrong, and he came to get his friends — and us — to help. Can we go after them? Please?" She held her breath waiting for his answer.

He gazed at her keenly. It was obvious he understood how important this was to her. "Of course," he said at once. "I'll go and give the order to follow that dolphin!"

8

For a while, all went smoothly as *Daisy Mae* easily followed in the wake of the dolphins. Maddie and Cam joined Jody and the others at the rail of the foredeck, where they all shared the excitement.

After about ten minutes, a line of coast came in sight, and as the dolphins raced ahead into a rounded bay, the big yacht slowed and hung back.

"What's wrong?" Jody asked as they came to a stop. "We're going to lose them!"

As the dolphins vanished from sight, Hal began to

moan. He jerked away and hugged himself when his mother tried to comfort him.

Rob Holdstock came dashing up to Gavin Davis. "I'm sorry, sir," he said breathlessly. "Captain says we can't go any closer without running aground. It's very shallow here, and there's a sandbank marked on the chart."

"Does that mean we've lost them?" Lauren asked.

Jody bit her lip in dismay.

Gavin Davis glanced at the girls' anxious faces, but spoke to Rob. "Where are we?"

"Just beside an uninhabited key. No name given for it on the navigation chart," Rob replied.

Jody looked over the side, trying to judge the distance to the shore. It was a calm day, and she thought she'd swim it easily. Depending on where the sandbank started, she reasoned that she could probably walk more than half the way.

She looked around at Gavin Davis again, and made her suggestion. "I could swim over and find out where the dolphins have gone."

"Oh, there's no need to swim," he said. "Rob can take

you in the motorboat. That way, if you find anything wrong, you can phone us for help."

They quickly got ready to go. Maddie said she would go along, and Cam seconded her. Jody was surprised when Brittany announced that she was coming, too, since she'd seemed so at home on the yacht. But maybe she felt a bit shy without the other girls around, especially since Janet Davis was now too busy looking after Hal to pay much attention to her.

Soon after they left the yacht in the motorboat Apollo reappeared, leaping out of the water and making a lot of noise to make sure he had their attention.

Jody grinned. "We see you, Apollo!" she yelled. "We're coming!"

"What does he want with us?" Cam wondered, scratching his head. "Isn't it pretty strange for a wild animal to act like that?"

"I've heard stories of wild dolphins approaching complete strangers when they've needed help," Maddie said. "Dolphins have been known to help people in distress — like Apollo rescuing Jody when she fell overboard. Since they help us, maybe they figure we will help them. And, of course, we're not strangers to Apollo."

"I'm sure Apollo knows I'd do anything to help him," Jody said fervently.

"Yeah, but there doesn't seem to be anything wrong with him," Cam pointed out.

"No, he must want our help for someone, or something, else," Maddie concluded.

"I think we're about to find out the answer," said Rob, raising his voice above the roar of the engine. "Look, the dolphins are all together there in the bay. End of the line, folks," He switched off the engine, and peace descended.

They'd come to the sandbank. "You can wade to shore from here," Rob pointed out.

Kicking off her shoes, Jody was the first to leap out of the motorboat and onto the sandbank. There, the shallow warm water rose only to her ankles. A few yards away, the sandbank dropped again to form a slightly deeper pool where the dolphins all were.

"Are they trapped?" asked Lauren, concerned, splashing up behind her.

Jody shook her head. "I don't think so, but . . ." She was puzzled to know how the dolphins had gotten to where they were — until she noticed that the sand-bank was not quite the total barrier it had seemed at first. One of the dolphins was swimming back and forth at the other side of the bay, between the shallow pool and the open sea. There the sandbank dropped away to form a narrow channel that the dolphins were using as a passage. They could easily get in and out. So what was the problem?

Maddie and Cam waded out to join Jody and Lauren, but Brittany announced that she didn't want to get her dress wet, so would stay in the boat with Rob.

"Give us a yell if you need any help," he told them.

Jody nodded distractedly, staring at the dolphins and trying to figure it out. The scene was idyllic: a curving half-moon of gleaming white sandy beach, brilliant blue water reflecting back a clear blue sky, and a group of dolphins frolicking in the shallow bay. Except these dolphins weren't playing. They were swimming rap-idly back and forth in a worried way, and their whistles and clicks didn't sound happy to Jody.

She shook her head as she waded forward, going to meet Apollo. "What's wrong?" she muttered to herself.

"Just that big pile of garbage somebody dumped," Lauren answered, her voice disgusted. "I just hate the way some people dump all their litter on the keys where nobody lives. Look at that."

Jody followed Lauren's pointing finger and noticed the heap of sodden cardboard boxes, newspapers, empty cans, plastic bags, and other junk at the edge of the beach and spilling over into the water. Some green plastic bottles bobbed about, and there was a heap of bright blue netting tangled up with something. . . . At first Jody thought it was a dark gray plastic bag, more unwanted rubbish, but then she realized what she was looking at, and gasped, "It's a dolphin, trapped in all of that junk!"

Both girls broke into a run, pounding through the water that became first knee- and then thigh-deep.

As they came nearer, Jody could see that it was definitely a dolphin that had become tangled in the dumped netting, and that the animal was lying frighteningly still in the shallow water.

Jody hoped they had arrived in time to help.

Lauren got there just ahead of her, and crouched down in the water. "It's Rosie," she reported breathlessly. "And she's still breathing, thank goodness! Oh, Rosie, my poor darling," Lauren went on, a catch in her voice. "Let me get this horrible stuff off of you!"

"I'll help," Jody offered. Both girls tried tugging gently at the plastic netting, but it was hard to even loosen it. In places the netting was wound so tightly around Rosie that it dug deep into her skin.

"She must have been struggling to get away, and just got herself tangled up even more," Lauren said. "Oh, Rosie, Rosie!" She was crying.

Tears came to Jody's eyes as well, but she blinked them away. "Just hang on, we're going to get you out of it," she promised. "Lauren, I think we're going to have to cut the net to set her free."

Cam and Maddie had just splashed up to join them. "I've got a knife," said Cam, unhooking the bulky Swiss Army knife from his belt.

"If that has a scissors attachment it might be better — safer," Maddie suggested. "Do you want me to do it?"

At Cam's nod, she found the small scissors and carefully set to work.

Lauren unwrapped a strand from Rosie's jaw, talking in a low, soothing voice all the while, and Maddie clipped away the tightly wound netting from her body and tail. Although she longed to help, Jody kept back, out of the way.

Within a few minutes, it was done. Rosie was free.

But she didn't move. Her eyes were open, and Jody could see the gentle movement of her blowhole as she breathed, but the dolphin didn't even try to swim away.

Lauren stroked Rosie's sides, careful not to hurt her. The net had left many welts, and she was bleeding from several cuts, including one very deep one in her fin. "Come on, sweetie," Lauren said softly. "It's okay to move now. That nasty old net is gone — there's nothing to tangle you up now. Why won't you try to move?"

Rosie did not respond. Lauren bit her lip. Jody could see she was battling against tears.

"Maybe we should call your folks and ask them what to do," Jody suggested.

Lauren nodded, looking more hopeful.

"Rob has a phone on the motorboat," Maddie reminded them. "I'll run back. I can call them, if you like, tell them where we are, and ask them to phone the vet."

"Thanks, Maddie," Lauren said gratefully. "I'd really like to stay here with Rosie."

"I'm sure that's the very best thing you can do for her," Maddie agreed. "You keep her comfortable, tell her everything's going to be all right, and hang on till your folks get here."

Maddie and Cam waded back to the motorboat where Rob and Brittany were waiting. Not wanting to disturb Lauren's quiet communication with Rosie, Jody moved away a little, into the warm, shallow water of the natural pool. She looked at the wild dolphins who were still swimming back and forth through the channel, whistling and clicking to one another. Jody thought they must be calling to Rosie, too, and it was even more worrying that the injured dolphin did not reply.

Apollo came gliding through the water and rubbed against Jody's legs. She smiled at the feel of his smooth skin against hers. Looking down, she met his eye. As always, there was a feeling of connection when their gaze met, and she felt calmer. Apollo made her feel peaceful, as if everything was going to be all right.

After about a quarter of an hour, Jody could hear the sound of motorboats approaching. A few minutes later, two boats came into view. Jody recognized Alice and Jerry in *Princess*. The second boat bore the letters "D.O.B." as its name, and was driven by a sturdy, dark-haired, middle-aged woman. Leaving the boat, she came splashing through the shallows with a medical bag in one hand.

"Maria Gomez," she identified herself briskly as she approached Jody. "I'm the vet. Now, what seems to be . . . my goodness, this isn't Rosie!" The woman looked in surprise at Apollo, who was still swimming around Jody's legs.

"No," Jody agreed. "This is Apollo, and there's nothing wrong with him! Rosie's over there, with Lauren." She half turned and pointed to where Lauren was crouched in the water with Rosie.

Maria Gomez looked puzzled. "Apollo? I haven't met him before."

"He's a wild dolphin," Jody explained. She saw Alice approaching, a worried look on her face. Jerry, moving a little more slowly and carrying a bucket of fish, was not far behind. Jody continued, "It was Apollo who led us to Rosie."

The vet's eyes widened. "I want to hear all about it — later," she said. "But now I'd better go see about Rosie."

"How is she?" Alice asked anxiously as she hurried up.

"She's alive," Jody assured her. "And we can't see any really deep cuts or anything, just little ones, but she just seems worn out. Lauren can't get her to swim at all. We think maybe she was struggling to get out of the net for a long time and just used up her strength."

Alice sighed. "Hopefully Maria can tell us more when she's examined her."

The vet was talking to Lauren and squatting in the shallow water to run her hands all over the injured dolphin as she listened to what the girl had to tell her.

Apollo had decided to swim away with the arrival of

Alice and Jerry. Happy to have Jody's company in the shallow pool, he'd obviously decided there were too many people around for his comfort. Jody watched him swim over to join his friends on the other side of the sandbank, then turned as she heard Jerry speaking to her.

"Your folks stayed behind to look after the twins and hold down the fort for us," he explained. "I still had one more patient to see this afternoon, but Kim convinced me she can handle him herself," Jerry went on, rubbing his face with his free hand. "I was too worried about Rosie to wait behind," he added. "I care about her almost as if she were my child!"

The vet finished her examination and beckoned Jerry to approach. Jody followed.

"I can't find anything seriously wrong with her," Maria Gomez said, a slight frown creasing her forehead in concentration. "It's my guess that her problem is shock and exhaustion. The whole situation must have been pretty traumatic for her, poor thing. Trapped and in pain, far from her own home and family. And if she's been struggling against that net for most of a day and night she's probably starving, too." She looked around. "Where's that fish?"

"Right here," said Jerry, stepping forward with the bucket. "And there's another just like this in the boat!"

"Good." Maria Gomez nodded her dark head approvingly. She looked at Lauren. "Rosie probably knows and trusts you better than anyone else. You try hand-feeding her. Maybe after she gets some fish in her belly she'll start acting more like her old self."

Lauren nodded seriously. Taking the bucket from her father, she looked at Jody. "Want to help me, Jody?"

"Sure!" Jody rushed forward, eager to help.

Rosie was lying still in the shallow water, in the same position as before. Only the brightness of her eyes, and the faint motion of her blowhole as she breathed, showed that she was alive.

"Got a treat for you, sweetie," said Lauren in a low, musical voice. She waved a fish in front of Rosie's beak. "Open wide!"

For a moment it seemed the dolphin would not respond. Jody held her breath.

Then, with a faint creaking sound, Rosie's jaws

parted. Lauren dropped in the fish. "Good girl! Want another?"

Rosie definitely did. This time, she opened her mouth as soon as the fish appeared.

Gradually, she began to perk up, and was soon eating greedily.

The vet's pager began to beep and she apologized for having to rush away on another emergency. "As far as I can see, your dolphin is on the mend. Give her all she wants to eat, and try to coax her to swim. If she doesn't seem much better by the evening, give me a call and I'll come back, all right?"

Alice and Jerry agreed, and thanked her for coming so swiftly. They began to walk her back to her boat. "I can see I'm going to need that second bucket of fish after all," Jerry said with a grin.

Now, Lauren and Jody took turns feeding Rosie. Shortly after the vet's motorboat roared away, Jody heard another motor and looked up to see that the motorboat from the *Daisy Mae* had gone.

Returning with the bucket of fish carried between them, Alice and Jerry explained that Rob had gone back to pick up the Davises. "They're eager to see Rosie, and I know he wants me to have a look at his boy," Jerry said. He shrugged. "I think I owe him that much for helping us to find Rosie! Maria thought that since Rosie is physically okay, and is used to meeting people, it would do no harm."

Rosie chomped her way through most of the second bucket of fish before deciding she'd had enough.

"There's nothing wrong with her appetite," Jerry said cheerfully.

"Maybe after she's had a little rest she'll feel like a swim," Alice said hopefully.

The motorboat from the *Daisy Mae* returned carrying Janet, Hal, and Gavin Davis, as well as Brittany, all wearing swimsuits. Jody noticed that Hal also wore a life jacket — obviously this time his mother had decided to take no chances, even in the shallowest water.

And she was right to be worried. As soon as they were out of the boat, Hal was struggling to pull away from his parents' restraining hands, his eyes fixed on the deeper water beyond the sandbar, grunting wordlessly as he tried to fling himself into it.

"We're going into the water together, Hal," his mother said loudly. "You must stay close to Mommy and Daddy."

He kept struggling and grunting as if she hadn't spoken.

Jody felt sorry for both parents and child, who couldn't seem to communicate. She began to walk toward the little boy, trying to get his attention. "Look at the dolphin, Hal," she said. "This is Rosie."

Rosie meets Hal

Whether her words had gotten through, or he'd just happened to notice the animal lying in the shallow water, Jody didn't know. But when he finally saw Rosie, a change came over Hal. Suddenly, he became quiet. He stopped struggling and simply stared. Then he said, "What's wrong?"

Janet Davis gasped.

Jody was amazed. Short as it was, this was the first clear sentence she'd ever heard the little boy speak. Slowly and carefully, Jody told him, "Rosie got caught in a net and couldn't get out. We helped her get free, but I think she's still kind of tired."

"Tired," the boy echoed. Still staring intently at the resting dolphin he asked, "Go sleep?"

"No, she's awake," Jody said.

"Play with Hal?" Again, the boy seemed to speak more to the dolphin than to Jody, even though she was right in front of him.

Jody looked questioningly at Hal's parents and found that they were looking to Jerry for the answer.

Jerry Rozakis nodded. He waded into the water and stood directly in front of Hal. Then he crouched, putting himself on a level with the boy, and spoke directly to him. "Rosie is a friendly dolphin. She's not feeling too well right now, but maybe you can make her feel better, Hal. You can go into the water with Rosie, but you must listen to the grown-ups, and do what we tell you. Nod your head if you understand me."

For a moment, as Hal went on gazing beyond Jerry at the dolphin, Jody was afraid he hadn't heard, or that he would act as if he hadn't heard. But after a second's delay he nodded.

"Good boy," said Jerry approvingly. "You must keep your life jacket on while you're in the water, and you must always have two people with you. You choose who you want to be with you, Hal."

Expecting the little boy to choose his parents, or maybe Jerry, Jody was astonished when Hal pointed his finger at her, and then at Lauren.

"Jody and Lauren," Jerry said. "That's fine. Remember to do what they say. If you don't, you'll have to come out. Now Jody and Lauren will take you to meet Rosie."

9

Standing on either side of Hal, Lauren and Jody walked him off the sandbank and into the slightly deeper water. As they went, Lauren kept up a soothing stream of talk. "Now we'll just go splash, splash through this water here until we come to Rosie. Look, she's watching us! See her eye, there? She may be still, but she's awake. She's wondering who you are, Hal. She knows me and Jody, but she hasn't met you before, has she? She doesn't know you."

"Hal," said the boy.

"Yes, that's right," Lauren agreed. "You're Hal, and this is Rosie."

"Rosie," he repeated, staring intently as they brought him close to the animal resting in the shallows near the shore.

"Do you want to touch her, Hal?" Lauren asked in a gentle voice. "You can stroke Rosie if you like."

Jody demonstrated by running the palm of her hand firmly along Rosie's flank.

Hal nodded. Moving stiffly, he stretched out one hand. After a moment's hesitation, he brought his hand down through the water to rest on Rosie's side. Then, slowly and gently, he began to stroke her.

Jody stood in silence, watching. The sun beat down on her head, and the air was still except for the hum of a few insects and the endless ebb and swell of the sea beyond the quiet little bay. She felt that she was witnessing a minor miracle, as this isolated little boy made contact with another creature.

"You can talk to her, you know." Lauren made the suggestion as she watched him stroking Rosie. "You

Best of friends!

can talk to her while you're touching her — she'd like that. Would you like to try it?"

Hal went on patting the dolphin, showing no sign that he had heard what Lauren said. Then suddenly, unexpectedly, he nodded. And then, to Jody's astonishment, he opened his mouth and made a sound like a creaky hinge — an excellent imitation of a dolphin sound!

Although Rosie had not made a sound since they'd found her, Hal had obviously remembered hearing this noise from Apollo or some of the other wild dolphins he had watched from the yacht.

Then Jody was even more amazed. Rosie responded. She moved a little, and poked her beak out of the water. Hal walked toward her head and peered down at her eye. He made the creaking noise again, a little louder this time.

Rosie creaked right back at him!

Jody looked at Lauren. Her eyes were wide with astonishment — she looked as stunned as Jody felt. Their eyes met and they grinned happily at each other.

Hal showed no sign of happiness or excitement. He looked as stiff and solemn as ever. But he stroked

Rosie's beak and made the creaking noise again. When she gave out a string of rapid-fire clicks, he tried his best to imitate them.

From behind her, Jody heard Hal's mother give a stifled cry. In tones of wonder, Gavin Davis said, "He's actually trying to talk to that animal."

Suddenly, Rosie flexed her tail. A moment later, she was gliding through the water between Jody and Hal, rubbing against their bare legs. She swam in a circle around the three of them, poking her beak out of the water to make creaking and clicking noises in the air.

Hal followed every move the dolphin made, watching her intently. When she rolled onto her back, offering her belly, he seemed to understand at once that she was asking to be stroked.

Gradually, as he responded to Rosie, Hal's expression began to change. His whole body relaxed. The terrible, stiff blankness of his face became peaceful.

Jody was thrilled. Through some sort of animal magic, Rosie was able to reach Hal as no person could. And by concentrating on reaching the boy, Rosie was healing herself at the same time. It was wonderful.

Far too soon, it seemed to them all, Jerry called time.

Hal started to get upset, making the strange wordless groans that Jody had heard before.

But Jerry was right there, his hands on the boy's shoulders, his piercing eyes commanding attention. "Hal," he said firmly. "Rosie needs to rest. She's had a bad time. You've helped her feel better but she needs to rest now. You can come and see her again tomorrow, if you like, but you have to be good. That means no fussing. Go with your parents, do what they tell you, and they'll bring you back tomorrow."

The groaning stopped. Hal stared into Jerry's eyes, saw that he meant it, and nodded.

Gavin Davis seemed less sure. "You really mean it?" he asked Jerry.

"Of course." Jerry gestured around at the little bay. "I don't mean *here*, though. Rosie seems to be okay now, so I think we can get her back to CETA all right. Come there, tomorrow. Five o'clock? Stay and have dinner with us afterward, if you don't mind potluck."

"That's very kind of you," Gavin Davis said slowly.

"But I know you're overworked already. I don't want to put you under more pressure, just because —"

"Don't worry about it," Jerry cut him off. "I can't offer you my full professional services, but if you're happy for Hal to be looked after by my two talented young assistants . . ." He gestured at Jody and Lauren.

Feeling herself blush, Jody concentrated on watching Rosie, who was swimming idly around the small bay.

"I'm sure Hal wouldn't want anyone else," Gavin Davis said warmly. "No one could have done a better job than they have today."

Jody glowed with happiness. She couldn't believe how lucky she was, to be allowed to work with dolphins this way. She exchanged a glance with Lauren and saw that the other girl was looking thrilled, too.

Everyone said their good-byes, and the Davises headed back on their motorboat for the *Daisy Mae*, taking Maddie and Cam with them. While Lauren and Jody had been busy with Hal and Rosie, Cam had managed to convince Maddie to let him show her the sights of Key West that evening.

"Tell your folks I may be back late," Maddie told Jody, smiling broadly.

"And that I've promised to take good care of their assistant," Cam added with a wink. He looked very pleased with himself Jody thought as she waved good-bye.

"What's going to happen to Rosie?" Brittany asked Alice Rozakis as she climbed on board *Princess*.

"We're hoping she'll follow us back to CETA," Alice said quietly, exchanging a glance with her husband.

"She certainly seems to have recovered," Jerry said, shading his eyes as he gazed out to where Rosie was now playing with the wild dolphins. He added, "We're only a few miles from Cedar Key. I don't think such a short journey will wear her out, but you girls can keep an eye on her. If she seems to be flagging at all, I'll slow down."

"You can count on us," said Lauren. Now that she realized Rosie was okay, Lauren had recovered her usual calm, cheerful good nature.

Not wanting to upset her, Jody didn't mention what she was thinking: What if Rosie decided to stay with her newfound friends in the wild, rather than return to her old life at CETA?

However, as soon as *Princess* began to motor away from the sandbank, Rosie came leaping through the water to follow the boat.

Jody, Lauren, and Brittany all leaned over the back to watch her, but Rosie was not content to stay behind. As if to prove how fit she was, the dolphin shot through the water, streaking past the motorboat and then returning to leap in and out of the water on either side of the prow.

Laughing with delight, Lauren called to her father, "I think she wants us to go faster! She's looking for a wave to ride!"

"I think you're right," Jerry agreed. He was laughing, too.

Jody could see that Rosie's recovery had lifted a great weight of worry off his shoulders.

"Okay, girls, hang on!" The engine roared as he powered it up. As the boat cut through the water it created a foam-crested wave that Rosie rode. Soon the other dolphins joined in, butting and jostling each other for the best place.

After about ten minutes, Jody recognized the familiar buildings of CETA and realized they were approaching Cedar Key.

Jerry slowed the boat. The dolphins began to drop away. Apollo poked his nose up out of the water near the back of the boat and looked at Jody. He made his creaking sound.

Jody reached out her hand and briefly touched his nose. "See you later?" she said hopefully.

The dolphin butted her hand and gave a series of chattering clicks in reply before diving down and swimming away after the rest of his group.

Now, only Rosie remained beside the boat. She pushed her beak out of the water and looked at them.

Alice picked up the cell phone as Jerry idled the motor. "I'm going to call the office and get Kim to open the sea gate," she explained as she punched the buttons. "It looks like Rosie is ready to come home."

Sure enough, Jody saw that Rosie was speeding

through the water toward the fence. They could hear her whistling and clicking, and, moments later, there was a response from the dolphins on the inside.

Alice got through to Kim and quickly explained the situation. "See you in a few minutes," she promised. Breaking the connection, she exchanged a relieved smile with her husband. "Thank goodness this has all ended so happily," she said with a small sigh.

Jerry nodded. "Shall I take the boat around to the dock?" he suggested.

"Can we wait to see the gates open, and Rosie go in?" Lauren asked. She was peering toward the gate with a slight frown.

"Okay," her father agreed, smiling. Then his smile faded. "I can't see her, though, can you?"

They all looked. They could still hear the faint, excited sounds of dolphins, and the familiar shape of the bottle-nosed beaks on the other side of the fence, but there was no sign of Rosie.

"She's probably just underwater," Alice said when a splashing sound drew their attention to the side of the boat.

They just caught sight of a curved dorsal fin and a flip of the tail as Rosie surfaced just long enough to take a breath before shooting away underwater — away from the boat, away from them, away from CETA.

"Rosie!" Lauren cried out in anguish. "Please come back! Please!" She turned to her parents. "Do you think she thought she was locked out?"

With a metallic shriek, the sea gate creaked open. Looking toward CETA, Jody saw her dad and Kim waving at them.

"She'll have heard that, surely," Alice said.

They all gazed in the direction Rosie had gone, waiting for her to return, hoping against hope. But the minutes ticked past without Rosie.

Finally, Jerry called an end to their wait by starting the engine.

"Oh, Daddy, please, just a little longer." Lauren begged.

"Sweetheart, Rosie will either come back, or she won't. Our being here doesn't make any difference. And I can't hang around on the water all day — I've got work to do," Jerry added, sounding weary.

Lauren looked close to tears. Jody knew how she felt, but could think of no comfort to offer.

Dinner that evening was a gloomy meal, even though Alice pointed out that the important thing was that they knew Rosie was well and happy.

"We've always known that some day she would probably want to live in the wild — it's just happened a little sooner than we'd expected," she reminded them quietly.

Lauren nodded sadly, pushing mashed potatoes around her plate. Then she looked up at her father. "Could we leave the sea gates open tonight, just in case she comes back?"

"Oh, no," Jerry said. "Absolutely not! The way my luck is running, the other three would decide to swim out and never come back! I'm sorry, sweetheart. But Rosie's made her choice; she's not going to come back now."

"Anyway, she could jump over the fence if she wanted to," Sean said suddenly. "Dolphins can jump really high. I know — I've seen them."

Jody stared across the table at her little brother. "Yeah, so have I," she said slowly, thinking about it. "I'm sure I've seen Apollo jump higher — much higher — than that fence. So how come your dolphins don't jump over it? Why do you need a gate at all?"

"I guess they could if they really wanted to," Alice said. "But they never have."

"Yes, it's odd, but although dolphins can be trained to leap over things, you'll almost never see a wild dolphin jump over any kind of barrier," Gina agreed. "No one knows why, but if a dolphin can't swim under, through, or around something, they act as if they *can't* jump over it. So even a very low fence will keep them in one place."

"That's weird," said Jimmy.

"May I be excused?" Lauren said quietly. "I'm not very hungry."

"Yes, of course, sweetheart," said her mother, giving her a concerned look.

"Me, neither," said Brittany, pushing aside her plate.

Jody watched unhappily as the two girls hurried away together.

June 30 — evening.
I hope Lauren doesn't blame me for losing Rosie, but I

wouldn't be surprised if she does. If Apollo hadn't followed us here, Rosie would still be living happily at CETA with her mother.

I felt so close to Lauren when we rescued Rosie, but now I feel like I'm just in the way. Maybe Brittany can cheer her up. I wish

Jody broke off and shut her diary hastily as the bedroom door opened. Lauren came in with Brittany right behind her.

"Okay, if we're not going to watch TV, let's put some music on," Brittany said. Ignoring Jody, she marched across the room to Lauren's stereo and began to go through her CD collection. "What do you feel like?"

"I don't feel like listening to music right now," Lauren said quietly. "I'm going to take a bath and go to bed."

"It's too early to go to bed," Brittany objected, scowling.

"Well, I'm tired," Lauren said.

"You can't be, not yet," Brittany said crossly.

Jody stood up. "Come on, Brittany," she said firmly. "Let's leave Lauren in peace."

Brittany turned on her. "Be quiet," she snapped. "Lauren's my friend, not yours!"

"If you were really Lauren's friend, you'd do what she wants, instead of just thinking about yourself," Jody replied fiercely.

"I'm more important than some silly animal," Brittany shouted, her face turning red. She glared at Lauren. "I thought you were different at first, but you're as bad as *she* is." She tossed her head to indicate Jody. "Just another boring dolphin fanatic! Why did I ever waste my time on somebody who thinks it matters on which side of a fence some stupid dolphin wants to live! You two were just *made* for each other!" Then she stormed out of the bedroom.

Lauren's eyes were wide. After a moment she turned to Jody and spoke. "You don't look surprised. Have you seen her like that before?"

Jody nodded.

Lauren looked thoughtful. "I don't suppose there's any chance that *she* might decide she'd rather go live in the wild instead of staying with us?"

10

Next morning, Jody and Lauren breathed a sigh of relief when Brittany demanded to be taken back to *Dolphin Dreamer*. But they were still worried about how Hal Davis would react when he found Rosie wasn't there.

Jerry tried to reassure them. "He probably won't notice that it's a different dolphin. Bottle-nosed dolphins look so much alike that even experts can find it hard to tell them apart."

"But Rosie has that scar over her eye," Lauren pointed out. "It's pretty distinctive."

"Well . . ." Her father shrugged uneasily. "All right, he

might notice the difference, but as long as he's allowed to get into the water and play with a dolphin, I'd be amazed if he made a fuss about which one. None of the other children have minded."

"I guess you're right," said Lauren. "Which one should it be?"

"Take your pick," Jerry told the girls. "They're all free. I'll be in the office, having a conference with some parents to discuss ways of teaching their child at home. I'm sure you'll do fine, but give me a yell if you need any help."

Jody and Lauren looked at each other when Jerry had gone. After a brief discussion they decided on Nora, who was also female, and the nearest in age to Rosie. They decided they wouldn't say anything about the change unless Hal asked. Once he got to know Nora they were sure he'd be fine, but if they warned him beforehand that Rosie was missing, he might throw a tantrum.

The Davises arrived promptly at five o'clock. They looked happy and excited. Jody thought she had never seen the little boy looking quite so alert and friendly. Somehow, that made her feel worse than ever.

"Cheer up," said Gavin Davis, smiling at the two girls. Then he cocked his head quizzically. "Is there something wrong?"

"We're just worried in case we do something wrong," Lauren said hastily. She was blushing. "Even though I've watched my dad hundreds of times, I can't help feeling nervous. . . ."

The shadow of suspicion quickly cleared away. "You girls have nothing to worry about," he said firmly. "You were absolutely brilliant with Hal yesterday. And, anyway, I understand that Jerry says the dolphins are the teachers here, so you don't have to worry too much about keeping Hal's attention — that's up to Rosie! And after what we saw yesterday, I can't believe she'd let us down."

Jody gulped and smiled weakly. "Come on, Hal," she called to the little boy. "Let's just check your life jacket . . . then we'll go into the shallow pool with . . . uh, with the dolphin."

Although he was obviously excited, Hal waited patiently for the girls to tell him he was allowed to get into the water.

As soon as they had slipped into the water, Nora came swimming up to investigate.

Staring intently at the sleek gray shape beneath the water, Hal opened his mouth and made the same creaking nose he'd made the day before.

Nora poked her head out of the water to look at the boy.

Hal frowned. He leaned forward, staring intently. Jody held her breath and exchanged a glance with Lauren. Was he looking for Rosie's scar? He didn't say anything. After a moment, he made the creaking noise again.

Unlike Rosie, Nora didn't respond with sounds of her own. But at least she seemed interested in Hal, Jody thought.

"Do you want to give her a fish to eat, Hal?" Lauren suggested. She tapped her fingernails against the metal bucket beside the pool.

Hal didn't take his eyes off Nora.

"Dolphins love fish," Jody added. "Hal, she'd like it if you gave her a fish."

Hal ignored her, too. He made the creaking noise, paused, then tried again. It was as if he was alone in the pool with the dolphin.

Suddenly, he started to shake. "This dolphin's not my friend," he shouted. "I want my friend!"

Lauren and Jody exchanged a swift glance. "She *is* your friend, Hal," Lauren said urgently. "But she needs to get to know you. You're right that this isn't Rosie. This is one of Rosie's friends, and she wants to be friends with you, too. Her name is Nora."

"Rosie," Hal cried. "Rosie! Rosie! Rosie!" He paused, but it was only to draw breath to scream.

"What's wrong?" Alarmed by the screaming, Hal's mother peered down into the water at them.

"Hal!" Lauren spoke sharply. "Listen to me! If you don't calm down, you'll have to get out of the water this instant."

It got through to him. He stopped yelling. But now, Jody noticed in dismay, Nora was deserting them, swimming away out of the shallow pool, and making for the sea pen. She realized that Maxi and Nick were making an unusual amount of noise out there.

"I want Rosie," Hal said flatly.

Jody's heart sank. What could they say to him, how could they possibly control him now?

Lauren seemed to be thinking hard. Then, into the silence, came a dolphin's whistle. She turned in astonishment to gaze out toward the sea. "Rosie?" she cried.

"Rosie," Hal repeated. He threw his head back and began to make his creaking noise as loudly as he could. Then he paused. They all heard the whistle again. Hal tried to imitate it.

"It *is* Rosie. She's come back!" Lauren exclaimed. "Oh, Jody, please — can you manage Hal? I've got to open the sea gate before she leaves again!"

With that, Lauren hauled herself out of the shallow pool and went racing toward the storeroom where the controls were. Jody watched anxiously as her friend tried the door and discovered it was locked. She turned and ran toward the office.

Jody had her hands full trying to keep Hal under control. He was determined to fling himself further out into the water, seemingly drawn by the sound of Rosie's whistle.

Janet Davis slipped into the water, much to Jody's relief, and took charge of her son. "Hal, you have to do what the girls tell you, or they won't let you see Rosie," she said firmly. Then, frowning quizzically, she looked at Jody. "But I don't understand. Wasn't that Rosie in the pool with Hal? What's going on?"

Blushing, Jody told her what had happened. "I was afraid if we told Hal, he'd be too upset. . . . We hoped he wouldn't notice."

"Well, I couldn't tell the difference between them myself," Janet confessed. "But it's different for Hal. He really bonded with the one you call Rosie. Listen!" They both listened to the amazingly accurate whistle Hal was producing now. "It's eerie, isn't it? I would never have imagined he could do that. He sounds *exactly* like a dolphin," Janet said in wonder.

Lauren came running out of the office with her parents close behind. They were heading for the sea gate controls in the storeroom.

Before they reached the door, though, something happened that Jody knew she would never forget in her whole life.

Suddenly, Rosie came rising out of the water, her sleek body arching to make one fabulously high leap. It carried her straight over the fence, into the sea pen, where she splashed down, and disappeared beneath the water.

Jody gasped in astonishment.

"That dolphin just leaped over the fence!" Janet Davis exclaimed. "I had no idea they could jump that high!"

Rosie had yet another surprise in store.

As Jody stared in wonder, Rosie appeared, swimming through the narrow underwater passage that connected the shallow pool with the sea pens. She emerged into the shallow pool, swimming right up to Jody, Hal, and Janet, expelling a gust of air through her blowhole.

Hal began to click and whistle more urgently than ever. As soon as he paused for breath, Rosie replied with a long series of chattering clicks and trilling

Rosie returns!

whistles. If you closed your eyes, thought Jody, you wouldn't be able to tell from the sounds alone which came from the boy and which from the dolphin.

"I can't believe it," murmured Hal's mother. "It's like they're really talking to each other."

"They are," said Jody. She was suddenly sure of it, and she felt awed and moved by the obvious affection between them. "Rosie loves Hal. That's why she came back. Not just for her mother and Nick and Nora, but for the people at CETA as well. She thinks they're all part of her family." She turned as Lauren slipped into the water beside them.

Rosie broke off her conversation with Hal to swim up and butt gently against Lauren's legs.

"Yeah, I'm glad to see you, too, Rosie," said Lauren. There were tears on her cheeks, but she was smiling broadly as she slipped down into the water to hug the dolphin. "Welcome home!"

July 1 — bedtime.
We've been invited to spend the Fourth of July on board the Daisy Mae. *Gavin Davis has promised the most spec-*

tacular fireworks display we've ever seen. It will be a great celebration . . . and we have so many things to celebrate! It will also be a going-away party for us, since in a few more days we'll be setting sail on Dolphin Dreamer *for the Bahamas.*

It will be hard to say good-bye to the friends we've made on Cedar Key — both dolphin and human! — but it is good to know that Rosie is safely home again, and, with the help of Gavin Davis, the future of CETA seems secure.

Dolphin Diaries™

RIDING THE STORM

1

July 15 — mid-morning.
Atlantic spotted dolphins!

My first sighting of Stenella frontalis. *We were still eating breakfast when Cam gave a shout from on deck. I went racing up to see. There were four of them swimming very close together, and they came right up to the side of the boat. When Dad and I leaned over to look, they poked their heads out of the water and looked right back at us! Their backs were an almost purplish color under the masses of white spots, with lighter sides and whitish underneath. In size and shape they seemed a lot like the bottle-nosed dolphins I've known, and every bit as friendly, fast, and playful. But they didn't stick around for very long . . .*

Jody McGrath sighed and leaned back in her bunk, letting her pen and diary fall into her lap. The latest dolphin sighting had been exciting, but all too brief. *Dolphin Dreamer* had left Key West nearly a week earlier, heading for the Bahamas, and the days at sea had been long, slow, and uneventful.

Sean and Jimmy, Jody's mischievous twin brothers, were being especially troublesome today. She had come down to her cabin to escape their pestering, but now that she had brought her diary up to date, she didn't know what to do with herself.

Back home in Fort Lauderdale, she would have picked up the phone and called her best friend Lindsay. The thought gave her a pang of loneliness. She longed for someone to talk to. Instead, she picked up her diary again.

Sometimes I feel so stuck on this boat! I wonder what Lindsay's doing now? She promised she would e-mail me every day, but it's been nearly a week since her last message. Maria and Devon haven't answered my last e-mails, either. I have this horrible feeling that they're all out having fun together and have forgotten about me completely . . .

Tears welled up and she had to stop writing and grope for a tissue.

"What's wrong with you?" The voice was loud and impatient.

Jody was startled. She had been too caught up in her own thoughts to notice her bunk mate entering the cabin. Brittany, daughter of Harry Pierce, *Dolphin Dreamer*'s English captain, stood staring at her, looking unfriendly, as usual. She was the one person on board who had nothing to do with the Dolphin Universe project and didn't want to be there. However, she'd been left by her mother in her father's care at the last minute, and with no one else to look after her, she'd had to come along.

"Nothing," Jody said hastily. She turned to stow away her diary and quickly wiped her eyes.

"You were crying. I saw you," Brittany persisted. She sat down on Jody's bunk. "Tell me what you were crying about." She still didn't sound that friendly, but it was obvious she expected an answer.

"I was just feeling kind of homesick," Jody confessed. She didn't expect any sympathy, and she was right.

"You?" Brittany sounded disbelieving. "How could you be homesick? You're right here with your whole family, and you've told me about a million times how much you love being part of this dumb dolphin research project! Nobody forced you to leave home and live with a bunch of strangers — what have *you* got to cry about?"

"I miss my friends," Jody replied. She bit her lip as tears threatened again. How different things would be if she was sharing this cabin with Lindsay, instead of with spoiled, unfriendly Brittany!

Brittany's expression softened. "So do I," she said quietly. "I miss hanging out at the mall with the other kids. And I miss my own bedroom, and my own computer, and watching TV, and our swimming pool . . ." A yearning look came over her face. "But mostly I miss my

330

mom." She looked directly at Jody, leaning confidingly close. "It's just so awful not hearing from her, not even knowing if she's gotten any of my messages. I need to talk to her. Can I use your computer to e-mail her again? Please?"

Jody's heart sank. She really did sympathize with Brittany's desperation, especially as she'd been feeling lonely, too. She couldn't imagine her own mother flying off to another country without even telling her when she'd be back! But they'd been through this before. "You know we have to ask my parents before going on-line while we're at sea," she replied, as gently as she could. "Phone calls and computer link-ups have to go by satellite, and that costs a ton of money."

Brittany frowned impatiently. "This is important! Just let me check my e-mail — I'll be on-line for less than a minute. My dad will pay for it!"

Jody knew that Harry had tried to contact his ex-wife by phone and e-mail many times already. "Maybe you'd better ask your dad, then," she said. "I wanted to check my e-mail last night, but Mom told me to wait till we reach Port Lucaya. It won't be long."

Tension had been building in Brittany as she listened. Now she snapped. "Thanks a lot! You wouldn't have to tell your mom what I'd done! You're such a goody-goody, Jody McGrath. I don't know how you can stand yourself!" With that, Brittany stormed out of the cabin.

Jody winced. It was so unfair to be blamed for things that weren't her fault — but that was just typical of Brittany. She waited a minute, so Brittany wouldn't think she was following her, and then left the cabin.

Jody's parents, Craig and Gina McGrath, were in the main cabin with Harry Pierce, looking at a navigation chart spread out on the table. Brittany was nowhere to be seen.

"*Honey Bee* should be on Little Bahama Bank, right about here," Craig said, tapping the chart with his finger.

"What's *Honey Bee?*" Jody asked curiously, going to join her parents.

Her mother smiled and put an arm around her. "That's the name of Matt Anderson's catamaran — his boat."

Jody recognized the man's name. "You mean Dad's old friend from college?"

Craig nodded. "That's right. Matt came out here right after graduation to pursue his own research. He's been studying the same group of dolphins for more than a dozen years — he's an expert on the Atlantic spotted dolphin, and he's built up a huge database," he went on enthusiastically.

"Sounds perfect to add to the Dolphin Universe database," Jody said. "I can't wait to meet him."

"Don't you mean, you can't wait to meet his dolphins?" Her father's blue eyes twinkled as he gave her a teasing smile.

Jody grinned back. "Mind reader! So when does this happen?"

"I've just made radio contact, and he's given us his coordinates," Craig told her.

"We're already on course," said Harry from across the table. He straightened up. "I'll need to check the wind speed, but my guess is that we should be approaching *Honey Bee* in about half an hour."

"Matt said his boat is right in the middle of a large,

333

friendly group of Atlantic spotted dolphins at this very moment," her father added.

"Great!" said Jody. "I hope they stick around till we get there!" She felt excitement rising like bubbles inside her. The last few days at sea had been a little too quiet for Jody. But now that was going to change. "I'm going up on deck," she said eagerly. "Maybe I'll be the first to see them!"

Her mother gave her a quick hug and let her go. "You watch out for pirates, now," she said mysteriously.

Jody understood what her mother had meant as soon as she emerged on deck and caught sight of her twin brothers.

Sean was wearing an eyepatch and a painted-on, curling black moustache. He was standing with his hands on his hips. Jimmy, with a red bandana tied around his head, was brandishing a cardboard sword. "You'll walk the plank for that, matey!" he roared at his brother.

Jody rolled her eyes. She wished she had someone to share her feelings with and thought again, with a pang, of Lindsay. Why couldn't Brittany have been somebody nicer, somebody she could have been friends with?

She looked at Cameron Tucker, the second mate, who was at the helm while the captain was below. "I hope these pesky pirates aren't bothering you, Cam," she said.

He shrugged and winked at her. "Just one of the hazards of sailing in the Caribbean," he said. "I've seen worse."

"You've never seen worse pirates than us," Jimmy objected. "We're the worstest pirates that ever there was!"

"Yeah — the worst eight-year-old pirates," Jody replied. She went to lean against the side, as far away from her brothers as she could get, and gazed out at the sparkling blue waves. The sun blazed down out of a clear blue sky, as it had every day that week, but the wind that now filled the sails also kept them cooler than they would have been on shore. As always, Jody scanned the surface of the water, searching for a curved fin, or a splash, or the wonderful sight of a glis-

Sean and Jimmy fooling around—as usual!

tening, streamlined body leaping joyfully into the air. But there was nothing to disturb the endless waves of the sea around them.

From behind her, Jody heard one of her brothers shout, "You're my prisoner!"

Then Maddie's voice, sounding cool and amused, said, "Do you know who you're talking to? I'm nobody's prisoner — I'm the Queen of the Pirates, and I've just commandeered this vessel!"

Jody turned to watch. Maddie was her parents' assistant, but before she'd decided to study marine biology she had worked as an elementary school teacher. Maybe that was why she could handle Jody's younger brothers so well.

Sean scowled. "Girls can't be pirates," he objected.

Maddie's eyes widened disbelievingly. "Don't tell me you've never heard of Anne Bonney? Or Mary Read?"

Sean looked at Jimmy, who shrugged.

"For real?" Sean asked Maddie.

She nodded solemnly. "Nearly three hundred years ago, Mary Read, Anne Bonney, and her pirate husband

Calico Jack sailed in these very waters making daring raids on merchant ships."

Jody found herself getting interested, even though she thought her brothers' pirate obsession was silly.

The boys were fascinated, bombarding Maddie with questions:

"Where?"

"What was the pirate ship called?"

"Did they bury their treasure?"

Maddie laughed and held up her hands in surrender. "Come below and I'll tell you everything. Your mom says you've been playing out in the hot sun long enough."

When they had gone, Jody leaned over the side again. The water was very clear here, and seemed shallow. She could see right down to the soft, white, sandy bottom. It was easy to imagine herself down there, gliding effortlessly through the water, as free and easy as a wild dolphin.

"Ship ahoy!" Her father's voice, amplified by the bullhorn, boomed out in the quiet air, rousing Jody from her dreams.

"Ahoy, *Honey Bee!*" As Craig spoke into the bullhorn again, Jody straightened up and hurried over to the other side of the deck where her parents were standing. They were approaching a twin-hulled boat with yellow sails. There was a crowd of people on board, most of them gazing down into the water.

Jody gasped as she saw what they were looking at. In the water around *Honey Bee* there must have been at least twenty dolphins bobbing, diving, and frolicking.

Cam was busy dashing about, hauling in the sails to slow *Dolphin Dreamer*'s speed while the captain changed course.

Craig raised the bullhorn and spoke again. "Request permission to approach!"

Another amplified voice came echoing across the water. "Ahoy, *Dolphin Dreamer*! Permission granted! Welcome aboard! What took you so long?"

Craig chuckled. "Good old Matt," he said fondly.

Jody grinned and hugged herself with excitement as their boat drew nearer to *Honey Bee* and the crowd of dolphins. Unlike the bottle-nosed dolphins she knew, the Atlantic spotted dolphins had obvious differences between them. Some had lots of distinct spots, some had only a few; the spots were clear and separate on some, and blurred together on others; even their colors were different. It was going to be easier to recognize and keep track of this group than the bottle-nosed dolphins, and she couldn't wait to get to know them.

But as they drew nearer, the dolphins began to leave. At first, only a few swam away, but soon, as if the word had spread quickly, all the dolphins took off, swimming rapidly away from both boats.

Jody stared at them in dismay. "What's wrong?" she asked her parents. "Why are they all leaving? Did we scare them?"

Her father looked as concerned as she felt. "I don't know, honey," he said slowly. "I hope not, but . . . it certainly looks that way."

From the other boat there came a buzz of disappointed voices, cries of "Come back!", and whistles that seemed to be attempts at the dolphins' own sounds. But the dolphins responded to none of it. Within minutes, they had all vanished from sight, as if they had never been there.

2

"I'm really sorry if we scared away your dolphins," Craig said after they'd boarded *Honey Bee* and he'd introduced Maddie, Jody, and the twins to his friend Matt.

Matt Anderson was a tall, thin, deeply tanned man with a long, friendly face. "It's not your fault," he assured Craig, including the whole group with his quick, warm smile. "The dolphins are just kind of wary of strange boats right now, that's all. Stick around for a while, and they'll come back."

"Actually, we *were* hoping to stick around for a

while, to see what you're up to," Craig replied. "But the captain and crew would like to get into port pretty soon to take care of business. Mei Lin, our cook, is desperate to buy some fresh fruit and vegetables. But if you don't mind, we could stay here with you on *Honey Bee* for a few hours, and then Harry could sail back to pick us up —"

"They don't have to come back for you," Matt interrupted. "We're spending the afternoon out here observing dolphins, then sailing into Port Lucaya in time to have dinner, so we'll take you back."

Gina, Maddie, and Jody all nodded enthusiastically when Craig looked at them.

He grinned. "That sounds great," he told Matt. "I'll tell Harry that we're staying and he can go."

Suddenly, Maddie gave a gasp, her eyes wide.

"What's wrong, Maddie?" asked Gina.

"We forgot somebody," Maddie replied softly.

Jody thought that Maddie must mean Brittany. "Oh, Brittany's sure to want to go into the port with Harry and Cam and Mei Lin," she said.

Maddie shook her head. "Who else?" she prompted.

Then they got it. Craig groaned, Gina laughed, and Jody named the person they'd nearly forgotten: "Dr. Taylor!"

Dr. Jefferson Taylor was a scientist who worked for PetroCo, the oil company that was providing much of the funding for Dolphin Universe. The funding had come with a catch, though: PetroCo had insisted that Dr. Taylor come along as part of the research team. He was on board to get good publicity for the oil company, showing that they were interested in dolphin conservation. But so far, Dr. Taylor had not proved to be much use as a dolphin research scientist!

"I'd better go find him," Craig said with a sigh. "He'd never forgive us otherwise."

Jody noticed that her brothers were talking to a boy who looked about eight or nine. "Is that your son?" she asked Matt.

For a moment Matt looked startled. "No, I don't have any children — my girlfriend Anna hasn't even agreed to marry me yet! Why, do you think he looks like me?"

Jody felt herself blushing slightly at the misunderstanding. The boy was sturdily built, with very pale blond hair, and looked nothing at all like the lean, dark man smiling down at her. "No. Only, he's too young to be a crew member, so I thought he must be family."

"Oh, of course," Matt said kindly. "No, he's neither crew nor family — he's here with his parents. They're tourists, like the rest of the people on board today — apart from my assistant Adam. That's how I finance my research: people pay to come out on *Honey Bee* to learn about dolphins, and even get to know them a little."

"That sounds great!" Jody exclaimed enthusiastically.

Matt smiled again. "Glad you think so. Come and meet everybody — I see your brothers got a head start on that already!"

Matt introduced the boy Sean and Jimmy were talking to as Logan Schroeder. He and his parents were visiting from Colorado. The rest of the tour members were Anita and Kim Lapidus, a mother and her teenage daughter from Florida; Bob and Kathy Moran, an older couple from Vermont; and Jim and Megan Hobb, from Texas.

Adam Jones, Matt's assistant, was from nearby Freeport. He seemed to be a quiet young man with a sweet smile.

"Excuse me, Mr. Anderson, but do you think that the dolphins will come back today?" Logan asked. Everyone waited intently to hear Matt's reply.

"I hope so, Logan," Matt said. "I'm gong to put some special music on — it often attracts them when they hear it playing from the underwater speakers. The boat our friends arrived on is about to leave, and once it's gone there shouldn't be any reason for the dolphins to stay away. They know they have nothing to fear from anyone on *Honey Bee*."

Jody frowned. Matt had said that it wasn't their fault, yet it sounded as if their arrival *had* scared off the dolphins — but why? Dolphins were not timid creatures, and were usually curious about the boats they met.

Jimmy obviously thought the same thing, because he spoke up loudly. "They don't have to be scared of *Dolphin Dreamer.* We *love* dolphins. And we've got lots of dolphin friends back in Florida to prove it!"

There were chuckles from a few of the adults.

345

"I'm sure you do, Jimmy," Matt said. "And once the dolphins of Little Bahama Bank get to know you, I'm sure they'll love you, too. The problem isn't with *Dolphin Dreamer*, but another boat, called *Stormrider*, and the obnoxious college kids who've chartered her for their summer break." He looked very serious. "A lot of people don't understand the damage a motorboat can do to a dolphin. They haven't seen a curious dolphin get badly cut by a propeller. I have."

Jody caught her breath, shocked.

"Those guys are worse than that," said Jim Hobb with a frown. "Ignorant is one thing — cruel is another. We've run into them before. They think it's funny to tease and torment animals."

Matt nodded. "I'm afraid Jim is right," he said. "I was told they even caught one dolphin in a net, and although they let it go, it must have been a terrifying experience for the poor creature. Anyway, the result is that recently the local dolphins are getting a little nervous whenever a strange boat turns up."

Listening to this, Jody was horrified. She knew that not everyone shared her passion for dolphins, but how

346

could anyone want to hurt such wonderful animals? "Who are they?" she demanded.

Matt shrugged. "Some brats with more money than sense. They really should know better."

Just then, Craig arrived with Dr. Taylor, who was looking distinctly rumpled and sleepy-eyed. He yawned as he was introduced to Matt Anderson, and then apologized, sounding rather sorry for himself. "Excuse me, Dr. Anderson, but I wasn't expecting this meeting. It *is* siesta time, you know."

"Ah, yes, the wonderful Spanish tradition of a nap in the afternoon," Matt replied politely. "We've got too much going on to want to stop for siesta on *Honey Bee,* but there are bunks down below if you'd like."

"No, no," Dr. Taylor said quickly, waving his hand. "Of course I'll be fine with what everyone else wants to do! I'm always glad to meet fellow scientists and learn about their work. Er, what *is* your work, exactly?"

Just then Jody heard Logan give a glad cry. "The dolphins! They're coming back!"

Jody rushed to join her brothers and Logan at the side of the boat. A herd of spotted dolphins, at least nine or ten of them, was swimming rapidly in their direction.

Logan leaned eagerly over the side. "Look! Look, there's Cressy. And that's Debby — she's real friendly. And see the little one without any spots? That's her calf, Dobbin. He'll be one year old next month. Matt told us he got to see Dobbin when he was just born."

"Why doesn't he have any spots?" Jody asked, surprised. "His mother is covered in them!" Debby's spots were so numerous that they blurred together and looked more like several large patches.

"Oh, that's 'cause he's just a baby," Logan explained. "They're born without any spots at all, and only start getting them when they're about four years old. They get more and more every year, and when they get old the spots all run together into one huge gigantic blur."

"That sort of pattern helps us know how old they are," said Matt, coming up behind them. "But the way their appearance changes from year to year makes it really hard to keep tabs on who's who, unless they have a scar or some other permanent mark."

"Just like the bottle-nosed dolphins," said Jody. She

thought of Rosie, a young dolphin she had met in the Florida Keys. A knot of scar tissue over one eye, where she'd once been snagged by a fishhook, had made her easy to recognize.

"Anyone want to swim?" asked Matt.

Jody whirled around and gazed up at him. "Really? You mean we can go in with them?"

Matt cocked his head and looked down at the dolphins swimming close to the stationary boat. "Yeah, it looks to me like those guys want company." He grinned at Jody and her brothers. "I hope you kids brought your swimsuits!" When they nodded eagerly, he said, "Maybe Logan will show you where to get changed."

"You guys are in for a big treat," said Logan as they hurried down below to change. "This is the best vacation I've ever had. My folks think so, too. Swimming with wild dolphins is just . . . the best!"

"Yeah, we know," said Jimmy, with a bored attitude. "We do it all the time."

"Oh, sure." Logan grinned, disbelieving.

"We do so," Jimmy insisted.

"Not *all* the time," Jody corrected him. "We've only

swum with bottle-nosed dolphins a few times. You see," she explained to the open-mouthed Logan, "our parents' job is to study dolphins. We live on a boat and we just go wherever the dolphins are." Then, hoping to make him feel better, she added, "But we've never been swimming with Atlantic spotted dolphins before!"

They were soon ready to go into the water with Kim and her mother, Logan's parents, the Hobbs, and Gina. The older couple decided they would just watch from the deck and take photographs.

Matt was also going to stay on the boat to bring Craig and Dr. Taylor up to date on his work. He explained that if there were more people than dolphins in the water, the dolphins would probably leave. "We don't want to overwhelm them," he said. "We like to keep things equal, so everybody has fun."

"I'll stay on board, too," Maddie volunteered. "That way, I can videotape everything that's going on below."

"That's great, Maddie, thanks," said Gina warmly.

Matt looked over the group assembled on deck and grinned. "I can see you're all ready now, and I know you're all experienced, so I won't go through the whole drill this time. But just to be sure — what are the two most important things to remember when swimming with dolphins?"

Logan's hand shot up. When Matt gave him a nod, he said, "Don't grab!"

"Absolutely right," Matt agreed. "Until a dolphin gets to know and trust you, even the friendliest touch could seem like a threat. Don't even reach out to them. Let them come to you, if they want to. The second thing?"

"Don't cover their blowhole?" Sean suggested, giving his brother a sideways look. Jimmy had once gotten into trouble for doing that.

"You got it," Matt said with a smile. "Okay, end of lecture. Have some fun!"

Gina grabbed the twins before they could get away. "No war cries, boys," she informed them sternly. "And no yelling."

Jimmy looked crestfallen. "So we can't be pirates?"

"Play something quieter," his mother advised.

"I know," said Sean. He jabbed his brother in the arm. "We'll be sharks. Silent, but deadly!"

Jimmy's face lit up. "Yeah, cool!" he agreed.

Jody slipped over the side and into the water. It felt absolutely wonderful, even warmer and calmer than the ocean off the coast of Florida. It was also the clearest water she had ever seen, so transparent it was like nothing at all. The brilliant white sand on the bottom, less than ten yards down, reflected the sun so brightly that it was like having another light shining upward. Everything in the water, even her own arms and legs, seemed to gleam and sparkle.

She looked around at everyone else and thought that it was like being in a huge swimming pool — except that most swimming pools didn't have dolphins in them!

The nearness of the dolphins almost took Jody's breath away. And there were so many of them! She remembered seeing nine or ten approaching *Honey Bee*, but more must have arrived when she wasn't looking. There might have been as many as twenty, but it was impossible to count as they kept moving.

It was like an ocean party. People were laughing and murmuring to the dolphins, and the dolphins gently clicked and whistled back. There was even music floating out of the underwater speakers — Jody's mother told her it was Handel's *Water Music*, and she thought that was the perfect choice!

A trio of lightly spotted dolphins suddenly glided past, so close Jody could almost reach out and touch them. She gazed down through the crystal-clear water and saw them flip over and swim back toward her, this time on their backs. Were they inviting her to play? Jody swam after them, trying to imitate their movements, but when they dived down to the bottom, to balance on their noses on the white sand, she had to give up. Perhaps she could have joined them if she'd had diving gear on, but that would just have to wait for another time.

Suddenly Jody noticed two dolphins together, one bigger than the other. The bigger one was heavily spotted; the smaller one had no spots at all, just a purplish-black back that faded to gray on the sides, and a white belly. Although this was not the pair that Logan had pointed out from the boat, Jody was certain that this was another mother and calf. They seemed interested in her, so she swam closer. When she was only inches away, she stopped.

The two dolphins lay almost still in the water, facing her. The calf was underneath its mother, cuddling under her fin.

Jody smiled. It looked so sweet! Then she saw something that surprised her. The mother had some sort of little fish on her back. It was about six inches long, and it was moving. Jody couldn't tell if it was crawling or swimming, but as she watched, the little creature made its way along the dolphin's back and down her side, to settle just above one of her fins. Now Jody could see that the fish seemed to be *attached* to the dolphin in some way — it had some sort of sucker or something on its head. She wondered if the dolphin knew it was there, and if she minded.

She had been so still while she was watching that the baby dolphin lost all nervousness and came away from its mother to investigate this new visitor. It swam right up to Jody and then swam all around her, coming as close as possible without actually touching her. Jody

Me and some spotted dolphins!

held still, not wanting to frighten it, but then she heard a cry from someone else:

"Oh, look, there's a baby one — isn't it cute!"

Suddenly there were two or three people swimming in their direction. It was too much for the calf, which scooted back to its mother in alarm. She immediately swam away, shepherding her calf to a safer distance.

Jody felt disappointed, but not for long. There were plenty of other dolphins around. Time went by swiftly. She could hardly believe it when it was time to get out. Only as she pulled herself up the ladder back onto *Honey Bee* and felt the trembling in her arms and legs did she realize that she really had been swimming for long enough!

Everyone sat around on the deck, snacking on dried fruit and nuts, candy bars, and soft drinks while they shared their experiences. Jody told about the odd little fish she'd seen attached to the mother dolphin. "What could it have been?" she asked.

"It's called a remora," Matt said. "Sometimes known as a suckerfish."

"I've seen that dolphin, too!" Logan exclaimed.

"Yes, Mary seems to be especially drawn to younger people since she became a mother," Matt said.

"Why do you call her Mary?" Jody asked curiously.

Matt grinned. "Mary and her little lamb," he explained. "Everywhere that Mary went, the lamb was sure to go!"

"So you call the calf 'Lamb'?" Jody guessed. It sounded odd to her, since the calf wouldn't always need its mother that much.

Matt laughed. "No, no," he said. "The calf is known as Skipper! It's the remora that is her lamb. Nobody knows why some dolphins have them when most don't, but those who do tend to keep them for years — as if they were pets."

Dr. Taylor snorted loudly. "That's ridiculous! Animals don't keep pets. The remora is a parasite, and that's all," he declared.

"What's a parasite?" Jimmy demanded.

"It's a creature that lives off another animal," Gina explained quietly. "Like a flea or a tick on a dog."

Dr. Taylor frowned and shook his head at Matt. "Would you say that a dog with fleas was keeping lots of pets? It's bad enough to see a scientist having to work as a tour guide, but to hear a man with a Ph.D. telling such sentimental stories to tourists is disgraceful."

Jody held her breath and looked quickly at Matt to see how her father's friend would take this sudden attack.

Matt kept calm, although there was a slight flush to his cheeks. "I think you misunderstood me, Dr. Taylor," he said quietly. "I didn't say that the remora was a pet, just that we don't know very much about the relationship between it and dolphins. I don't claim to understand everything I see. And I don't regret being a tour guide, as you put it. I simply couldn't afford to do my research if I didn't take paying passengers on board *Honey Bee*, but I happen to think that it's just as important to educate the public about my work as it is to do the research itself."

Dr. Taylor looked uncomfortable now. "Yes . . . public education . . . very important," he muttered. "Kind of what I do myself." He took a deep breath. "Well, perhaps I spoke out of turn. But I think giving personal names to specimens encourages an unscientific attitude."

Jody remembered hearing this same argument from Dr. Taylor when she had wanted to name the first dolphin she'd befriended Apollo.

"Well, I find names help my recognition," Matt said. "But if it makes you feel better, all the dolphins in my catalogue have an ID number as well."

Dr. Taylor nodded, satisfied with the reply.

Jimmy piped up suddenly, "I think Lamb is a stupid name for a remora. They don't look anything like lambs!"

"No," Jody agreed, remembering. "Actually, it looked more like a tiny shark."

"Then I'll call him Jaws," Jimmy announced. He beamed with triumph as the others laughed. "Baby Jaws!"

3

*H*oney Bee dropped off the McGraths, Maddie, and Dr. Taylor at Port Lucaya's marina just after sunset. They quickly found their way to where *Dolphin Dreamer* was docked.

Jody couldn't believe her eyes when she went into the galley to say hi to Mei Lin. There was Brittany, smiling as she chopped up a pile of melons, pineapple, mango, and bananas.

"Hi, Jody," she said cheerily. "You missed a great afternoon — they have the coolest marketplace here — and lots of stores selling everything you can think of.

It's got to be the best place in the world for shopping! I can't wait to go back tomorrow. How about you? Want to come?"

Jody was still staring at the pile of fruit Brittany was preparing. Brittany hardly ever did any chores. And she'd *never* been this friendly with her before.

Mei Lin looked up from the fish fillets she was preparing and smiled warmly. "Yes, why don't you come with us, Jody?" she suggested.

Jody shook her head. "Um, thanks, but not tomorrow," she said apologetically. "Maybe another time. My folks still have business with Matt, and I really want to see more of those dolphins!"

Brittany wrinkled her nose, but her tone was pleasant as she said, "Well, suit yourself. I'd have thought you would have had enough of being on a boat all day! But guess what," she went on enthusiastically. "There's a really great diving school right here in the port. My dad says it's probably the best in the world! We went to check it out this morning, and he's signed me up for a course. And — guess who's going to teach me?" She paused and waited expectantly.

Jody couldn't imagine why Brittany thought she might know. She was still reeling from surprise that Brittany was going to learn how to scuba dive! "Is it somebody famous?" she asked.

Brittany laughed. "No, but I think you've heard of her — she's named Anna, and your parents' friend Matt is her boyfriend! And guess what?" Brittany went on happily. "She said that if I work hard, I might be able to get my diving certificate within a week!"

"Great!" Jody said. It *was* great that Brittany was going to learn to dive. Maybe she'd come to appreciate the dolphins more while she was underwater! Jody shook her head again. She wasn't used to Brittany talking to her like this!

She reached out to snag a tempting chunk of fresh pineapple and munched it. "But getting your certificate in one week sounds really fast," she mused. "It usually takes much longer — there's an awful lot to learn!" Then she turned to Mei Lin. "Anything I can do to help?"

"No thanks, Jody, we've got everything under control now," Mei told her. A delicious smell rose up as the fish fillets began to sizzle in the pan.

July 15 — evening — Port Lucaya.
I just love it here!

Lucaya is a modern, busy resort town, just a few miles from Freeport, which is the main town on Grand Bahama Island. It doesn't look all that different from Florida to me, but it sure feels different. I haven't seen much of the is-land yet since we spent most of today out on Honey Bee, *but we saw a little bit of the marina area on the way back to* Dolphin Dreamer. *Everyone is so friendly. They all seem laid back and happy. It's like even the people who live here are on vacation. Even Brittany seems to have changed her tune. She's going to learn to scuba dive — and she couldn't wait to tell me all about it a few minutes ago! I hope her good mood lasts!*

Later, at dinner, Brittany cocked her head and gave Jody a calculating look. "How long did it take you to get your diving certificate?" she asked.

"I guess I took lessons and did coursework for about three months," Jody replied. "But —"

"Well, it won't take *me* that long," Brittany interrupted. "I'm a fast learner, all my teachers say so!"

Jody stopped herself from explaining that she'd had to fit her diving sessions into the rest of her life rather than taking an intensive weeklong course. She bit her lip and kept quiet, reminding herself that she didn't need to compete with the other girl.

"My mom's going to be amazed when I tell her," Brittany added.

"Have you heard from her yet?" Jody asked cautiously. She didn't want to dampen Brittany's unusually good mood.

Brittany laughed. "Well, of course, silly! I knew there'd be an e-mail waiting for me, and there it was! She apologized for being out of touch, and not telling me what was going on, but there was something she just had to do. She's promised to phone real soon and explain everything. She says she's got some wonderful news to tell me!" Brittany concluded with a big grin. "I'm dying to know what it is!"

"I'm really glad for you," Jody said warmly. That was true. Life would be better for everyone once Brittany was back where she really wanted to be, she thought.

July 15, continued

At last! A long, juicy e-mail from Lindsay! She hadn't for-gotten me at all. Turns out her grandmother wasn't very well, so she went up to Winter Park with her mother to look after her for a few days. No computer in the house, so she couldn't write. But we're back in touch now, and while we're in port we can stay that way. She also re-minded me of something I'd forgotten — no e-mail from Devon or Maria because they've gone away to camp!

Next morning, the McGraths and Maddie were up bright and early to join Matt and his tourists on *Honey Bee.*

"No Dr. Taylor today?" Matt asked, eyebrows raised, as they came on board.

"I think he's planning to *research* the . . . *non-marine* . . . attractions of the Freeport/Lucaya area to-day," Craig explained. He pursed his lips in an imitation of Jefferson Taylor's prissy style. "But he wanted me to tell you that he's downloaded a copy of your dolphin ID catalogue, and he intends to study it closely."

"Is he? I'll test him on it, to make sure," Matt said with a mock scowl.

Jody and her brothers joined Logan and Kim at a prime lookout spot near the front of the boat, each one eager to be the first to spot a dolphin. It was another hot, sunny day, and Jody knew there was nowhere in the world she'd rather be than on a boat gliding through the crystal-clear waters of the Bahamas — unless it was actually *in* the water, with the dolphins!

At first there was a lot of water traffic to get through. All sorts and sizes of boats were departing from Port Lucaya for a day of sailing, fishing, diving, or exploring. But gradually *Honey Bee*'s course took them out to a more peaceful area where they were at last on their own.

"Look," said Kim suddenly, pointing.

Jody followed the direction of her finger, shading her eyes against the sun. Her heart beat faster as she recognized the unmistakable dorsal fins emerging from the waves. Her father had once pointed out to her that they had the same shape as a thorn on a rose. Then she caught sight of graceful, curved bodies as three dolphins broke the surface at the same time before diving down again. Moments later, they were swimming alongside the boat.

Logan gave a yell to let everyone else know the dolphins had arrived. Jody leaned over the side to keep watching. As always, the sight of their beautiful, curious faces, wearing what seemed to be a permanent smile, made her smile back. She couldn't help feeling happy whenever there were dolphins around.

Someone on the other side of the boat called out that there were several more dolphins fast approaching.

"Seems like a good place to stop," said Matt. "We'll take it slow . . . remember, always be careful in the presence of dolphins. A sudden, unexpected stop could be as harmful as too much speed or a sudden change of direction."

The dolphins jostled one another in the water, nudging and rubbing against one another as they bobbed up and down, turning their heads to eye the humans curiously.

Jody counted five. She couldn't tell if any of these dolphins had been among those she'd met before, but she was sorry to see no calves in this small group. "Do you recognize any of these?" she asked Logan.

The boy shrugged uncertainly. "I'm not sure. Oh yes! That one with a kind of swirly pattern at the back of

And then there were five!

his head, that's Nebula. But I don't know about the others."

"Well, these guys are all between six and eleven years old, I'd say," said Matt, coming up behind Jody.

"Can we go into the water with them?" Jody asked eagerly.

"Not just yet," Matt replied. "Remember, easy does it. We'll watch them first, get a feel for their mood. You can talk to them from the boat, I'll play some music, then, if they seem interested, I'll let one or two people get into the water at a time. You build a better relationship that way."

Jody nodded, accepting his experience.

"Can I give them a toy to play with?" Logan asked. "I brought something along." From his backpack, he pulled out a bright green frog that squeaked when he squeezed it.

"That looks like a dog toy," said Jimmy.

"It is," Logan agreed. "But I thought the dolphins might like it." He looked hopefully at Matt.

Matt laughed and shrugged. "Sure, why not? They play with things they find in the water all the time."

Everyone crowded around to watch as Logan leaned over the side with the toy frog in his hand. He squeezed it, making it squeak, and the dolphins responded immediately, whistling and chattering.

"Here you go — it's a present," Logan called, and tossed the toy overboard.

One of the dolphins — Nebula — shot straight up into the air and nabbed the frog.

Kim clapped her hands. "Way to go!" she called.

"He won't swallow it, will he?" Jody asked, concerned.

"No, dolphins know what they like to eat, and plastic is not on their menu," Matt assured her.

Soon the other dolphins were mobbing Nebula, determined to get the frog away from him. He bit down on it, making it squeak, and then dashed away, the others in hot pursuit. Then one of the other dolphins captured the frog, and became "it."

Jody and the others watched the game and cheered happily as the dolphins leaped and dived, passing the frog from one to another.

"Uh-oh, here comes trouble." Matt spoke quietly to

Logan's parents, but Jody heard him, and then became aware of the drone of a powerful engine, and the pulsing beat of dance music blasting at top volume.

A boat came speeding past, dangerously close. *Honey Bee* lurched on the wave the passing boat left in its wake.

Jody gasped and clutched the side rail for balance. She gazed down into the water, concerned for the dolphins. But they'd been aware of the approaching speedboat long before she had, and had slipped well below the surface to safety. She could see them gliding along in formation near the bottom.

There were angry exclamations from some of the other passengers. Jody stared out at the speeding launch and read the name in ornate black script on the back: *Stormrider.* She could see four people on board, around nineteen or twenty years old — the college kids Matt had described.

The launch turned in a wide circle and headed back toward *Honey Bee.* The rocking caused by their first pass hadn't even settled down when *Stormrider* plowed the ocean on the other side, making *Honey*

Bee lurch again. Shrieks of taunting laughter carried to them on the breeze.

"They're doing it on purpose!" Jody exclaimed indignantly.

"Try and catch us, little bee," shouted a girl with curly red hair as they zoomed past.

They all had bottles in their hands. One of them, a dark, muscular young man, finished his drink and hurled the bottle over the side.

"Hey! Don't litter!" Kim shouted angrily.

"Why don't you get your dolphins to pick it up?" was the reply, causing the passengers on *Stormrider* to shriek again with laughter as they sped away out of sight in a haze of foam and spray.

Gradually the sound of the loud music and the launch's powerful motor died away, as did the huge waves it had left behind.

"Let's hope we've seen the last of them," sighed Craig.

"Unfortunately, I don't think we're that lucky," Matt said grimly. "They've leased that boat for a whole month. Rumor has it that they're here in search of sunken treasure. And even though they seem to spend most of their time zooming around, annoying everybody on or in the water, they have diving equipment, and I've even seen them using an underwater metal detector."

Jody saw the word "treasure" catch Jimmy and Sean's attention.

"Treasure? What kind of treasure?" demanded Jimmy, his blue eyes glowing. "You mean like pirate treasure?"

"Could be," Matt agreed. "Hundreds of ships have gone down in these waters, and only a fraction of them have been salvaged. The Bahamas have always been popular with pirates — Captain Kidd, Henry Morgan, Blackbeard, practically every pirate you've ever heard of. If your parents are going to stop off in Nassau, you should visit the Museum of Piracy and learn all about it."

"Can we go there, Mom? Dad? Please?" Sean begged, gazing beseechingly at his parents.

Gina smiled. "Well, we're certainly going to visit Nassau sometime this summer," she said. "I'm sure we could manage to fit in a visit to the pirate museum, as a treat for you boys."

"But what about *real* sunken ships, like the one those guys on *Stormrider* are looking for?" Jimmy asked.

"Well," said Matt thoughtfully. "They certainly do exist. But you guys are too young to dive yet."

Jimmy scowled. "Kids aren't allowed to scuba dive until they're twelve. That means we have four whole years to wait. I can't wait that long to find treasure!" He sounded outraged.

Jody tried not to laugh.

"Well, maybe you'll get lucky," Matt said kindly. "This part of the world is full of stories of people who found gold or jewels while they were beachcombing, or snorkeling, or just floating along in an inner tube looking into the shallows."

"They just sound like stories to attract more tourists," said Gina with an indulgent smile.

"No, the stories are true," Matt declared. "I know, because it happened to my friend Ismay Collins! She came to Grand Bahama Island on vacation, found some pieces of eight on a deserted beach, and it changed her whole life!"

"What are pieces of eight?" Logan asked with a puzzled frown.

"Pirate coins," Jimmy told him.

"Actually, they're coins made from one ounce of pure silver, minted by the Spanish in the New World from the 1530s onward," Maddie put in.

They all looked at her in surprise. "Are you a treasure hunter, too?" asked Matt.

Maddie shook her head, smiling. "No, but history is a hobby of mine. With the boys so interested in pirates, I've been reading up on the subject. Now I'm puzzled: how did finding a few silver coins change your friend's life? Pieces of eight aren't *that* valuable!"

"The find didn't make her rich," Matt agreed, nodding. "But it gave her the itch to find more. She teamed up with her brother, Alex, to buy a boat, and they come out here every summer to look for the lost pirate shipwreck. It's all legal. They call themselves The New Treasure Seekers, and they've got a salvage permit from the government, but so far, they haven't found another piece of treasure." He stopped and looked around at his audience.

Jody realized that everyone on board *Honey Bee* had gathered around Matt to listen to him.

"And . . . believe it or not, I haven't gotten as far off the subject of dolphins as you might think," he told them. "There's a very famous wreck called the *Maravilla*, a Spanish galleon which sank in the Bahama Channel on New Year's Day of 1656, while carrying a load of treasure back to Spain. Divers at the time managed to recover some of it, but the rest was thought to be lost forever . . . until, in the early 1970s, a man found an old document in a Spanish library. It was an eyewitness account of the wreck. From it, he figured out exactly where the ship must have gone down, and started diving in the area until he found it. Since then, many thousands — possibly millions! — of dollars' worth of treasure — gold, silver, jewels, even a complete elephant tusk — have been found. Divers are still hunting for more."

"Is there anything left?" Maddie asked curiously.

Matt nodded. "There's a record of everything the

ship was carrying, and lots of it has never been found. Like a life-sized, solid-gold statue of the Madonna, for example!"

Craig let out a low whistle. "How does something that big get hidden?" he wondered.

"The same way whole ships are lost," Matt told him. "It's buried somewhere under the sand. A storm comes along, high winds, waterspouts, whirlpools — you can't believe how fierce they are if you've never experienced a tropical storm! Of course, the damage when they move inland is awful. We all know about that. But the storms also tear up the seabed, places most people never see. All that soft sand under the water is stirred around like somebody took a gigantic spoon to it. Afterward, nothing is the same. Stuff lying down there gets broken up, thrown around, and buried ten, twenty, thirty yards deep."

Jody tried to imagine it. But she found herself distracted by something Matt had said earlier. "But what does all this have to do with dolphins?" she asked.

Matt laughed. "Thanks for bringing me back to my point, Jody! I'm an awful rambler when I get going.

Okay — except for the famous dolphins of Monkey Mia in Australia, the spotted dolphins of Little Bahama Bank are among the friendliest in the world!"

He paused, then went on. "In my opinion, it's the divers we have to thank. For years, people have been diving into the wreck, and the dolphins have been watching them. Because divers have their own work to do, they don't have the usual grabby response when dolphins come near. They just continue their work. They respect the dolphins, and the dolphins respect them." He looked around at everyone. "When you all go away from here, I want you to remember that these are special dolphins."

"They sure are!" Logan said enthusiastically, and there was a general chorus of agreement.

Matt raised a hand for silence. "I mean, if you happen to encounter wild dolphins somewhere else in the world, or even somewhere else in the Caribbean, don't expect that they'll be as interested in you and as friendly as the dolphins here. Maybe they will be, but chances are that if you get into the water hoping to swim with them, any other dolphins would be outta there!"

Gina raised her hand like someone in a class. Matt pointed at her. "Here's another dolphin expert to confirm what I say!"

"It's true, I've encountered a lot of dolphins, and I've been surprised by how especially friendly yours are," she told him. "I thought it must be because they were used to you, and trusted you."

"I wish I could claim all the credit," Matt replied. "But when I first arrived, the dolphins welcomed me with, er, open fins, as it were. They were already used to people, and had a good impression of us, thanks to the divers working on shipwrecks in the area. Especially the *Maravilla*."

He looked very serious as he spoke, but now he relaxed and a smile lit up his face. "End of lecture. I hope you understood the lesson. Now, let's get back to looking for dolphins!"

4

July 19 — evening.

Met some bottle-nosed dolphins today. Five of them came up to Honey Bee *with ten Atlantic spotted dolphins. Then people started getting into the water. The spotted dolphins were as friendly as always, but the bottle-nosed kept their distance, and swam away after a few minutes.*

It made me think about my first dolphin friend, Apollo. I wonder how he is. Does he ever think of me? Will we meet again when we get back to Florida — and will he remember me? Matt says dolphins have excellent memo-

ries, and seem to be able to remember people they have met years before. I hope so.

Brittany is real busy learning to dive — and that has definitely been a good influence on her! I don't think she is finding it as easy as she expected, and maybe that has given her a little more respect for me. Anyway, she's a lot nicer, and sharing a cabin with her isn't such a hardship anymore — even though I'd still swap her for Lindsay in a second!

"Hey, Jody? What do you think of this lipstick?" Startled, Jody looked up from her diary to discover Brittany pouting dark red lips at her.

"Oh, I don't know," she said cautiously. "What's the point?"

"The point is to look more grown up," Brittany explained, examining herself in a small mirror.

"Will your dad let you wear it?" Jody asked.

Brittany hunched her shoulders, sighed, and began to wipe her lips with a tissue. "Probably not, the old dinosaur. Some of his ideas are positively prehistoric!" She rolled her eyes.

Jody liked Harry too much to take sides against him. "Does your mom let you wear makeup?" she asked.

Brittany wriggled uncomfortably. "Well . . . I think she would . . . at least, on special occasions . . . it hasn't really come up," she confessed. Then she added quickly, "She did give me this lipstick, though. It's one of her old ones." She brightened. "Did I tell you she sent me another e-mail? She's going to call next week for sure!"

"That's great," Jody said warmly. She closed her diary and stowed it away. "Have you told her about learning to dive?"

"No, I'm saving that for when she calls. Hopefully, I'll have my Open Water Certificate by then! That'll *really* surprise her!"

There was a knock on the cabin door, and then Gina looked in, smiling. "Hi, girls. Come on out — we have visitors."

Harry and Craig were in the main cabin with Matt and Anna — a short, strong-looking young woman with curly black hair and a calm, self-confident manner.

Anna shook Jody firmly by the hand and gave Brittany a brief hug. "How's my star pupil?" she asked.

Jody was surprised to see Brittany blush and duck her head shyly. "I'm not really . . . " she muttered.

"Sure you are!" Anna declared. "You went through the theory like it was a bag of candy! I've never known anybody to learn so fast. You've got it all up here." She tapped her head. "Now we've got to bring it out there." She stretched out her arms as if to embrace the world. "You need more self-confidence. Say 'I'm a star' — go on, say it!"

Brittany giggled and rolled her eyes. "I'm a star," she muttered self-consciously.

Jody felt very glad nobody was putting her on the spot like that. Anna seemed nice, but she was rather theatrical!

"And you're ready to dive in," Anna announced. "That's why I'm here." She looked at Craig and Gina. "Matt tells me you're not going out on *Honey Bee* tomorrow, but you're going on your own boat to look for dolphins?"

"We want to do some underwater filming," Gina explained. "Matt gave Harry the coordinates for a spot where he's pretty sure we'll find some dolphins."

"Yes, he told me," Anna replied. "Of course, there's never any guarantee with dolphins, but it's a perfect spot for diving and filming," she went on. "Clear water, great visibility, and well under ten yards deep."

"Sounds ideal," Gina said, smiling.

"Ideal for an inexperienced diver, too," Anna said. "If you agree, Brittany and I could come along for her first experience of diving from a boat."

"Sure, that will be fine," Gina agreed.

Jody heard Brittany gasp. She looked and saw that Brittany had gone pale and wide-eyed.

"I can't — I need more practice," Brittany said nervously. "I'm not ready for deep diving yet!"

"Of course you need practice," said Anna. "Practice is what you will get! It's not deep diving — the water will be very shallow. I will be there beside you always, don't worry about that, honey."

"But — I don't think — I'm not really —"

"If you're not happy about it, dear, then of course

you don't have to go," Harry added, sounding concerned.

Anna gave a little frown and shook her head at him
before turning her attention back to Brittany. "It's the
next step," she said firmly. "You can't learn any more
from swimming pool practice. If you don't want to
take the next step, the lessons stop here. That would
be too bad, because you've been doing so well. Do you
want to continue with your lessons and learn to dive,
or are you going to give up now?"

There was a silence. Jody didn't know where to
look. She saw Harry looking, uncomfortably, down at
his shoes. She felt sorry for Brittany, and also surprised.
Brittany had sounded so enthusiastic, she could hardly
believe she'd been hiding fear behind her confident
words.

Finally Brittany spoke. Her voice sounded small but
determined. "I'll do it."

"Of course you will, sweetheart, of course you will!"
Anna boomed cheerily, smiling broadly.

Jody sighed with relief.

* * *

It was another beautiful day. The brilliantly blue water sparkled in the sun, and *Dolphin Dreamer* raced smoothly along under full sail. Jody stood by herself on the forward deck, leaning against the side and scanning the waves for any sign of dolphins. She thought how peaceful it was to be without the twins for a change. Sean and Jimmy had gone out on *Honey Bee* that morning. It was their last chance to see Logan, who would be flying home with his parents the next day.

Soon she heard Harry call, "Prepare to come about!" and she scrambled to get out of the way as Cam and her father began pulling on lines and taking in the sails to slow the boat's progress.

She joined Harry at the helm. "Is this really the place Matt suggested?" she asked, feeling a little worried. "I haven't seen any dolphins at all."

Harry Pierce scowled. "Are you questioning my ability to navigate, young lady?" he said in his gruff English accent.

"You'd better not doubt the captain," Cam laughed as

he fastened down the mainsail. "*Dolphin Dreamer* has all the most up-to-date navigational aids, but if he had to, Harry could find his way at night in a thunderstorm!"

"I just hope I never have to prove it," said Harry.

Jody looked out at the empty expanse of bright blue water. "How can Matt know they'll be here?" she wondered aloud.

Gina came up and put a hand on her shoulder. "I'm sure they'll turn up," she said. "Matt knows what he's talking about. He's been keeping track of the local dolphins for a long time. Over the years he's managed to build up a really good picture — a sort of 'dolphin map' of the Little Bahama Bank, showing changes over the course of the year."

"That's why he's able to provide such great tour service," Craig said. "He can pretty much guarantee dolphin sightings every day he goes out. But it has much greater implications. The sort of map Matt has drawn up could help people avoid dolphins as well as find them. That could cut way down on the deaths of dolphins caused by fishing or any sort of undersea industry, like oil exploration."

Dr. Taylor had been sitting in the shade, reading a book. He looked up at Craig's last words. "That's very interesting," he said. "But how accurate is this map? If we don't see any dolphins today, we'll have to wonder!"

"Oh, I don't think there's a need to worry about that," said Craig softly. He was gazing out to sea, a big smile on his face.

Jody turned to follow her father's gaze and was thrilled at the sight of about a dozen Atlantic spotted dolphins swimming directly toward the boat.

"Come on," said Gina urgently. "Let's get a move on before they get bored and leave!"

A short time later Jody rejoined her parents, Anna, and Brittany to discuss their dive plan and check all the equipment.

Brittany was looking pale and nervous, chewing her lip. Anna patted her arm. "Let's run through those hand signals and make sure you remember them all. How many are there?"

"Nine," said Brittany in a small voice. "This means, *Are you okay?* or, *I'm okay.*" She demonstrated the sign with her hand at head level, finger and thumb joined to make a circle, the other three straight. She went through the rest of the basic signals every diver must know, seeming to gain confidence as she proved she could communicate with her dive partner and the others underwater.

Meanwhile, Jody's father was double-checking her equipment. He would be her dive partner, although he would also be alert for any signals from Gina.

"This air tank is awfully heavy," Brittany complained after Anna had helped her put it on her back. "I'll be exhausted in about five minutes!" She made the fingers-spread *out of breath* sign that divers use when they need to rest and recover.

Anna chuckled. "Maybe, if you were running around on land. Remember, it'll feel a lot lighter in the water! Okay, partner, I think we're ready to dive!"

Craig McGrath was the first to "giant-stride" into the water, followed soon after by Jody. Then came Brittany, then Anna, and finally Gina. Cam handed down the video camera to Gina. They all swapped *okay* signals after they were submerged, and then Anna pointed out the direction she and Brittany would take.

As always, Jody was thrilled to be in the undersea world. She loved having the same view of things as a dolphin. Here, in the shallows of Little Bahama Bank, where the water was so clear, and the brilliant white sand reflected back so much light, it was more magical than anywhere else she'd ever been.

She saw a brightly colored parrot fish hovering in the water to her right. On her left, a small school of yellow-and-blue angelfish were passing, indifferent to her presence. Something nudged her arm and she turned her head. To her astonishment and delight she saw the familiar, perpetual smile and warm, round eye of a curious dolphin.

Jody knew immediately that it was a calf from its smaller size and lack of spots, so she looked around for the mother. As soon as she turned her head she saw three adult dolphins swimming in close formation. They circled her, swimming smoothly around until the calf joined the group.

Riding the Storm

Jody saw that one of the adults had a remora clinging to her side, and knew that this was Mary with Baby Jaws, and that the calf, now nuzzling affectionately against Mary, was certainly Skipper. She felt happy to meet them again, and as she looked more carefully at the other two adults, she thought she recognized them as Cressy and Nebula.

Nebula had a long strand of seaweed draped over his tail. He swam past Mary and Skipper, the long green fronds waving gently in the water. Mary suddenly flipped onto her side and shot away. Jody blinked in surprise. Now the seaweed was hanging from Mary's tail!

Skipper raced after his mother. He tried to grab at the seaweed with his mouth, but Mary kept it out of his reach. Then he swam under her. Mary dipped her tail and the strand of seaweed floated for a moment before Skipper caught it on his tail and swam directly toward Jody.

Jody was thrilled as she realized Skipper was inviting her to play. She finned closer to him and stretched out her arms to take the seaweed. But Skipper kept it out

Skipper having fun with seaweed

of her reach; Jody guessed it was cheating to use either mouth or arms in the seaweed game. But she did think she was a bit handicapped in not having a tail like the other players!

Still, she would do her best. She kicked herself closer to Skipper and tried to hook the seaweed with one of her fins. But it was harder than it looked, especially since Skipper wouldn't stay still. In fact, all of the dolphins were constantly in motion, swimming over and under and around each other.

After three or four failures, Jody was feeling awfully clumsy. She was getting ready to try again when she realized that the seaweed was no longer hanging from Skipper's tail. Somehow, Mary had it again. She swam past Jody . . . and Jody, startled, felt the soft fronds of the weed land gently across her ankles. She'd barely realized it was there before Nebula, swimming past her on her other side, flicked his tail and claimed it back.

Whatever the rules were in this game, Jody realized she couldn't compete. But that didn't matter. She had a wonderful warm feeling inside from knowing the dolphins accepted her as a friend. She was happy just to watch them play, and to admire their grace and beauty.

Her undersea experience seemed to have transformed Brittany. Back on deck, she was bubbling over with emotion. "Gosh, it's so gorgeous down there! It's wonderful! I wish we could have stayed longer, though. I was so nervous at first, but then, just when I felt like I was starting to get the hang of it, we had to come up!" Then her excitement gave way to anxiety. "Did I do okay?" she appealed to Anna, who smiled at her warmly.

"You were fine," Anna assured her. "There are some things you need to work on. We'll talk about those when you fill in your logbook. Now, let's get this equipment safely stored away."

Jody felt pleased for Brittany as she hurried away to get changed and jot a few notes in her own logbook. She would fill in more details later, she decided. Right now, she wanted to watch the dolphins while they were still close by.

As she leaned over the side, Jody saw that a crowd had gathered, clicking and whistling to each other as they swam under and around *Dolphin Dreamer*. She grinned happily as she counted fifteen dolphins. A few she recognized right away — Mary and Skipper, of course, and Nebula, Debby, and Dobbin — the others she couldn't be sure of so quickly. She wondered if *Honey Bee* was having as much luck, wherever she was today. This was obviously *the* best place for dolphin-spotting!

Somewhere in the distance was a low, droning sound, gradually getting louder. Jody recognized it as the motor of an approaching boat.

When she turned to look, she saw that the boat was *Stormrider*. And it was heading straight for them.

5

Stormrider came roaring by, churning the water into a foaming wake. Jody was not surprised when the dolphins scattered. But then she saw that while most of the dolphins were swimming rapidly away, four or five were now heading directly toward the motor launch. And one of them was Skipper.

"No!" she cried out, clutching the side rail and staring in horror. In her mind was what Matt had told her about dolphins being badly hurt by propellers.

Dolphins liked to play in the wake of fast-moving

boats, she knew. But she was afraid that this time their playfulness and curiosity would get them into trouble.

She held her breath. Mary and Nebula were racing after Skipper. They closed in on the young dolphin from both sides and firmly steered him away to safety.

Jody sighed with relief. But the other dolphins continued on their course. She watched as three adult dolphins began to leap about in the spray and "surf" the wave left in *Stormrider*'s wake.

The *Stormrider* crew must have noticed this activity, because they began to clap and cheer. They were very close now, and the sound carried clearly. Then, with a suddenness that could have been dangerous for the dolphins who followed them, the motor cut out, and the launch rocked and slowed to a halt just behind *Dolphin Dreamer*.

Jody saw her parents exchange puzzled looks with Harry and Cam.

"I'll see what they want," said Harry. "Ahoy, *Stormrider*!" he called.

"What's going on?" Brittany came up beside Jody.

She stared over at the other boat, and her expression brightened with interest. "Ooh, those guys are cute," she said admiringly. "That boat looks expensive, too!"

Jody shot a withering glance at Brittany, but the other girl was too fascinated with the *Stormrider* crew to notice her disapproval.

There were four people on board the launch, all standing and staring at *Dolphin Dreamer* in a most unfriendly way. They didn't respond to Harry's greeting.

A blond girl in a bright pink swimsuit said, "Marcus, tell them to go away." Whether or not she meant to be overheard, her voice was loud and carried clearly.

The dark, muscular young man shrugged and muttered something.

The blonde frowned angrily and looked at the other boy. "Jay, can't you do something?"

"Yeah," said Jay. He spoke so loudly Jody thought it had to be deliberate. "I am going to party! Heather, put on some music. Loud as it'll go!"

The red-haired girl nodded enthusiastically and scrambled into the cabin. Moments later, loud, pounding music began to pulse out into the peaceful air.

Jody saw Harry wince as, next to her, Brittany was moving her body in time to the beat.

Jay and Marcus put their heads together for a moment, and then Marcus yelled, "Bring me beer! Lots of beer!"

Jay gave an ear-splitting yell — "Yeee-haaaa!" — grabbed the blond girl, and started a clumsy dance.

"We might as well leave," said Gina, sighing.

"Yeah, that's what they want us to do," Craig said. He nodded at Harry to pull up the anchor. His blue eyes narrowed thoughtfully. He spoke very quietly. "Funny, if they didn't want company, why'd they come here?"

Gina's eyes widened. "You mean, they came to chase us away?"

Jody frowned, and stared across at the launch. They were all making a lot of noise, whooping and yelling, as if they were having a great time, but something about it didn't ring true. Then she noticed the diving equipment. There were four air tanks standing neatly in a row. The party was just a pretense. They had come here to dive, and for some reason, they didn't want anyone to know.

July 20 — bedtime.

They're looking for treasure! And they seem to think it's in that area. But we didn't see any sign of a shipwreck, so they're wrong. Or are they? It could be hiding somewhere close by . . . now their dolphin-chasing behavior makes a weird kind of sense . . . that's one of Matt's favorite spots to take Honey Bee. Chasing the dolphins away chases him away, so there are no witnesses if they find anything. Matt told us that all finds in the Bahamas have to be reported and shared with the government (they take twenty-five percent). I bet these guys are planning to keep it all for themselves.

Brittany is so silly sometimes. She has decided that the one called Jay looks just like her favorite TV star, and thinks that the girls are cool because they were wearing expensive swimsuits and designer sunglasses. She doesn't care that the things they do could hurt dolphins; she says I'm the one who is silly — about dolphins! I am totally fed up with her.

"There they are!" Brittany's whisper buzzed in Jody's ear as they entered the air-conditioned coffee shop.

"What? Who?" Jody frowned, puzzled. Some time had passed since their encounter with *Stormrider*, but it was far from her mind. She'd just spent an exhausting hour with her brothers at the adventure playground near the marina, and was looking forward to sitting down and having a cool drink before heading back to *Dolphin Dreamer*.

"Shh! Pretend you haven't noticed them!" Brittany giggled behind her hand and darted her eyes in the direction she wanted Jody to look.

Jody's heart sank as she recognized the four college kids who'd chartered *Stormrider*. They were sitting around a table crowded with coffee cups and pieces of paper, including a big navigational chart.

Marcus was holding something that looked like an old-fashioned parchment and jabbing his finger at the chart as he argued with the others.

Jody didn't want to sit anywhere near them. Unfortunately, the twins had already dashed ahead and settled into a booth directly opposite the *Stormrider* party, so she had no choice.

Brittany sat up very straight and licked her lips. She

toyed with her hair. Jody even saw her check her appearance using the back of a spoon as a mirror!

When the waitress came, Jody, who had been given the money by her father, ordered ice cream sundaes all around, and Cokes for herself and the boys. She looked at Brittany inquiringly.

"I'd like a coffee with mine," Brittany said loudly.

Jody raised her eyebrows, surprised. "You don't usually drink coffee!"

"Yes I do. I love coffee," Brittany declared.

Jody shrugged and didn't argue. She guessed Brittany was trying to act grown up in the hope of attracting the college kids' attention. But they were much too preoccupied with their own discussion to notice anyone else. Jody didn't want to eavesdrop, but as the argument grew louder, she couldn't help but overhear.

"It's right here," Marcus was saying, jabbing a spoon at the chart. "We *know* that. This spot absolutely fits the description to a T. It's lying buried under the sand. I say we rent a bigger boat and a prop wash and blow that baby out!"

"It could be anywhere within a twenty-mile radius. No sense wasting more money till we've narrowed it down," Jay objected. "We've already got the metal detector, so let's use it some more. Another week of diving, maybe less — we're bound to get lucky!"

"You talk like we've got forever," the blond girl said, frowning. "We've got to go home in less than two weeks. If we don't find something soon . . ."

"Calm down, Ally," said the red-haired girl, patting her hand. "Why don't we take a vote?"

"Okay," said Marcus. "I vote we rent a bigger boat and prop wash tomorrow."

Jay frowned. "Easy for you to say. Don't forget who's paying for this . . ."

"Yeah, rich boy, and don't forget who did all the research into the sinking of the *Elvira* and found the eyewitness accounts, and the map! We wouldn't have gotten very far without this!" Marcus rattled his parchment in Jay's face.

Sean and Jimmy looked at each other, their eyes big and round. Before Jody or Brittany could even try to stop them, both boys had scrambled out of the booth and were leaning across the next table, struggling with each other to be the first to get a good look at it.

"Is that a treasure map?" Jimmy demanded.

"It looks like a real pirate's map!" Sean crowed excitedly. "Please, can we see it? Please, we know lots and lots of stuff about pirates."

"We could help you!" Jimmy added.

Marcus held the piece of parchment high out of the boys' reach.

"Now look what you've done," Jay snarled, glaring furiously at Marcus. "Telling the whole world . . . if you'd keep your lips sealed —" He snatched the ancient map out of his friend's hand and stashed it in a briefcase lying open on a chair beside him. Ally, meanwhile, was busily rolling up the navigational chart.

"Aw, they're just kids," Marcus said.

"So are we," said Ally. "Just big kids." She smiled broadly at Sean and Jimmy. "It's just pretend, you know. Just a little game we're playing, to make our vacation more fun."

Jody could see her brothers weren't fooled.

"Didn't look like a pretend map to me," said Sean, frowning.

Jimmy attempted his own sly approach. "We've made up treasure maps, too. You show us yours, and we'll show you ours, okay?"

"No deal," said Jay firmly. "But I'll tell you what. You be nice to us, and we'll be nice to you. All you have to do is be quiet, don't tell anyone what you've heard today, and then, if we *do* happen to find any treasure, we just might share it with you. To prove it, I'll give you a little advance on that treasure, right now." He dug into his pocket and pulled out a handful of crumpled bills.

Jody was furious. But she didn't have to say a word. At the sight of the money, Sean and Jimmy backed away, shaking their heads.

"Aw, come on, don't be like that — what's wrong, isn't it enough?" Jay wheedled.

"We aren't allowed to take money from strangers," Jimmy said firmly.

"You're right, you shouldn't even be talking to us,"

What's Brittany up to?

said Ally swiftly. "Better not tell your parents — they might get mad! We'll just pretend this whole thing never happened, okay?"

"Fine with me," Jody said coldly, and steered her younger brothers back to their table.

"Don't worry," she heard Brittany say. "We won't tell anybody. I figure if somebody is smart enough to figure out where to find a treasure, then they ought to be allowed to keep it."

"You sound like a smart kid," said Jay.

Then the waitress arrived with their order, and the next few moments were taken up with exclamations from the boys about the size of the sundaes, before settling down to the serious business of eating.

Brittany strolled over to pick up her coffee and ice cream. "Ally invited me to go and sit with them," she said, smirking proudly on her return. "And guess what? Heather's cousins live in West Palm Beach. I bet we even know some of the same people!"

Jody watched her go, feeling uneasy. She didn't like the *Stormrider* crew, and she didn't like the idea of Brittany getting involved with them. But she couldn't think of any way to stop her from doing as she pleased.

6

Matt and Anna joined them on board *Dolphin Dreamer* for dinner that evening. Mei Lin had decided to try her hand at some local Bahamian specialties. She served up conch salad as a starter, followed by some sort of local fish cooked in a spicy tomato sauce, accompanied by huge helpings of golden brown peas and rice. For dessert there was fresh fruit salad.

"Hey, Matt," said Sean, pushing aside his bowl after picking out the banana, which was the one fruit on hand that he was willing to eat, "you were right about those guys on *Stormrider*. They *are* looking for sunken treasure. They've even got a map! Hey, do you think we could get there ahead of them and find the treasure first?"

"You little tattletale!" Brittany exclaimed, frowning fiercely. "You weren't supposed to tell anybody!"

"We never said we wouldn't," Jimmy answered for his brother.

"You're the only one who said you wouldn't tell," Jody reminded Brittany. "And I don't see why we shouldn't. They don't have any special right to that treasure."

"Well, I think they do. They're the ones who did the research and found the map. And they've paid for the boat and diving equipment and everything. And I like them," Brittany finished, her chin high.

Jody shrugged. She didn't trust that group. And she thought Brittany only wanted to make herself seem more grown up by pretending she had older friends.

"Unless you can sketch the map from memory, I'd

say there's no chance of us finding this mysterious wreck," Matt said to Sean.

Sean looked disappointed. He shook his head. "I hardly saw the map," he confessed. "But I know the name of the ship. It's called *Elvira.*"

"Elvira!" exclaimed Anna. She looked at Matt. "That's the name of the shipwreck Alex and Ismay are looking for!"

"You're sure of the name?" Matt asked Sean. Both twins nodded vigorously.

"It must be the same ship," Matt said, exchanging a glance with Anna. "So they've found a map. Well, well . . ." He shook his head. "My friends spend three summers searching for the wreck without any luck, and then these guys come along with a map! It probably won't do them much good, though. They don't seem to be very organized about their search. I think they're time-wasters, really. Amateurs. Even knowing the general area where a ship went down doesn't mean you'll be able to pinpoint the spot where it is now. There've been centuries of storms to smash it to bits and bury those pieces deep under the sand."

"But didn't you say your friends found some coins that came from it?" Jody asked.

Matt nodded. "They found them washed up on a beach right after a big storm. Possibly some part of the ship was uncovered then. Unfortunately, it was hurricane season, and there were even bigger storms to come. By the time Alex and Ismay had a chance to start diving, *Elvira* must have been completely buried again."

"Coffee, anyone?" asked Mei Lin as she began to clear away the plates with Cam's help.

Brittany frowned at Matt in a puzzled way. "Don't your friends know about using a prop wash?" she asked. "That's what *my* friends are going to use. Ally and Heather explained it to me. The prop wash fits over the boat's propeller and sticks down deep in the water. They anchor the boat so it can't move, and they run the engine, and the prop wash creates like a whirlpool that blows away the sand and uncovers the wreck."

"Yes, if the wreck is there," Matt agreed. "Otherwise, all you end up with is a nice, empty hollow in the sand.

There's an awful lot of ocean floor to just dig at random! But if your friends have a good map, they may get lucky."

"Your own friends must have some idea where the wreck of the *Elvira* might be," said Craig, leaning across the table, his eyes bright with interest. "Did they ever tell you where they thought it was?"

Matt looked back at his old friend and laughed as he shook his head. "Don't tell me the treasure-hunting bug has bitten you, too!"

"No, no," Craig protested, unconvincingly. "I just thought it might be interesting for the kids . . ." His voice trailed off, and he rubbed his face, looking a little embarrassed.

"As a matter of fact," said Matt slowly, "you've been there. It's the same place where you got that great underwater footage of the dolphins playing the seaweed game with Jody."

"You mean where I had my first open-sea dive?" Brittany asked, sounding startled. "I never saw anything that looked like a shipwreck!"

"Neither did I," said Gina. "But it's a great spot for

412

filming — shallow, great visibility, and popular with dolphins. In fact, I really would like to go back, only . . ."

Jody thought she knew what her mother was thinking, and finished her sentence for her: ". . . if *Stormrider* is there they'll scare off the dolphins. And if they think that's where the wreck is, they're bound to be there every day." She exchanged a resigned look with her mother.

Craig sighed, and took a sip of coffee. "No point in looking for trouble," he agreed. "We'll find another spot for filming . . . or maybe just spend tomorrow analyzing some more of Matt's files. You've collected enough raw data to keep half a dozen graduate students busy for ten years!"

Matt grinned. "It's to give you something to do during those long winter nights at sea," he said. "I don't think you should spend your time on it while you're here. Get in as much underwater filming as you can before the weather turns. After all, there's plenty of other places you could try."

Brittany spoke up unexpectedly. "*Stormrider* won't

be there tomorrow," she said. "They're taking a day off from treasure hunting. The boys are going deep-sea fishing. Ally and Heather think fishing is boring, so they're going shopping in Freeport." She turned to her father, who had said almost nothing throughout the meal, and gazed at him appealingly. "They said I could go with them. Can I, Daddy? Please?"

"I need to meet these girls first, and have a chat with them," Harry said cautiously.

Brittany beamed confidently. "I thought you might say that! They told me they'd be in the coffee shop to-morrow morning for breakfast. You could go and meet them then."

Harry must have decided that Ally and Heather were trustworthy, Jody thought, because when *Dolphin Dreamer* cast off the next day, it was without Brittany. But Mei Lin also stayed behind — she would travel to Freeport with the three girls, do her own shopping, and then meet up with Brittany later in the day.

Jody leaned against the rail and watched the sails fill

with wind as she inhaled the warm salt air. The sun shone down out of a clear blue sky as it had every day they had been here. Gazing out at the gentle waves on the turquoise water, she found it hard to believe that there could be hundreds of shipwrecks lying down below.

Behind her, she could hear Cam talking to the twins: "Yeah, I've been treasure hunting. Never found anything, though. But I always used to hope. See, my dad found seven gold coins on the beach when he was a little boy, so I was always on the lookout."

"Was it pirate treasure?" Jimmy asked. Both boys were listening with breathless attention.

"No, nothing to do with pirates. These were Spanish coins from about 1700, and my dad was pretty sure where they came from. Back in 1715, a convoy of twelve ships were carrying treasure from the Spanish colony in Cuba, back home to Spain. A hurricane struck as they were sailing up the Straits of Florida at the end of July, and . . ." he slapped his hands together. "Four ships were sunk."

It was nearly the end of July now, Jody thought. She turned away from the calm sea to ask Cam, "Isn't the end of July early for a hurricane?"

Cam nodded. "Hurricane season's really not supposed to start before the end of August," he agreed. "But you can get a big storm any time. Out here, they can boil up fast and fierce. And back in the old days, sailors didn't have the benefit of satellites, weather tracking stations, or radio to warn them to get into shelter."

Although he could obviously hear this discussion from his place at the helm, Harry Pierce was keeping very quiet.

Jody noticed a slight frown on the man's bearded, weather-beaten face. She wondered if he was worried about Brittany. Hoping to distract him, Jody asked, "Harry, have *you* ever seen a shipwreck?"

"Yes, I'm sorry to say I have," he answered in a low voice. "And it's not something I'd like to see again." Then he gave himself a little shake. "But that's not what you meant, is it? I'm sorry — I can't get excited about sunken treasure. It feels unlucky to me. I guess I'm just

416

a superstitious old sailor! But when I hear about a ship-wreck, even if it happened hundreds of years ago, I can't help imagining the people who were on board, and what it must have been like for them."

Jody felt as if a game of pretend had suddenly turned serious. She didn't know what to say. She was glad when a sudden cry from her mother, on the foredeck, grabbed their attention:

"Dolphins approaching to starboard!"

Jody forgot all about pirates, treasure, sunken ships, and everything else as she raced to the side and looked. A group of about a dozen Atlantic spotted dol-phins were swimming rapidly toward them. Occasion-ally, one at a time, they would leap through the air, seemingly for the sheer joy of it. But even when they were swimming entirely beneath the water she could see them clearly.

Soon, they had reached *Dolphin Dreamer* and be-gan to compete with each other to ride the wave pro-duced as the sailboat cut through the water. Now they were near enough to be identified, especially as they jumped up, playfully knocking each other aside.

Jody stretched out her hand, and one of the leaping dolphins just brushed it with the rounded top of its head. She wasn't quite sure, but she thought it was Nebula.

She watched carefully, trying to recognize some of the dolphins she had met before. Was that Cressy? And Mystic and Oberon? Scar-fin's damaged dorsal fin was unmistakable. When she'd spotted him she was pretty sure she was right about the others. She was sorry not to see the ones who had become her favorites — Mary, with her "pet" remora, and her calf, Skipper. All of the dolphins now playing alongside *Dolphin Dreamer* were adults; there weren't any babies in this group.

Jody was careful to keep out of the way as Cam and her father scrambled about, pulling on lines and taking in the sails to slow the boat's progress. She was worried at first that the dolphins would abandon them once the boat was no longer moving, but these dolphins were used to visitors. They knew what to expect, and from the way they hung around, it seemed that they were as eager to play with humans as Jody and her family were to swim with them.

"We're ready! Can we go swimming now, please?" Sean and Jimmy's voices chimed together. Jody stared at her twin brothers in disbelief. They must have raced below and changed into their swimsuits in literally half a minute, she thought.

"You boys know you can't go in on your own," Gina said. "Your dad, Jody, and I are going diving, so —"

"I could go in, too, and keep an eye on them," Cam volunteered.

"Oh, Cam, that's very kind of you," Gina replied with a warm smile. "Thank you. Okay," she went on, as Sean and Jimmy began to cheer, "you'll get to swim, but remember to do exactly as Cam tells you."

"And try not to act like you outnumber me," Cam advised them sternly. "Even though you do."

"Maybe I could even things out by joining your team," Maddie suggested. She looked at Gina and Craig. "If you don't need me for anything, that is."

"I was only going to ask you to keep an eye on the tape recorder," Gina said. "But maybe Dr. Taylor would do that?"

At the sound of his name, the portly scientist, who

419

had been resting in the shade of an oversized straw hat, suddenly jerked upright, as if startled awake. "Er, what was that?" he asked.

Gina explained that they would be using the hydrophone — an underwater microphone — to record sounds made by the dolphins, and needed someone on board to monitor it and change the tape if necessary.

"No trouble at all — only too happy to contribute," he exclaimed. "And if there's anything else — you will let me know if there are any other little jobs that need to be done?"

He sounded grateful to have something to do, Jody thought — as if Gina was doing him a favor instead of the other way around. For the first time it occurred to her that maybe he wasn't exactly thrilled about being a sort of tagalong, instead of a vital member of the Dolphin Universe team.

It was not much longer before Jody and her parents were dressed and in the water. As she descended, Jody was aware of being watched by a group of dolphins. Beyond the hiss and bubble sounds of her own underwater breathing she could hear a rapid clicking noise coming from the dolphins.

Four heavily spotted dolphins peeled away from the larger group and came swimming toward her. They moved in harmony, like perfectly trained dancers. Just before they reached her, they all pointed their heads down and sank gently to the bottom. For a few moments they balanced with their noses resting in the soft, white sand. Only their tails moved, waving very slightly. Then, one by one, they shot up and circled Jody before rising back to the surface. She felt honored and pleased by this attention. She was sure this was their way of saying "hello" and welcoming her to their underwater world.

As they swam slowly around her, Jody was able to recognize Nebula, Dottie, and Cressy. She wasn't sure about the identity of the fourth.

Looking over at her dad to check that it was okay, Jody finned after the dolphins. After a quick visit to the surface, they came back and glided beside her, two on each side. She was thrilled. They matched their speed to hers, so it felt like she was part of the group, traveling slowly through this magical, underwater world.

Everything was clear and brilliantly lit. In this sheltered, shallow bay there was no hidden danger, nowhere to hide. Gazing down, Jody tried to imagine the wreckage of a ship buried beneath mounds of gently rippled white sand. If it really had been there for nearly three hundred years, surely it was gone for good by now and would never be seen again, she thought.

When she looked up toward the surface, Jody saw four pairs of legs churning the water. She recognized the shorter, paler legs — they belonged to her brothers — and Maddie and Cam were just as easily identified. But it was certainly a strange view to have of people! She realized she was seeing them just as the dolphins did.

Suddenly the clicking sounds made by the dolphins, which had faded away into the background, became louder and much more intense. Jody could feel it against her eardrums. She turned, and saw three more dolphins arriving. She recognized Mary and Skipper at once. They were accompanied by another adult. All three were swimming very close together, the two adults pressed tightly against the calf as if to keep Skipper from getting away.

Happy to see her friends, Jody swam forward to greet them.

Then she stopped and stared in horror at poor little Skipper. Wrapped tightly around the baby dolphin's tail, cutting deeply into the flesh, was a fishing line. She could also see several yards of the line trailing behind him.

The three dolphins circled Jody, rising up until they were above her head. As she looked up, she saw that the tightly wrapped fishing line was not the worst of the calf's problems. A large fishhook was sunk into his flesh.

A lump came to Jody's throat. She felt horrified and fearful for poor little Skipper, but she knew that wouldn't help him. She had to stay calm and think clearly.

Suddenly she realized that Mary and her friend had

brought Skipper to her because they knew she could help. They couldn't free the baby dolphin from the fishing line and hook, but perhaps Jody could.

I'll try, she said to them silently, hoping they would sense her feelings. *It might hurt, but I will get it off.*

She made herself be calm, and tried to communicate that sense of calm to them. It was so important that the calf should be still while she worked on the line! If he moved suddenly she knew she might hurt him even more.

Jody sank down to kneel on the bottom. For a moment she stayed very still, waiting. Then the dolphins came down after her. The two adults guided Skipper until he was resting on the soft sand right in front of her. They stayed, one on each side, keeping him still.

Jody reached out a hand to stroke the calf's side. His round eye watched her trustingly, and he didn't move as she touched him gently. She moved her hand along his body to find the fishhook. She felt a little sick as she saw the damage it had done. It had torn the skin, leaving a raw, jagged cut about an inch long. She knew the hook would have to be pulled out or the calf might

Skipper in trouble!

die from an infection, or be snagged on something by the trailing line. If that happened, he could become trapped and, unable to rise to the surface for air, he would drown.

Suddenly all three dolphins let out a chattering stream of clicks. Jody pulled her hand back and watched, bewildered, as they rose together, moving away from her, up through the water. Had she done something wrong? Had she frightened them?

Only when they returned, less than a minute later, did Jody understand that they'd had to go up to the surface to breathe. She knew then that she would have to work fast, and wondered if she could really do it.

But just as the dolphins arrived, so did Jody's parents, having noticed the dolphins' strange behavior. Jody breathed a sigh of relief.

Through his mask, her father's eyes were concerned. "Are you okay?" he signaled.

Jody pointed to herself and made the "I'm okay" signal. Then she pointed at the baby dolphin and waved her forearm to and fro, fist clenched. This was the divers' signal meaning "Need immediate help!"

Craig moved to get a better look at Skipper. Seeming to understand, the adult dolphins shifted their position, moving away so he could examine the calf.

Jody saw her father's lips tighten. She knew he felt as angry as she did at the careless fisherman who had let this happen. She watched as he reached for the knife that he wore in a sheath strapped to his left leg.

While Gina kept on filming, Craig used the knife to cut away the tightly wrapped fishing line. Jody held Skipper, stroking him gently, keeping him as calm and still as she could.

When Craig pulled away the fishing line, the calf wriggled and made some high-pitched noises. Jody saw dark droplets of blood flow out of the cuts left by the line. But although what Craig was doing must have hurt, it seemed that Skipper trusted him. He didn't try to get away. Mary made more clicking sounds, and Skipper calmed down.

Soon, all of the line was gone except for a short piece attached to the hook, which was still embedded in the baby dolphin's flesh. Craig grasped hold of the shaft and tried to pull it out. It moved slightly within the wound, and when that happened, the calf jumped and trembled with pain and fear. Jody held him tightly to stop him from swimming away, and heard urgent clicking noises coming from both adult dolphins. The calf settled down, although he was still trembling.

Jody looked at her father. He held up his knife. She nodded, and moved to hold the baby dolphin still as her father operated. It was hard to watch as her father slipped the blade of the knife right into the wound, especially as Skipper was wriggling and crying out in pain. She kept on stroking him and trying to keep him calm as Craig dug the barbed hook out as quickly as he could.

Jody saw her father pull the hook free. A gout of blood, greenish in the underwater light, escaped. Craig immediately pressed down hard on the wound with his hand, holding it closed. Jody felt the baby dolphin relax. It had stopped crying and wriggling. The worst of the pain was over.

After a little while, Craig cautiously moved his hand away. The wound stayed closed, and there was only a little blood now. Jody stopped holding Skipper and waited to see what the calf would do.

The little dolphin rose up slightly in the water. Mary came up close and looked at the cut where the fishhook had been, then ran her nose down the calf's tail, checking it out. Then she swam over to Jody and gazed at her, eye to eye. Jody felt a little shock of connection, as if Mary had spoken to her.

Riding the Storm

All three dolphins began to swim in a circle around Jody and Craig, clicking loudly. Jody could feel the sound they made not just in her ears, but throughout her body — a warm, grateful, friendly feeling.

A moment later the dolphins were gone, racing to the surface for a much-needed breath of air, then swimming rapidly away.

7

July 26 — late.

I've been so worried about Skipper, wondering if his wound would heal okay. But now I'm happy to say that he is fine! I finally got to see him today, when a big group of dolphins came up to Honey Bee. I spotted Mary and Skipper among them.

As soon as I got into the water, Skipper swam right up and rubbed against my legs. He made it clear he wanted me to stroke him, so I did. I could hardly believe it — I was scared that he'd be afraid of me after what happened. He might have associated me with the memory of being hurt.

Instead, it seemed like he wanted to thank me . . . rubbing against me like a big cat . . . just the way dolphins do with each other! He and his mother stayed close to me the whole time I was in the water.

Matt said that Mary and Skipper have accepted me as an "honorary dolphin"! I almost burst out crying . . . does that sound silly? I was so moved . . . thinking about it now brings tears to my eyes. It isn't that I want to be a dolphin or anything like that, but to know that these wonderful creatures trust me is . . . well, I can't really find the words to express how thrilled and honored that makes me feel.

Skipper let me check out his wound without any fuss. It looked okay to me, but just to be sure, I asked Matt what he thought. One of the guests on board was a vet, so she had a look, too. She said she didn't get many (actually, not any!) dolphins at her practice back home in Norman, Oklahoma, but her professional opinion was that the wound was healing nicely, and the scar probably won't even be noticeable after Skipper gets his grown-up spots in a few years.

Better wrap this up and get some sleep. Brittany is

bound to get up early tomorrow because that's when her mother has promised to call with her exciting news . . .

"Wait'll Mommy hears that I've got my diving certification," Brittany said breathlessly, brushing her well-brushed hair yet again. "She won't believe it! It's funny, you know — she's not very good at sports herself, so she never thinks I will be, either."

Putting the hairbrush down, she turned to look at Jody, who was sitting on the edge of the bunk, lacing up her sneakers. "All that stuff I said about how it was going to be so easy for me . . . I was really trying to convince myself! I didn't want to admit how scared I was."

Jody could see it was hard for Brittany to tell her this, and she gave her an encouraging smile. "The main thing is that you did it anyway, in spite of being scared!" she said. "And now you know how much fun it is, right?"

Brittany nodded enthusiastically. "Yeah. You know, I hope Mommy doesn't want to take me home *too* soon . . . Anna was telling me about all the great dive sites around here. I'd love to get the chance to check some of them out."

"That would be fun," Jody agreed. She stood up. "Come on, let's get some breakfast."

"I'm too excited to eat," Brittany objected, but she followed Jody out to the main cabin. The air was fragrant with the smells of fried bacon and eggs, toast, and freshly brewed coffee. Jody's mouth watered, and she hurried up behind Maddy and Cam to get her food from Mei Lin in the galley.

As she sat down, Jody noticed the sleek black shape of a cell phone resting beside Harry's plate. She was just digging into her bacon and eggs when the phone's merry little tune pealed out.

Brittany gasped, and jumped up.

Harry picked up the phone and answered it. "Yes . . . Hello, Gail . . . yes, she's right here." Harry handed the phone to his daughter across the table.

Jody put down her fork and crossed her fingers.

"Hello?" Brittany spoke almost timidly. Then her voice changed, becoming warm and excited. "Mommy!

Oh, Mommy, I'm so glad you called! I've missed you! Wait'll you hear what I've been doing!"

Jody relaxed and picked up her fork again, exchanging a smile with her own mother.

"Now you tell me your news," Brittany demanded cheerfully, after explaining all about her new scuba-diving skills in a breathless rush.

In the silence that followed, Jody glanced at Brittany, and was shocked by the abrupt change in her. All happiness had drained from her face.

"*Who* wants to marry you?" Brittany demanded into the phone. Blank disbelief gave way to a furious scowl as she heard her mother's reply. "Jacques! You have got to be kidding! No way! I hope you told him — what do you mean you said *yes*? No! I refuse to have that creep as my stepfather! He can't live with us. I won't live with him. You can't do it! I won't let you!" Brittany's voice went sliding up the scale in anger, and her face flushed beet red.

Suddenly she pushed herself away from the table. "No!" she shouted into the phone. "I won't stay here! You can't make me! You're ruining my life!"

Bad news for Brittany

Looking very concerned, Harry got up and moved toward his daughter.

Brittany flung the cell phone at her father. "Tell her!" she shouted. The color had drained out of her face as abruptly as it had come, and she was now very white. "Tell her she can't get married! Tell her she has to come back and look after me!"

Harry put the phone to his ear. "Gail?" He spoke gruffly. "We need to talk —" Then he looked startled. He pulled the phone away from his ear and stared at it in disbelief. "She hung up!"

Brittany stared into space. Her lips were parted and she was panting slightly. Jody thought with concern that she looked ill, and wondered if she was about to faint.

Suddenly Brittany charged toward the hatchway. Harry stepped forward, blocking her way. She managed to stop just short of running into him.

"I'm going out. Let me go!" she cried.

"No." Harry spoke gently but firmly. "You're not going anywhere just now, dear. Calm down. You've had a shock. I'm going to call your mother back and have a talk with her, and then — we'll get this sorted out, I promise."

Brittany looked at her father. Then she nodded tersely, turned on her heel, and stalked out. A second later, Jody heard the sound of their cabin door being slammed shut.

Riding the Storm

July 27 — after breakfast.
This is awful!

*Brittany won't talk to anyone. I tried my best, but she's
locked the cabin door — my cabin, incidentally! — and
has been sulking inside for hours.*

*Harry got hold of his ex-wife and learned that she is
planning to get married in the spring. She says that B.
can go to Paris for the wedding. She thinks that by then
a) Brittany will have "come to her senses" and be happy
about it, and b) they will have decided where they are
going to live and figured out a school for her. But until
she is actually married, she doesn't want her daughter
around . . . probably figures B. would scare off her fiancé!
She told Harry that if it was absolutely impossible for B. to
stay with him on Dolphin Dreamer, she would find her a
good boarding school.*

*I feel bad for Brittany, but I honestly can't stand the
thought of having to put up with her until next spring! I
know she has been so much nicer lately, but that's because she was enjoying her vacation. I haven't forgotten
what she was like at first . . . and if she is forced to stay*

with us, it will be an absolute nightmare! Especially once we are at sea, with no escape . . . How many more times will I get locked out of my own cabin? I am sure Brittany would fit right in at some snobby boarding school, but Harry doesn't think so. Despite all the trouble she has been so far, he wants her to stay with him rather than send her off to a strange school. So Mom and Dad have agreed: the twins and I are going to have home schooling (with a little help from the Internet!) from September onward, and B. could have the same. But I could hardly believe my ears when Mom went on to say how great it was for me to have "a friend her own age" on board. Okay, I know she was trying to make Harry feel better, but honestly. That spoiled brat my friend?

And when Brittany has a problem, it throws a monkey wrench into all our plans. I missed the chance to go out with Matt on Honey Bee and now Mom and Dad are so concerned about helping Harry sort this out they can't even think about anything else. Here it is nearly midday and we are still tied up in Port Lucaya, with no plans to go sailing, or diving, or anything today. It is all Brittany's fault!

Jody was sitting by herself on the forward deck, hunched miserably over her diary, when a sound made her look up. She saw Brittany emerge from below, and tensed wearily. But Brittany didn't notice her. Even though she'd put on makeup, Jody could tell that she'd been crying.

As Jody watched, puzzled, Brittany left the boat, swinging across to the boardwalk and then marching away, shoulders hunched, without looking back. Her face wore a hard, determined expression.

Jody stared at her, frowning. Maybe it was perfectly innocent. Brittany might be headed for the coffee shop, or the diving school, or running an errand for her dad — but in that case, why the makeup? And Brittany had been so upset this morning — Jody couldn't believe she'd calmed down yet. Something was wrong here.

What was she up to? Jody knew Brittany would probably be furious at her for following, but somebody had to look out for her. Stowing her diary in the sail locker, she got to her feet and hurried after her.

For once, the sun was not shining. The sky was heavily overcast, and there was a strong, warm wind blowing. As she felt it on her back, pushing her along, Jody thought it would be a good day for sailing — the sail would billow and fill and a boat would absolutely race along, driven by the winds that buffeted her now. What a bore, to have to stay ashore! Rigging rattled and clanked noisily as the boats she hurried past bobbed and shifted in their berths.

Brittany had disappeared. Jody paused and wondered where to look for her. The coffee shop or the diving school?

Then she saw the *Stormrider.*

Jay was on the pier, passing shopping bags full of food and drink across to Marcus and the girls on board. Jody was about to turn away when she realized that there were three girls, not two, on board — and one of them was Brittany.

"Hey, Brittany, here's your friend," called Jay as he noticed Jody standing and staring.

Brittany scowled. "She's not my friend." Turning to stare down at Jody she asked angrily, "What do you want?"

440

"I'll bet she'd like to help us find the treasure," said Ally. There was an amused, superior smile on her pretty face as she gazed down at Jody. "Funny how everybody wants to get in on the act." She shook her finger at Jody. "Sorry, honey, but you'll just have to go find your own shipwreck. We're not sharing with anybody else."

Jody shrugged impatiently. "I don't care about that. I came to see Brittany."

"Well, now that you've seen me, you can run along," Brittany snapped.

"Please, I need to talk to you," Jody said urgently.

Jay leaped into the boat. "Come on, let's get moving," he said.

"Wait!" called Jody. "Brittany, does your dad know where you are? Did he say you could go with these guys?"

Brittany shrugged. "I can do what I like," she said. "Nobody cares about me."

"That's not true!" Jody said, but Marcus was revving the engine now, and she didn't know if Brittany could hear her. She chewed her lip unhappily, trying to think of something else to say.

Brittany tossed her hair back and turned to murmur something to Ally. As *Stormrider* pulled away, the tall blond girl gave her a mocking wave. Jody could only stare after them, helpless.

As she walked slowly away, Jody wondered what to do. She didn't want to be a tattletale. Harry might not be bothered, anyway — he might even have given Brittany permission to go. Although Jody thought the whole *Stormrider* crew was obnoxious, Harry had met Heather and Ally and had let Brittany go to Freeport with them.

She was still turning it all over in her mind when she heard a familiar voice call, "Ahoy, Jody!"

She looked up, astonished to see the yellow sails of *Honey Bee,* and watched as Matt and Adam maneuvered the catamaran into the slip reserved for it.

When they had docked Jody asked, "What are you doing back? I thought you'd be out looking for dolphins today."

"Not in this," replied Matt with a glance at the cloudy sky.

Jody felt a clutch of apprehension in her stomach. "Why? It's so breezy . . . isn't it good sailing weather?"

"It is right now," he agreed. "We made record time! But haven't you heard the forecast? Why do you suppose *Dolphin Dreamer* stayed in dock today? Harry heard the warnings."

"Warnings?" she repeated weakly.

"All sailors are being told to seek shelter. There's a major tropical storm brewing. Winds of over a hundred miles per hour are predicted. There's no way anyone with any sense would want to be out at sea today!"

8

There was no time to waste. Jody spun on her heel and ran away from a bemused Matt. "Gotta go!" she called.

She ran as fast as she could back to *Dolphin Dreamer*, leaped on board, and scrambled down through the hatch.

Cam was alone in the main cabin leafing through a yachting magazine while reggae music played on a local radio program.

"Where's Harry?" Jody gasped. "I've got to talk to him!"

"I think he's in his cabin," Cam said calmly. "We have different tastes in music, you know." He was relaxed, grinning, unaware of any problem.

Jody hurried along to the captain's cabin and rapped sharply on the door. "Harry? Are you there?"

"Come in," called Harry's voice.

Jody entered and saw that he was playing a computerized chess game and listening to music.

Harry took the headphones off, and a worried line appeared between his eyes as he saw the anxiety on Jody's face. "What's wrong?" he asked.

"I just saw Brittany go off on *Stormrider*," Jody blurted out. "They said they're going treasure hunting," she added. "I don't think they realize there's a storm coming."

Harry quickly got to his feet. "Those young fools," he muttered. His blue eyes searched Jody's face. "How long ago was this?"

"I don't know . . . ten, fifteen minutes?" Jody replied. "I should have come sooner . . . but I saw Matt coming in and stopped to talk to him. I'm sorry. I didn't know about the storm until Matt told me."

"Okay, dear," Harry said. "None of this is your fault. Come on. We've got to make radio contact with *Stormrider* and convince them to turn around and head straight back."

The ship's two-way radio was on, as it always was, in the small control room. Jody knew that it was important, especially when out at sea, to hear about any potential dangers or changes in the weather. It was also vital for vessels to be able to communicate with each other, whether sending a distress call or exchanging information.

But none of Harry's attempts to reach *Stormrider* met with success.

He slammed his hand down on the chart table in frustration. "Why don't they respond? They must have their radio switched off!" he said angrily. "People like that shouldn't be allowed to rent boats. They don't have a clue what they're doing . . . and they put other people in danger with their stupidity."

Harry's next call was to alert the police and the Coast Guard. "I don't suppose you have any idea where they would be headed?" He looked at Jody without much hope.

"Yes, actually I do," Jody said, leaning forward earnestly. "They're still looking for the wreck of the *Elvira*. I'm sure they'll be going back to that little bay where we went diving a few days ago."

Harry sat up straighter when he heard this. "So at least I know where I have to go."

"You're going after them?" Jody asked.

"One way or another," Harry said. He had a determined look on his face. "If this was my boat, there'd be no question about it. But if your dad doesn't want to risk *Dolphin Dreamer*, I'll rent or borrow another boat. That's my little girl out there. I have to go and bring her back."

"And I'll be there to help you," said Jody's father.

Startled, Jody turned and saw that her dad and Matt were both standing in the doorway, where they'd obviously been listening.

"We'll take *Honey Bee*," Matt announced. He held up a hand to silence the protests from Craig and Harry.

"A catamaran like *Honey Bee* is much more stable in rough weather," he explained swiftly. "Also, her engine is more powerful, which is useful if it gets too fierce for sails. Plus, I know these waters like the back of my hand, so you'll want me to navigate. And finally, we can leave right away. *Honey Bee* is ready to go."

"You're on," said Harry. "Thank you." His voice was gruff with emotion.

As soon as Cam heard what they were planning, he said he would come, too. Craig turned to Jody. "Your mother's taken the twins to the adventure playground," he said. "When she gets back, tell her —"

"But I want to come, too!" Jody exclaimed. She stared anxiously into her father's eyes, willing him to understand. "I can't help feeling that I could have stopped Brittany from going, if only I'd thought of the right thing to say! Please let me help!"

Craig hesitated, then nodded his agreement. "I'll have a quick word with Maddie, so she knows what's up. But with luck, we may be back before they are."

Jody sighed with relief, glad to get another chance. Even though she'd been careful to hide her annoyance

in the private pages of her diary, she was afraid she had
added to Brittany's feelings of being unwanted.

Honey Bee was soon sailing out of Port Lucaya with
a crew of five. The wind was strong, and fortunately
blowing in the right direction, so they bounded swiftly
over the waves. It was a fast, rough ride. Jody kept a
grip on the railing and gazed at the horizon, searching
for *Stormrider.* She wondered if Brittany was feeling
seasick, and if she was wishing herself safely back in
port.

To the south and west, the sky was purple-black, and
Jody could see occasional jagged flashes of lightning
against the heavy clouds. Luckily they were headed
north. Jody kept her eyes fixed on the friendlier,
lighter gray sky and hoped they would be able to outrun the storm.

Even though they were moving much faster, the
journey seemed to take a lot longer than it had under
the calm, clear blue skies of last week. Minutes crawled
by and the ocean threw them around as they struggled
on with no end in sight. Jody chewed a piece of gum
given her by the sympathetic Cam, who had said it

might help settle her stomach. She was soaking wet, but at least it was warm. She couldn't tell if it was raining, or if the water that drenched her was only salt spray from the higher and higher waves that broke against the side of the boat.

"There she is!" shouted Harry suddenly.

Jody leaned out over the edge, narrowing her eyes against the wind and the sea spray. Then she saw *Stormrider,* and was startled by how small and fragile the sleek modern launch appeared as it was tossed up and down by the green-gray waves.

"She's riding awfully low in the water," Craig said, sounding concerned.

Harry held the bullhorn to his mouth. "Ahoy, *Stormrider*!" he called. "Ahoy! Put on your radio!"

As they drew nearer, they could see no one on the deck. Jody's heart lurched. For one terrifying moment she thought that the entire crew had disappeared.

Then a couple of figures appeared, wrapped in bright waterproof slickers. They were carrying plastic bowls full of water, which they poured over the side. Jody frowned, puzzled by this.

"Ahoy!" Harry hailed them again. "Are you in trouble?"

Marcus lifted a bullhorn to his mouth. "The bilge pump isn't working! We're splashing around up to our ankles! Do you have a spare pump?"

Harry looked at Matt, who shook his head.

"Tell them I'll try to fix it," Cam suggested. "It's probably just blocked."

Harry raised the bullhorn. "Request permission to approach and board. We'll try to fix it for you!"

Jody was sure Marcus would have agreed, but Jay snatched the bullhorn from him and shouted, "I'll fix it myself! We don't need any help! Back off, *Honey Bee*!"

Harry lifted the bullhorn. "Put your radio on! There's a tropical storm warning, all boats advised to get into port!"

"I'm not scared of storms!" Jay replied. "We'll ride it out — this boat was made for rough seas! Don't worry about us, Grandpa!"

Harry set his shoulders, determined to make them understand the danger. "Winds are predicted to reach

Harry to the rescue!

over a hundred miles an hour! That's more than a storm — it's practically a hurricane!"

Jay made a rude noise. "How dumb do you think we are? It's not hurricane season yet!"

As he was speaking, Ally and Brittany appeared at the side to pour more water overboard. Brittany was wrapped in an oversized, bright yellow slicker and didn't look happy at all. When she caught sight of *Honey Bee,* she gave a cry. Then she turned and tugged at Jay's arm, speaking urgently.

He tried to shrug her off, then spoke impatiently into the bullhorn again. "I guess you'd better take this little girl back with you. You'll be pleased to know you've managed to scare her!"

Harry turned to Matt, Craig, and Cam, who were waiting for his order. He spoke quietly. "Getting close enough isn't going to be safe —"

"I'll take down the sails," Matt said immediately, and he and the other two men got to work right away.

Harry lifted the bullhorn again. "Brittany — do you have a life jacket on?"

On the other boat, Brittany nodded, and opened the yellow slicker to show her father she was prepared.

"Good girl," he boomed back. "We're going to come as close as we can, but you'll have to climb across. Could be tricky. Keep calm. And don't worry, we'll get you home safely. Anyone else on *Stormrider* want to come with us?"

Brittany turned away and shouted into the cabin: "Ally! Heather! Come with me! It's not safe here!"

Red-haired Heather, wearing a blue slicker, popped out for a moment. "I need help, you guys!" she shouted. "The water's getting deeper!"

Ally tugged at Marcus's arm, pointing to the bowl, and the two of them vanished below.

Cam switched on the engine, and Matt maneuvered *Honey Bee* alongside *Stormrider.* Handing the bullhorn to Craig, Harry swung himself up onto the side and balanced there, one hand gripping the rigging.

Jody chewed her lip as she watched him. Even in calmer weather it would have been a risky position. What if he fell? She remembered how, back at the start of their journey on *Dolphin Dreamer,* an unexpected lurch of the boat in a rough sea had sent her overboard.

"Okay, sweetheart," Harry shouted. "Wait till I say so, and then step across to me!"

Brittany nodded.

Honey Bee lurched under the impact of a strong wave, and Harry swayed, but stayed where he was. Jody could hear Matt muttering under his breath as he grappled with the tiller, trying his best to hold the boat steady. The two boats drew closer still.

"Now!" Harry snapped. Wedging his foot between two lines, he leaned with outstretched arms. Jody held her breath. She could hardly bear to watch, but she couldn't look away. Brittany stepped off the side of *Stormrider* just as it was rocked by a wave. The gap between the two boats widened, and for a moment it seemed that the girl would plunge down into the water.

But her father grabbed hold of her, and pulled her onto *Honey Bee,* setting her down on deck. Brittany burst into tears.

Harry patted her back a little awkwardly. He looked

at Jody. "Look after her, please," he said quietly. He turned to Craig. "We can't leave them to drown," he said. Then, to Jody's astonishment, he leaped back to his perch on the side, and swung himself across to the other boat. They heard Jay give an angry yell as he landed.

Brittany screamed, "Daddy!"

Jody grabbed her, afraid she would try to go after her father. She stared across and saw Harry vanish into the hold, despite Jay's protests.

"If somebody doesn't fix that pump, *Stormrider*'s sunk," Cam explained.

"It may be too late already," Matt said, standing grimly at the helm, trying to keep the boats close without colliding. The waves were getting higher and higher; Jody felt as if someone was pouring buckets of water onto them, and she was dizzy from the pitching of the boat.

"You girls better get below," Craig said.

"Not without my daddy," Brittany said with a catch in her voice.

Craig didn't reply. His face was very pale and still. Jody had never seen her father look like that. She realized he was frightened. Suddenly, she was terrified. What if it was too late — not only for *Stormrider,* but for all of them on board *Honey Bee,* too?

The boat pitched wildly. Jody felt her stomach drop, as if she were on a roller coaster, and she grabbed at the side to steady herself. The sea lifted them up. They were above *Stormrider.* The motorboat seemed to nestle in the hollow of the wave. Then the movement of the sea brought *Honey Bee* down again, and a wave closed over *Stormrider.*

Sturdy *Honey Bee* found her balance again. But *Stormrider* wallowed. Before Jody's horrified gaze, the launch began to sink.

They could hear cries of fear from *Stormrider*'s crew. Jody and Brittany leaned forward together, holding on to each other, peering anxiously at the other deck, searching for Harry on the foundering vessel.

Cam lifted the bullhorn to his mouth. "Harry! Are you all right? Ahoy, *Stormrider*! Abandon ship!"

Matt brought his boat closer. There was a loud, grinding shriek as it scraped against the other boat's hull, and he winced. "Get ropes and life jackets," he shouted to Craig. "Some of those fools aren't wearing them!"

"Take it easy." Harry's voice, amazingly calm and re-assuring, boomed out from the bullhorn on the half-submerged boat. "We're all okay. Help us aboard one at a time."

Jody grabbed her father's arm. "Can I do anything to help?" she asked.

Craig shook his head, not taking his eyes from the other boat. "I don't think so. You and Brittany look after yourselves and keep out of the way."

She let go of him reluctantly. She wondered if it would be safer down below, but she couldn't bear to miss anything.

It gave her a strange, sick feeling to see *Stormrider* lying half-submerged, battered by waves that seemed determined to drag the boat under. Her crew was clinging on to whatever they could, and crying out for help. Only Harry, standing on deck waist-deep in wa-ter, seemed in control. Jody was amazed by how brave he was.

She had to clamp her jaws together to stop her teeth

from chattering as she saw her father climb up and balance himself on the side of the boat. He was wearing a life jacket, and had a rope tied around his waist. Cam was hanging on to the rope to keep from being pulled in along with the people he was trying to save.

Ally was the first person to come aboard. Her long blond hair hung in dripping rattails around her face. Her teeth were chattering, and her eyes were round and staring with shock. Moments later, Heather, shaking and weeping, joined her.

Jody cried out as she saw her father stumble and almost tumble down into the sea. But Cam had a firm grip on the rope he held, and pulled him back to safety. A few moments later, with Matt's help, they hauled the heavy Marcus on board. A minute or so later, Jay, the last member of the crew, had been saved. Only then did Harry clamber across to safety with Craig's help, out of breath and red-faced, but smiling reassuringly at Brittany.

She moaned and flung herself into his arms. "Oh, Daddy, Daddy, I was so scared!"

Jody, hugging her own dad, was startled by his reply.

"So was I, dear," Harry murmured, holding his daughter tightly. "Scared to death, I was. But we're okay. We're okay."

Matt shouted above the wind and rain. "Cam, give me a hand to batten everything down! Everybody else, get below now!"

The next hour was one of the longest of Jody's life. They all huddled below deck and waited for the storm to pass. She couldn't stop thinking about *Stormrider* sinking beneath the waves; how quickly the boat had filled with water, and how impossible it had been to stop. What if that happened to them? But *Honey Bee* was a sturdy boat, snug and sound. The only seawater inside was that dripping off everybody's wet clothes.

The *Stormrider* crew kept to themselves at the far end of the cabin, muttering and complaining together. Matt offered them towels, food, and drink, then left them alone. He began swapping sea stories with Cam and Harry. Their descriptions of comic sailing mishaps and near disasters took Jody's mind off what was happening outside. Even Brittany stopped shivering and perked up a little to listen to her dad.

The worst moment was when they felt a huge crashing bang right above them that shook the whole boat. Jody gave a yelp of fright, and felt her father's arm tighten around her reassuringly.

"Sounds like the mast is down," said Harry.

Matt was already on his feet. "I'll just check that it didn't block the hatchway," he said. He was back a few moments later to report that the broken mast had fallen clear of the door, and that the storm did finally appear to be passing.

Ten minutes later, he was back at the helm with the engine running, and *Honey Bee* was heading for home.

9

July 28 — late.

The Stormrider *crew is just unbelievable! Except for Heather — who insisted on giving everybody — but especially Harry and Matt — big kisses when she left! — they didn't seem at all grateful to be saved. Marcus complained because there wasn't any beer on board. None of them think what happened was their fault at all. Jay just talked about suing the charter company for giving them a defective boat.*

Hopefully we have seen the last of them.

Brittany has gone to the other extreme. She has apologized to everybody for causing so much trouble. She hangs around like a sad little ghost, all pale and quiet. She keeps offering to do things for people. It seems she can't stand to be alone for a minute. If she is not following her dad, then she's trailing after Maddie, or Mom — or me! Yeah, that's the worst thing. She's always trying to be nice to me now. She says it's because I saved her life. I told her it wasn't me, it was Harry and Matt she had to thank, but she insisted that it was all because of me. If I hadn't followed her, and then gone to tell Harry, he wouldn't have known to go after her, and she would have drowned. They all would have drowned.

This may sound weird, but I kind of miss the old, selfish Brittany. . . .

"And one more for Jody," said Brittany, putting the last blueberry muffin onto Jody's plate. Usually everyone lined up to get their own food from the galley, but this morning Brittany had insisted on serving.

Jimmy scowled. "That's not fair!"

"Thanks, but I don't need two," Jody replied. She pushed it across the table to her brother. "You guys can split it," she said, to stop any argument.

"Why are you being so nice to Jody?" Sean demanded.

"Because she saved my life," said Brittany, turning to smile at Jody.

Jody shrugged her shoulders uncomfortably and stared down at her plate. She wished Brittany would stop saying that.

"That's a heavy burden to put on Jody's shoulders, Brittany," said Mei Lin, slipping into the last place at the big table.

"What do you mean?" Brittany frowned uncertainly. "I just want to be nice to her."

"In China we believe that if you save someone's life, you become responsible for that person forever after," Mei Lin explained.

Jody felt the hairs on the back of her neck prickle. She stared at Brittany and saw the other girl's gaze reflect back her uneasiness. Obviously Brittany didn't like that idea any more than she did!

Harry suddenly spoke up. "I rather think that Brittany is *my* responsibility," he said firmly, but with a warm look across the table at his daughter.

Brittany nodded, flushing slightly. "I — know. I didn't mean — I just wanted everybody to know — I know what I did was wrong, and —"

"But just think," Jody interrupted as the thought occurred to her, "if you *hadn't* gone off on *Stormrider,* those guys would have all drowned! Nobody would have gone after them. So, in a way, *you* saved *their* lives!"

Brittany stared back at her, her eyes very round. Finally, she found her tongue. "Well, in that case, I'm glad we don't all live in China!"

Just as they were finishing breakfast, Matt arrived with a tall, slender, fair-haired couple, who looked so much alike they were obviously brother and sister.

"These are my friends, Alex and Ismay Collins," he said.

Jody remembered the names. "Are you the treasure hunters?" she asked.

Alex flashed a grin. "Yes . . . but we haven't had much luck so far this summer. Today we are doing some better-paid salvage work. The owners have hired us to find *Stormrider,* recover her if possible, and prepare a report for the insurers, if not."

"And since you all saw it sink," Matt said, "I thought maybe you'd be willing to help Alex and Ismay locate the wreck. I'm going to be too busy with the repairs to the *Honey Bee.*"

Brittany spoke up. "What happened to Jay and — I mean, what about the people who rented the boat? Couldn't they help?"

Ismay made a face. "Maybe, if they'd stuck around. but it seems they cut their vacation short and took the first available flight home, rather than stay and explain what happened."

Brittany scowled. "Cowards," she muttered.

Jody agreed. It was typical of them to think nothing of the damage they were doing, and leave it to others to clean up afterward.

"What do you want us to do, exactly?" Craig asked. "I

466

mean, obviously Matt could show you on a chart roughly where she went down . . ."

"True," agreed Alex with a nod. "And maybe it will be simple to find her right away. But maybe not. That storm will have churned and shifted the sand, and the boat may have broken up. The more people looking, the more quickly we should find her. Matt tells us you dive?"

Jody caught her breath with excitement. She could hardly believe it. She checked to make sure she hadn't misunderstood: "You want us to dive with you?"

Ismay's eyebrows went up. She looked apprehensive. "Only if you'd like to come along. I understand from Matt that the boat went down in an area where you've been diving before, so you'll be familiar with it. It's shallow, and the visibility should be good today. We wouldn't expect you to do any actual work, and we can't afford to pay you . . ."

Craig burst out laughing. "I think Jody would be prepared to pay *you* for the chance!" he said, when he could manage to speak. "Thanks for the invitation —

we would love to come along and help you look for *Stormrider*!"

Craig, Gina, Jody, and Brittany quickly collected their diving gear and everything else they would need for a day's dive. Harry said he'd go along to provide backup support on board. Sean and Jimmy were happy to stay behind with Maddie and Cam, after making their parents promise to tell them if they came across any sunken pirate ships.

"If we do, we'll get it all on videotape, I promise you," Craig said solemnly before waving goodbye and heading off to board *New Treasure Seeker,* Alex and Ismay's sturdy salvage vessel.

They soon reached the bay where *Stormrider* had gone down.

Brittany seemed startled when Alex cut the engine and dropped anchor. "Is this really the same place?" she asked, staring around in bewilderment.

Jody guessed she was remembering the slate-gray, storm-lashed sea beneath a purple sky. That terrifying vision had disappeared, replaced by calm breezes under a bright blue sky that now arched over crystal-clear waters. Staring down to the seabed — only about eight yards away — Jody thought that the smooth white sand looked as if it had rested undisturbed for centuries. But that was an illusion. The sands were always being moved and shifted by the weather, which could change in a matter of hours from calm to deadly.

There were still a few pieces of litter from *Stormrider* bobbing about on the waves — the Styrofoam lid of a cooler, a red plastic bowl, empty beer cans — but there was no sign of the launch itself. It had completely vanished.

Jody noticed that Brittany was shivering, despite the warmth of the day. Harry was watching her with concern.

"Why don't you stay here with me, dear?" he suggested. "I'll tell you some more sea stories." He smiled, trying to coax a response out of her.

She shook her head, staring out at the blue water. "No, I want to dive," she said quietly. "I hate the thought of seeing *Stormrider* down there . . . but I have to do it."

Harry nodded slowly. "That's up to you," he replied.

After they were all ready and their equipment had been checked, they paired off and discussed their dive plans. Jody's buddy would be her father, while Gina would look after the less-experienced Brittany.

"Remember, I'll be right beside you," Gina told Brittany, her brown eyes soft and concerned. "I'm sure there won't be any problems. But if you feel uncomfortable, or tired, or want to come up for any reason at all, just signal, and we'll end the dive."

"Thanks, Mrs. McGrath," Brittany said.

Gina smiled. "Why don't you call me Aunt Gina?" she suggested. "You could be my honorary niece! I've just about given up on my sister ever giving me a niece or nephew."

To Jody's surprise, this suggestion brought a flush of pleasure to Brittany's pale face, and she smiled shyly as she said, "Thanks . . . Aunt Gina!"

Once in the water, Jody descended two or three yards, keeping pace with her father. Gentle kicks with her fins propelled her smoothly through the water.

Craig, who had the camera today, went more slowly, and Jody soon outdistanced him. They had agreed beforehand that this was okay, as long as she didn't go out of sight. Visibility was so good in this clear water that Jody was sure this wouldn't be a problem.

It did seem puzzling that they had not managed to spot *Stormrider* yet. How could it just disappear, in such shallow water? She wondered if they were wrong about the spot. Maybe the floating litter that had seemed like a marker was misleading. It might have drifted away much farther than they realized. Without permanent landmarks, it was hard to know where you were at sea.

Jody's attention was distracted from the search when she caught sight of a group of dolphins. She swam toward them. Two peeled away from the group and glided rapidly toward her.

Even at a distance Jody could see that one was an adult, heavily spotted, and the other, smaller, just a calf. They came closer and, with a joyful leap of her heart, Jody recognized Mary and Skipper.

The calf zoomed right up to her and rubbed affectionately against Jody's side. He swam around her quickly several times and then darted away, back to his mother.

Mary swam closer to Jody. Jody could hear her clicking. Then she flipped over and glided away a short distance before swimming back again, circling Jody and again gliding away slowly, waving her tail in a beckoning way.

Jody had a strong feeling that the dolphin wanted her to follow. She looked around for her father and saw that he had the video camera pointed in their direction — he had seen the whole thing. She pointed to indicate she wanted to follow Mary. He nodded and signaled okay.

Jody swam after Mary and Skipper. She was a little apprehensive that Mary might be taking her to rescue another injured dolphin. Yet Mary's clicking sounds and her whole body language seemed to promise something very different this time.

They went deeper. Jody realized they were heading for the group of dolphins, who were hovering in the water with their noses down. Jody thought they were looking at something on the seabed. As she drew nearer, she could see that it was something very large sticking up out of the sand . . . something like the hull of a ship! Yes, it was definitely a wreck!

Jody finned harder, excited by the thought that she'd been the first to spot the *Stormrider*. But she was puzzled because what was lying there before her, half-covered by the shifting sands, didn't look anything like the modern launch she remembered. Two days at the bottom of the sea shouldn't have changed it that much. She swam closer, trying to make sense of what she was looking at, searching for a detail she could focus on.

The curious dolphins parted before her like a curtain, letting her through, and now she saw what they had been looking at.

Thrusting up out of the sand was the head and upper body of a woman. Not a real woman, but a statue carved of wood, a face with wide-open eyes, a straight nose, and smiling lips.

Jody reached out one hand and touched the old ship's figurehead wonderingly. She couldn't believe it, but as she felt the ancient wood, solid and real beneath her fingers, she knew it was true. Thanks to the dolphins, she'd discovered an ancient shipwreck!

Elvira, at last!

*   *   *

While Jody was busy with her discovery, Alex and Ismay had found *Stormrider,* still in one piece. The next step should have been to haul the launch to the surface and tow it into port. But when they heard Jody's exciting news, back on board the *New Treasure Seeker,* they decided that could wait.

"It must be *Elvira!*" Ismay exclaimed.

"If it's not, it must be something just as good," Alex added. "You wouldn't believe how many times we've been diving in this very spot, and never found a thing!"

"I guess we have the storm to thank for uncovering it," Ismay said with a grin.

"No, you have the dolphins to thank," Jody put in. "They're the ones who led me to it!"

"Honestly, Jody, you have to drag dolphins into *everything*," Brittany groaned.

Jody looked at her sharply, but was that a twinkle in Brittany's eye? Maybe she was teasing. "Oh, I don't know," Jody replied lightly. "I think in this case I'd say it was the dolphins who dragged *me* into it."

"And are we ever glad they did!" said Alex enthusiastically. "Do you guys need to rest, or are you up for a little treasure hunting?"

"Treasure hunting, definitely!" Jody exclaimed. She shot a pleading look at her parents and was relieved to see that they looked nearly as excited as she felt.

"Yeah, count me in!" Brittany agreed. She had obviously recovered her nerve, Jody thought.

"I think we could manage another dive, after a short rest," said Craig, a huge grin on his face.

Gina sounded a note of caution. "At least another hour before we dive again," she said. "And we'll have to set a strict time limit. I know how easy it is to get carried away and forget everything else when exploring something as exciting as this!"

"Sure," said Alex. "I suggest a dive of three-quarters of an hour. We'll take a look, and bring up any interesting small objects that we find. Everything else will have to wait for another day. After all, we still have to do the job we're being paid for, and haul up *Stormrider!*"

While *New Treasure Seeker* was being moved so that she would sit in the water immediately above the wreck of *Elvira,* Gina reminded the girls of the importance of keeping their wits about them. "Stay in constant visual contact with the rest of us. Don't go diving into any enclosed areas unless one of us has checked it out first, and be careful where you put your hands. Eels have a tendency to make their homes in wrecks, and if you disturb one you could get a nasty bite," she said.

"Anna warned me about camouflaged fish like stone-fish and scorpions, which have poisonous stings," Brittany said. "Don't worry, Aunt Gina, I'll be careful. I don't intend to grab anything unless it's made of gold or silver!"

Gina laughed. "We should be so lucky!" she said.

"But you are that lucky!" Alex exclaimed exuberantly, with a grin that seemed to split his face in two. "We're all that lucky! Today is our lucky day!"

The dolphins were still hovering around the old wreck. They seemed fascinated by what the storm winds had uncovered. The normally smooth, sandy bottom they knew had been transformed.

As she approached the site with the others, Jody was so excited she had to remind herself to breathe normally through her regulator.

Only a part of the ship had been uncovered by the shifting sands; most of it remained buried. As she swam closer, Jody tried to figure out which part of the ship she was looking at, and where any treasure was most likely to be. Could there still be a locked chest hidden away on board? Or would its contents have been scattered far and wide long before now? Her eyes scanned the seabed as she hoped to catch the gleam of gold or silver.

Jody saw the others busily fanning the sand with their gloved hands to uncover objects hidden there. She tried it herself, but found only more sand. She looked around at the others again and saw that they were all making discoveries, tucking found objects safely into the mesh collecting bags that Alex had handed out before the dive.

Ismay held up something flat and round, the size of a dinner plate. Craig was inspecting some lumpy object, and Alex's bag was already bulging. Even Brittany had made a discovery. Jody swam closer to look, and the other girl huddled protectively over her find. Jody thought the tiny things she was picking up looked like a bunch of pebbles, not interesting at all. Anyway, it was clear that Brittany didn't want to share them with her. She'd better find her own place to look.

Jody noticed something like a bottle sticking out of the sand, but decided against it. Bottles were boring.

She wanted to find something better! So she continued to search.

Yet when she saw her mother signal ten minutes to go, Jody was still empty-handed.

She gazed around, despairing, and noticed Mary and Skipper were close by, watching her curiously. Jody was startled to realize that she'd been too preoccupied with her search to pay any attention to the dolphins — that had to be a first! All of a sudden, she felt annoyed with herself for letting the treasure hunting fever overwhelm her like that. She'd been the first to spot the wreck. That should be enough.

She was sorry now that she hadn't just relaxed and played with Mary and Skipper. She swam toward them eagerly, determined to make it up to them in the few minutes she had left.

With a flick of her tail, Mary shot away, her calf swimming rapidly beneath her. A moment later, Mary doubled back to be sure Jody was following. She slowed down, letting the girl catch up. Then she did a somersault, ending by balancing on her nose on the soft white sand.

Jody wasn't sure what the game was, but she decided to imitate the dolphin. She shot down to the bottom and attempted a handstand there. As her fingers closed on the soft bed, she felt something hard and flat beneath the sand. Digging down a little deeper, she managed to hook her fingers into something and pull it up.

Looking at her find she saw that it was a dark, metallic disc, slightly bigger than her outstretched hand. Jody felt a moment's flare of excitement — that she'd *finally* found something — followed immediately by disappointment. It was man-made, and it *could* have come from the shipwreck, but whatever it might be, it wasn't a treasure! It was something like a wheel or cog; it probably came from some sort of machine or engine. And if so, then it didn't belong to the *Elvira* at all. It might even have dropped off *Stormrider.*

She nearly dropped it back into the sand. But then she stopped herself. Whatever it was, it didn't belong in the ocean. She stowed it away in her collecting bag, and then finned alongside Mary and Skipper until she received the signal to return.

10

"Anyone find any old or valuable jewels?" Ismay asked with a smile when they'd all gathered back on deck.

They all laughed and shook their heads.

"No, me neither," Ismay said cheerfully. "I haven't found any serious treasure yet, but I am absolutely certain that it's down there. Have a look at this!" From her collecting bag she pulled out two large discs made of some pitted and corroded grayish material.

"What are those?" Brittany asked.

"Dinner plates," Ismay replied, smiling. "I think they're

made of pewter, rather than silver, but they were marked with the ship's name, probably to discourage anyone from walking off with them. Look!" She rubbed the side of her hand hard against the flat rim and then held the plate up on display.

They all crowded close to see.

Jody read the name etched in curving letters on the raised rim: "Elvira!"

"Yes," said Alex, smiling as widely as his sister. "So there can be no doubt about it — we have definitely found the ship we've been searching for these past three years!"

"Anyone else want a drink?" Ismay asked. She gave the plate to her brother and went to open the cooler. "I'm parched!" She began to hand out soft drinks and bottled water.

Jody gulped down an orangeade thirstily.

"So what happens next?" Craig wanted to know. "Will you be able to stake a claim, or will it become a free-for-all, with lots of treasure-hunting divers turning up?"

"It would be best if we can keep the news to ourselves for as long as we can," Alex said cautiously.

"Don't worry — we won't tell anyone," Jody assured him.

Brittany snorted. "Not even your nosey kid brothers?" she asked.

Craig raised his eyebrows. "We'll tell the twins it's a secret. They won't want any bad guys beating our friends to the treasure!" he assured her.

"We will probably have to hire some more divers to help us — when treasure is involved, it's best to work as quickly as possible," Alex said.

"Especially with hurricane season coming," Ismay added. Finishing her water, she stowed the empty bottle back in the cooler.

"We'll apply for a salvage claim from the Bahamian government," Alex explained. "We've had them before, so there shouldn't be any problem. What happens is, we register our intent to salvage *Elvira* — since we've found something with that name on it. Then we dive and search like lunatics and hope to make our fortunes before the weather changes!"

"Could we help you look?" Brittany asked suddenly. Her eyes were bright, her cheeks flushed. Jody thought that this was the first time she had seen her looking happy since before the phone call from her mother.

"So you want to be a treasure seeker, too, do you?" asked Ismay. She smiled sympathetically at Brittany, then looked at Craig and Gina. "We certainly wouldn't say no to more help."

Craig and Gina exchanged a glance before nodding.

"We'll be sticking around for at least another week or two to help Matt out," Craig explained. "I've already told him that *Dolphin Dreamer* is his to command while *Honey Bee* is laid up. He's got insurance to cover the repairs, but it wouldn't be fair if he had to miss out on a couple of weeks at the height of the season!"

"And luckily, there are plenty of dolphins around here to study," Gina added. "After what Matt told us about dolphins and divers, I would really like to film the dolphins watching you while you work. I think it could make a fascinating project . . ." She broke off with a grin. "If I don't get too distracted by the treasure myself, that is! Hey, I haven't shown you all that I found!"

Reaching into her own bag, Gina pulled out a handful of blackened spoons and forks. "Silverware!"

"Probably the closest thing to treasure we found today," Ismay said. "Those should polish up very nicely, and then you could use them to eat off the plates!"

"We obviously stumbled into the pirates' dining room," Craig joked, displaying his own finds — two old bottles, and what might have been a cup, all heavily encrusted.

"I found a bottle, too," said Brittany. "And there's these . . ." She held out her cupped hand. Jody saw that what she had taken for pebbles underwater were actually blue beads.

"A necklace!" Ismay exclaimed. "Or possibly a rosary. Impossible to know now what they were when they were strung. They're really lovely! Clever you, to find something so small!" She looked at Jody. "What about you, Jody? What did you find?"

Jody felt embarrassed to show them what was obviously just some piece of machinery that had dropped off a modern boat. She shrugged. "Nothing."

"Nothing at all?" Ismay looked surprised. "Really? You didn't find anything at all?"

Jody shook her head, feeling herself blush. "Well," she said. "I did find something, but . . . it was just some piece of a machine, I think," she added, with a shrug.

"Did you leave it behind?" asked Alex.

"No, I brought it up," Jody replied. "Well, I figured, it's not important, but leaving it was like leaving litter behind," she explained. She reached into her bag and got out the metal disc, which she handed over to Alex. "There, see? It probably just fell off some boat that was passing . . ." Her voice trailed off as she took in the way Alex was examining her find. He looked genuinely interested — excited, even.

Craig leaned over to investigate. "What is it?" he asked. "It looks very old."

"It *is* very old," Alex agreed. His voice was solemn. "And it's complete. If this didn't come from *Elvira* then it must have come from an even earlier ship."

"But what *is* it?" Jody asked.

"It's a bronze astrolabe," Alex replied. "It's very rare."

Everyone stared at him blankly — except Ismay, who was nodding wisely.

"Clear as mud," Craig grumbled. "Have mercy on us ordinary folk and explain, please!"

Alex laughed. "Sorry," he said. "No reason why you'd know what an astrolabe was — nobody has used them for hundreds of years!"

A real find, after all!

He went on, "It's an early navigation tool. It works a little bit like a portable sundial." He held up the flat disc so they could see. "This little piece in the middle can be moved, like the hand on a clock. By pointing it in the direction of the sun or the brightest star at night, and figuring out how far it was from the horizon, you could figure out the local time and, roughly, where you were."

Jody stared at him, open-mouthed. She could hardly believe what she was hearing. To think she had nearly tossed it away! Finally she found her voice. "So it was a good find?"

Alex grinned widely. "You could say that," he replied. "In fact, it's a brilliant find — a museum piece! I know of only one other like it in this part of the world! Wait'll we get it cleaned up, and you'll see!"

August 7
Lucky seven! Today, the New Treasure Seekers struck gold! Alex and Ismay found the pirates' hoard — a great pile of jewelry, gold chains, gold bars, and silver coins ... Sean and Jimmy are absolutely ecstatic about

the genuine pieces of eight that Dad brought up for them. We each get to keep one as a souvenir of our stay here.

Alex and Ismay wanted to give us something more to thank us. They offered to contribute to the funding of Dolphin Universe. But we talked it over as a team and had a better idea. Since the treasure comes from here, it should help the dolphins that live in this area. Matt is doing as much as he can on his own. With more funding, he could set up a project to encourage more responsible tourism in the area, and educate people about preserving the local ecology, and not endangering the lives of the animals who live here — especially dolphins!

We will be leaving soon, now that Honey Bee is ship-shape again. I went for a swim this evening with Mary and Skipper and the others. It may have been for the last time, but I hope not. Surely we'll meet again. I hope they will always remember me. No matter how many more dolphins I come to know, I'm sure I will never forget them!